DATE DUE

Other Books by LAURA KALPAKIAN

Steps and Exes

Caveat

Graced Land

These Latter Days

Crescendo

Dark Continent and Other Stories

Fair Augusto and Other Stories

Cosette: The Sequel to Les Misérables

Beggars and Choosers

The Delinquent Virgin

LAURA KALPAKIAN

Graywolf Press
Saint Paul, Minnesota

Publication of this volume is made possible in part by a grant provided by the Minnesota State Arts Board through an appropriation by the Minnesota State Legislature, and by a grant from the National Endowment for the Arts. Significant support has also been provided by Dayton's, Mervyn's, and Target stores through the Dayton Hudson Foundation, the Bush Foundation, the McKnight Foundation, the General Mills Foundation, the St. Paul Companies, and other generous contributions from foundations, corporations, and individuals. To these organizations and individuals we offer our heartfelt thanks.

In slightly different forms, some of these stories appeared in:

USA:
The Iowa Review
Story Magazine
The Los Angeles Times Magazine
Good Housekeeping
Chuckanut Reader

UK:
Good Housekeeping
Home and Life
Winter's Tales (Constable)

Published by Graywolf Press
2402 University Avenue, Suite 203
Saint Paul, Minnesota 55114

www.graywolfpress.org

Published in the United States of America

ISBN 1-55597-295-0

2 4 6 8 9 7 5 3 1
First Graywolf Printing, 1999

Library of Congress Catalog Card Number: 99-60736

Cover design: A N D
Cover photo: Photodisc

For

Jay McCreary

from

Pancho y los muchachos

Acknowledgments

many thanks

Juliet Burton
Deborah Schneider
Anne Czarniecki
Janna Rademacher
Lisa Bullard
Fiona McCrae
And special thanks to Robin Baird-Smith

Also, I am grateful to the Hawthornden International Writers' Retreat in Scotland for their hospitality and to Susan Thames and Katherine Pierpoint for their camaraderie.

Contents

Lavee, Lagair, Lamore, Lamaird

THE MORNING MABEL JUDD left for France, bunting billowed from the railroad cars and from the station roof while the high school band oompahed lustily and recruiters for the Red Cross and the army took turns addressing the crowd gathered on the platform. The Mormon bishop, the Methodist pastor, and Otis McGahey representing the city council also spoke, waxed at length on behalf of sacrifice, unstinting valor, and Liberty Bonds. Their words caught on the same dry breeze that fluttered the American flag, intertwining it symbolically with a makeshift French tricolor and a British Union Jack. Admittedly, Mabel Judd looked rather odd amongst her France-bound compatriots, three dozen youths, "the cream of St. Elmo's young manhood," intoned the bishop, "who have volunteered their sacred blood to fight the Hun Over There." Also leaving for Over There were about a half-dozen volunteer nurses, girls of good character. And Mabel Judd. Mabel looked particularly odd because her character was (by St. Elmo standards) questionable, and by no means could she be considered a girl. Fortyish, stout, clad in a stiff blue traveling suit, she wore an out-of-date hat with a long rusty plume that blew about in the desert wind, occasionally tickling the cheeks of those who stood closest to her. Her face was round, reminiscent of a fishbowl, the effect enhanced by thick glasses over her heavy-hooded eyes. She listened to the speakers impassively, as though neither the grand words, nor the solemnity of the occasion, nor the prospects of the War itself moved her beyond her usual expression—benign, distracted, unsuitably wistful for a woman her age.

Her sister and brother-in-law and several of their children and grandchildren (the youngest a babe in arms) had brought Mabel to the station that morning in the clattering family Ford and they stood by her, listened attentively, clapping when applause was indicated. Mabel's sister Sarah (universally known as Dumpling) held her baby granddaughter, but cast baleful glances toward her fifteen-year-old daughter Cordelia, who had shamelessly thrown herself into the arms of Eldon Whickham, one of the departing recruits. Dumpling also kept an eye on her youngest son Clarence, who, at seventeen, seemed ready to bolt toward the army recruiter so that he too might be showered with flowers, bathed with praise, kisses, and tears from the bevy of admiring maidens. She told her husband Roy to watch Clarence and keep him away from the recruiters. If someone in the family must court death (for that's how Dumpling saw it), then let it be Mabel. This thought made Dumpling sniffle, and shifting the baby to her other ample hip, she took her sister's arm. "Oh, Mabel, if only Pa and Ma were here to see you. They'd be so proud of you."

"I think Miss Savage would be proud of me too. I think Miss Savage would be glad to know that finally, thirty years later, I can put her teachings toward a noble cause. At last I'm going to get to speak French."

"I'm just sure Pa and Ma are looking down from heaven on you this very day, Mabel," Dumpling replied, returning to her initial premise.

"Yes, and probably Miss Savage is dead too, by now. You suppose she's looking down from heaven as well, Sarah?"

"Probably not the same heaven," said Dumpling dubiously.

"Heaven is a singular place, Sarah," Mabel informed her sister. "Not plural."

Theological hairsplitting was not Dumpling's forte. She said, "We're all very proud of your sacrifice, Mabel."

"I haven't made any sacrifice. Yet," she added as an afterthought.

"Yes, Mabel," Roy chimed in, "we'll all of us, the family, the church, we'll remember you in our prayers. It's a long long way to Tipperary."

"About six thousand miles," she replied, speaking over the band's rendition of this very tune.

Irritated, Roy made an awkward noise, privately cheering the War, any war for that matter that would spare him Mabel Judd with her blunt ways and her book learning and her thumping alto-thrashing hymns in church on Sunday. He delighted, too, in any war that would spare him Dumpling's eternal dithering over her unmarried sister.

The mother of one of the nurse-volunteers came up to them, her daughter Ellie in tow. Her face awash in tears, Bertha Dewitt embraced Mabel and begged her to look after Ellie. "Oh, Mabel, you'll be her friend and companion, won't you? You'll look after Ellie. Oh, all those foreigners! My heart breaks!"

Mabel cast a frankly appraising glance to the twenty-three-year-old Ellie. Clearly, Ellie's heart was not breaking. Mabel turned to Bertha. "In France we will be the foreigners, Bertha. And don't forget the War."

"Oh, this terrible, terrible War!" cried Bertha, who, since 1914 had scarcely read beyond the headlines before confidently tucking her St. Elmo *Herald-Gazette* at the bottom of her canary's cage. Even after the April announcement of America's entry into the War, the European conflict remained mercifully distant till Ellie announced she was volunteering to be a Red Cross nurse, spurred romantically on by the uplifting song, "Rose of No-Man's-Land." Naturally Bertha (like every other parent of these girls of good character) had forbade her daughter even to think of such a thing. No unmarried girl of good character could dream of handling men's bodies, even men's blasted, bloodied bodies. But in wartime, values change; at least Ellie's values changed. Bertha's did not. "Oh, Mabel, I hope I can rely on you to look after Ellie and—"

"You can't," Mabel replied without blinking. (Dumpling always shuddered when her sister was so cruelly straightforward.) "I am going to France as part of the War effort, to translate for the Allies, and I shall certainly not have time to think of Ellie. You know I'm the only person in this town who can speak French, impeccable French, thanks to our governess Miss Savage. Isn't that right, Sarah?"

Dumpling murmured something vaguely affirmative. Bertha Dewitt—who, as a married woman, had every right to feel superior to Mabel Judd and who (democratically) snorted at the very idea of a French-speaking governess—muttered something, snatched Ellie's elbow, and led her away through the crowd.

"Oh, Mabel," Dumpling moaned, "did you have to say it just like that?"

"Like what? Was Bertha offended?"

The train whistle sliced through Mabel's question as well as the Mormon bishop's concluding remarks, and for an instant, before the high school band launched into "The Battle Hymn of the Republic," the buzz of conversation and farewell ceased and the platform was eerily quiet. Then the weeping began in earnest. The boys shouldered their bags and began boarding the bunting-draped train (especially provided as a patriotic gesture on the part of the railroad). This train would take the recruits and Red Cross volunteers to Los Angeles where they would be put on yet other trains, eventually on boats, braving the submarine-infested waters of the Atlantic to arrive in war-ravaged Europe where they would make short work of the horrible Hun. The speeches finished, the passengers boarded and waved out the windows. Railway workers began stripping bunting from the cars, wadding it unceremoniously, leaving the train shorn of gallant purpose. The look of manly pride in the eyes of the young men faltered; second thoughts flashed across the faces of the Red Cross volunteers.

Dumpling flung herself against her sister, weeping. Mabel held her and said they would all meet again in some undiscovered country. Dumpling wept the more and Roy picked up Mabel's bag, but she refused Roy's offer to carry her bag with the observation that in wartime women must shoulder new responsibilities as well as their own bags. She stepped onto the train.

"Oh, Roy," Dumpling wept against her husband, squeezing the baby between them as Mabel's broad back vanished into the car. "What if Mabel dies Over There?"

Roy patted her back ineffectually. "She's going to translate, Dumpling, not to fight."

"But so much can happen in wartime."

"Not to Mabel Judd," he replied with rather more emphasis than need be. "Nothing ever happened to her and nothing ever will."

"But what if she does die?" Dumpling wailed. "You know how the church feels about . . ." she daubed the baby's head where tears had fallen, ". . . marriage, Roy. I mean if Mabel dies unmarried, she won't . . . she can't . . . she'll be denied the Celestial Kingdom."

"Well, who knows, Dumpling. Maybe she'll get married." He chuckled. "A wartime romance. Why, just look at all these good Mormon boys in uniform!"

Dumpling drew away from him indignantly. "How can you make fun of my sister? How can you say such a cruel thing when Mabel is making sacrifices for her country and—"

"All I'm saying is that whatever your sister had to sacrifice, she gave it up a long time ago."

The whistle split the air again and the train heaved to life, its wheels making those first uncertain revolutions forward, gathering courage and conviction slowly. Just then Mabel Judd stuck her head out the window, the silly plume in her hat twitching in the wind, and cried out, "Good-bye St. Elmo! Hello Paree!"

Prior to that day, Mabel Judd was the librarian at the St. Elmo Public Library, a post she had held for many years and an occupation which suited her since she was educated, bookish, organized, unmarried, and required to earn her own bread. That she should be unmarried was odd because men outnumbered women in St. Elmo two-to-one, especially when Mabel was young, twenty years before. Even a plain girl could count on two or three (equally plain and probably poor) suitors, but suitors nonetheless. Mabel's spinsterhood was all the more remarkable because she was a Mormon; for Mormons, marriage is the only state imaginable, as much a church edict as a civil institution. Mabel's family was not a clan graced with beauty, and they were poor as well, but neither their poverty nor their plainness stopped her sisters from marrying. Nothing stops a Mormon girl from marrying. Before each of them was twenty, the other Judd girls had all wed: Agnes to the feckless Zeke (eight children), Esther to the dour Willis (six children), and Sarah to Roy who worked for the railroad and who had dubbed her early on with the name Dumpling and by whom she had five children.

When Mabel was a young woman (and even then, blunt and bookish) the Latter-day Saints would inquire lightly when she intended to marry, citing (sometimes subtly, sometimes not) her duty to God and the church. As time passed they reminded Mabel as well of her duty to all those soul-babies awaiting only flesh to come to earth, awaiting flesh and legally wed parents, naturally. To these inquiries, Mabel inevitably replied that she had her eyes on Higher Things (which accounts perhaps for her slightly befuddled expression). Whatever those Higher Things were, no one else in St. Elmo could see them and gradually Mabel grew, passed into ossified eccentricity, the object of both mirth and pity. Mabel alone seemed unaware of her incongruous, anomalous, impossible situation in the family, the church, the community itself.

Until their deaths, Mabel lived with her parents, Ephraim and Leona, in their little rented clapboard on C Street. When they died, rather than moving in with one of her married sisters, or taking a room in some respectable boarding house, Mabel continued to rent the C Street house, where she lived alone. That house was destroyed in the terrible flood of 1917. Even then Mabel declined the shelter of her sisters' roofs. She moved the few things she salvaged from the flood into the back room of the library, set up a cot, and lived there.

The Library Board decided she should not live there and they gave Mabel Judd sixty days' notice, which she ignored. When, more forcefully, two members of the Library Board came to call (after-hours so as to spare everyone embarrassment), they softened her eviction saying they would be happy to find suitable accommodation for a maiden lady. Mabel heard them out and then announced she would be giving up her post at the library, that she had volunteered to use her command of the French language for the betterment of the Allied Cause against the Hun. They didn't believe her. She assured them it was so, saying (as she had said to the recruiting officer—having anticipated his objections) that the Allies could ill afford to spurn her contribution merely on the basis of her age.

When she announced her decision to her sisters and their husbands, they were unanimously aghast and declared she could not do this. In her bland, blunt way, Mabel reminded them she had not asked for their approval. She added, "Of course I am eager to use my abilities and education to defeat the brutal Hun, but I must say, I'm looking forward to seeing England and France. Miss Savage always spoke of—"

"Don't say that woman's name in my hearing!" cried Agnes. "Don't mention that—that—" Agnes glanced to Esther and Sarah to supply the word, but even their faces were mute. Agnes colored. "I can't bear to hear that name."

As the eldest of the Judd girls, Agnes could well remember the day the impecunious Miss Savage entered their young lives. Agnes was seventeen that day in 1887 when the four girls and their mother, dressed in their finest, had driven the family rig down the single street of Leona, California, to the dock at the gold mine to meet the supply train that came twice-weekly bearing food, water, mail, payroll for the miners, liquor for the two saloons, and any other contact between this distant desert and the rest of the world. Any passengers had to squeeze themselves behind the engineer and the stoker as the narrow-gauge train only pulled a few supply cars and boasted no particular place for passengers. But then, not many people came to Leona, California. The clank and clatter of this twice-weekly train were the only punctuation to the incessant thump and throttle of the smelting mill and the gold mine. These sounds beat through the desert air, sunup to sundown, like a doleful tattoo and clanged behind Leona Judd and her four daughters as they got out of the rig and walked up the platform to the unshaded dock to await the train.

That Leona Judd should take the rig to meet the train was itself worthy of note. That she should take her four daughters with her was virtually a civic event. Leona Judd made every effort to shield her daughters from the rough-and-tumble life of this desert mining town, never mind the town bore her name, as did the gold mine itself, as did the dry goods store and the boardinghouse run by Mrs. Skaggs, wife of the mine foreman. Naturally the saloons and the grimy café were not graced with Leona's name. However feminine its antecedents. Leona, California, was a man's town, populated by a few taciturn Indians, a handful of industrious Chinese, and a great many miners, men who worked hard, drank hard, lived hard, and occasionally shot one another in brawls contesting the affections of a handful of whores who—other than Mrs. Skaggs, Mrs. Judd, and the four Judd girls—were the only white women in town. So new, so raw, so committed to gold was Leona, California, there was not even a church, Mormon or otherwise, and certainly there was no school. Even if there had been, Leona Judd could not possibly have sent her daughters (monied girls with gilded prospects) to be educated with the children of the unsavory Indians, the heathen Chinese, and the vulgar brats begot upon the whores. Clearly, the daughters of

Ephraim and Leona Judd required an education suitable to their gilded prospects, and through the mails, the services of a Miss Savage of San Francisco had been engaged.

Standing on the loading dock that day in 1887, Leona and her four daughters watched the supply train coming into view from a far distance, the sight wavering, slippery, silvery, slick as mercury in the waves of heat, congealing finally into a discernible shape that could only with certainty be called a train when the clack and rattle could actually be heard snapping down the narrow-gauge tracks. The train heaved in and disgorged its single passenger who climbed down the ladder, carrying a carpetbag and muttering, "Bloody hell. Bloody sodding heat," as she alighted on the dock. She turned and looked at the five Judds gathered to greet her, all surprised to hear such unusual, though unmistakable oaths. She blushed very slightly and then, tossing her skirt emphatically behind her in a theatrical manner, strode up to Leona with the words, "Mrs. Judd, I presume?"

Leona murmured in the affirmative.

"And these are the girls?"

Leona nodded. "Miss Savage?"

"Indeed, who else?"

Never in all their limited lives had the Judd women beheld anyone quite like Miss Savage. Of indeterminate age, Miss Savage was not particularly small, but so pathetically thin and bony that she seemed tiny, and the substantial Judd women appeared to tower over her. She had a small, sharp face, sharp nose, hollowed-out cheekbones, sharp little teeth in her small mouth. Her brown eyes were shrewd and narrow. From beneath her flamboyant (and now dust- and cinder-creped) hat, she had a crop of the reddest hair imaginable.

Miss Savage appraised them all quickly, from the

seventeen-year-old Agnes to the twelve-year-old Mabel. She turned from them and rested her gaze on the desert, which lay in every direction, the hot, wavering landscape encircled by distant mountains that looked like black ash heaps smoldering in the white distance. Her eyes traveled up the track that stretched back into the uncertain past and then her gaze turned down toward the collation of frame buildings, shacks along the single street that constituted the town of Leona. She brought her gaze back to the family and to the rhythmically thumping, throttling mine and mill emblazoned with the faded, ornate words, LEONA GOLD MINE. She was visibly, grossly, grievously disappointed.

"Have you had a long journey, Miss Savage?" asked Leona.

"How could it be otherwise?" Miss Savage replied in a manner the Judds would come to recognize: whenever possible, Miss Savage answered questions with yet another question.

In the family rig (Leona, Mabel, and Miss Savage in front, the other girls in the back) they drove down the single dusty street, past the Leona Gold Mine offices, Leona Room and Board, the Leona Post Office, Telegraph and Land Claims, past the Golden Grotto Café and the Gold Camp Laundry (both of these run by Chinese), past the Golden Nugget Saloon and the Golden Floss Saloon (this last named in honor of a misunderstood Golden Fleece). But for all this civic insistence on metallurgic substance, all that glittered was not gold. All that glittered were dust motes, raised by the rig as it traversed the unpaved street; dust gleamed golden in the sunlight as Miss Savage and the Judds rolled past tin-roofed shacks and blanket-domed lean-tos, and all the other squat, hastily assembled buildings that sheltered Indians, pigtailed Chinese, and miners, many of whom loitered in what shade there was to be had, smoking and spitting.

"Vulgar," Miss Savage announced.

"Ain't it?" said Mabel, breathing in the scent of Miss Savage's cologne, overripe and fruity despite the dust and dirt of travel. "That's our house, down yonder. Best house in the whole town."

To this Miss Savage offered a strange guttural snort.

"In the whole county," added Leona in a small voice.

They pulled into view of a grand, galleried, rambling, two-storied wedding cake of a house, set so high off the ground that sixteen shallow steps led to the broad encircling porch. The porch was shaded by a steep roof upheld by eight slender white posts, grooved and lovingly worked with pineapple formations at the tops. The cornices and balustrades of the porch balcony off the second floor were festooned with intricate bric-a-brac, half-hubs of lacy wheels so elaborate one might have believed them spiders' webs worked in wood. The eight windows fronting the street were graced with real glass and pale lace curtains, and the door was heavy with beveled, leaded glass that caught the light and ricocheted it everywhere.

A Chinese servant came out to hold the horse and rig while the ladies stepped down and went inside. Mabel hurtled forward to be the one to hold the door for Miss Savage. "My pa and ma say nothing's too good for us," said Mabel, ushering the governess into the large foyer, complete with gilded mirror and a coat tree of smooth, polished mahogany and a bin for workingmen's boots.

Miss Savage regarded the boots in the bin. "Bourgeois," she declared.

She moved into the parlor, decorated with leafy potted palms and rich, red velvet valances over the lace curtains. Despite the unmerciful heat, the Judds' parlor testified to the best of taste, everything clothed, dripping, mantled, downright shrouded in gold-tasseled velvet hangings, a red velvet settee and matching chairs equally gold-tasseled; gold tassels framed the mantel while the ornate, obese legs of the grand piano were swaddled in a white silk shawl, also heavy with gold tassels.

Miss Savage flipped open the keyboard and fingered out a little tune. "Lovely," she remarked.

Agnes was instructed to lead Miss Savage to her room and the other three followed. As they walked down the long hall toward the kitchen, they encountered a pigtailed Chinese man plucking a singed pullet and chattering to a Chinese woman peeling potatoes. The smell of burnt feathers lingered in the kitchen.

Miss Savage wrinkled her nose. "Disgusting," she stated unequivocally.

Off the kitchen, they opened the door to a small room papered in a faded gay rosebud print with a narrow bed, a spindly washstand, and a wardrobe with a cracked mirror. Miss Savage walked directly to the window and pulled aside the thin curtains that offered a view of the back porch jutting off the kitchen. There was as well a shack sheltering the washtub (also used for bathing), the privy, a clothesline strung between the shed that housed the horse and buggy and another shed where the Chinese servants slept, as well as a shaded chickenhouse and rabbit hutch. Miss Savage turned back and regarded the room. "Adequate," she said, baring her small white teeth, "but hardly inspiring."

As was his custom, Ephraim Judd came home for the midday meal. Although he owned the gold mine, Ephraim still wore heavy boots (which he threw into the boot bin and donned a more genteel pair of shoes), thick working-man's pants, and a collarless cotton shirt. He put on a collar and washed the ink and dirt from his hands before he was introduced to Miss Savage. Ephraim Judd was an unlikely rich man. Genial, tolerant, shiftless in his youth, his slack ways and uncertain means had made him the bane of his thrifty Mormon family. Ironically, his very lack of character and Mormon convictions had made him rich. He had won the gold mine in a poker game in Ma Grant's Saloon and Pleasure Palace nineteen years before, playing five-card stud with a gnarled prospector named Fitzhenry who had hunkered over his claim for years, shooting at trespassers. They were few. Who would claim-jump a worthless mine? Fitzhenry was reduced finally to gambling in a desperate attempt to secure more capital so that he might wrap his scrawny hands around those veins of gold, extract the gold he was certain lay underground. But the winning cards that day were in the loose, lazy rawboned hands of Ephraim Judd.

Of course, Ephraim could never so much as indicate to his Mormon relatives that he had been playing cards in Ma Grant's Saloon and Pleasure Palace. He moved out to the desert, lived at the old mine, and put off the family's inquiries with vague references to hard work and self-denial, which indeed were qualities he came to practice. Having won the gold mine with a royal flush, the full weight of his Mormon ancestry rose up within him and he was, in a manner of speaking, transformed by his wealth into an upright, hard-working, thrifty, steadfast man. On the basis of that single hand of cards, he not only acquired the gold mine, but sufficient prospects to ask Leona's father for her hand in marriage, and thus claim for a bride his true love. He named the mine and the town after her. For the first two years they lived in a tin-roofed shack. With the mine's modest initial success, they moved to a clapboard house with a real cookstove and glass windows. Ephraim parlayed that success into capital, the capital into machinery, supplies, and labor. He built an office and spent his days there overseeing his little empire. They had built their fabulous white wedding cake of a home when their youngest, Mabel, was two and moved in when she was three. Mabel remembered nothing of the earlier hardscrabble life and the other Judds quickly forgot.

For all his easygoing ways, Ephraim Judd was shrewd enough to hire (and pay well) the skilled mining engineer Skaggs to oversee the day-to-day operations of the mine and later, the mill. Ephraim was respected by his miners and beloved by his family; he had no airs and no affectations, and for a man whose mine brought in several hundred thousand yearly, he still sometimes put food into his mouth with his knife rather than his fork. A fact Miss Savage did not fail to note.

"I'd no idea you were this isolated," said Miss Savage in her crisp curling accent as the Chinese woman collected their plates and delivered dessert, a pudding of doubtful origin.

"Not nearly as isolated as we used to be before the telegraph," said Leona.

"I can see your daughters are certainly in need of the education befitting the children of a man who owns a gold mine." Miss Savage was appalled as she spoke these words to see Ephraim rub his nose with his napkin. "Otherwise, they would be forced to marry miners."

"Forced?" Leona's voice quavered slightly.

"Of course. A girl with money but wanting suitable education, refinements, and accoutrements, a girl who can neither play the piano, nor speak French, nor draw, a girl who knows no poetry or literature, who lacks manners and posture and social graces, who else can such a girl marry except a miner?" Miss Savage took a petite bite of the pudding. "She could marry a drover, I suppose. A clerk, possibly. A railroad man might suit. A farmer wouldn't be out of the question. A—"

"Oh no," said Leona hastily. "That would never do. Our girls must marry well."

"Latter-day Saint men," Ephraim added with an internal nod to his ancestors.

Leona was not as committed to the religion of her mythical sons-in-law as she was to their prospects. "We want our daughters to choose their husbands from the very best society."

"Exactly," Miss Savage daubed her lips. "I hope you will not think me too bold if I suggest we begin today."

"Oh, Miss Savage, you must rest today. It's such a tiring journey and—"

"I intend to rest today. I was not referring to beginning legitimate instruction." (She said the word *legitimate* with a sort of fierce affection.) "I meant I hoped you would not mind if I say to Esther that her elbows do not belong on the table, that Agnes ought not to bite her nails, and that Sarah ought not to chew her hair. Sit up, Mabel. You must sit up straight and carry yourself with a posture commensurate with your expectations in life."

"Whuh?" Mabel mumbled, her mouth full.

"You will never be a tall woman. That much is clear. You might as well enhance what you have. Sit up straight. Shoulders set. Do not allow your back to touch the chair. Carriage. Courage." Miss Savage turned to Leona. "I have a motto, Mrs. Judd, by which I have instructed girls of the best society from London to San Francisco."

"London? England?" said Agnes breathlessly.

"Isn't London the only civilized city in the world?"

"'Zat why your voice sounds so . . . so funny and curlied up?" Esther asked.

"Oh Contrare, that is why your voices sound so flat," Miss Savage replied coolly. "Your remark, Esther, further illustrates your need for suitable education. I shall imbue you all with my motto."

"And what's that?" asked Ephraim, leaning back gracelessly in his chair and picking his teeth with his fingernail.

"That young ladies may best advance themselves in this world by keeping their backs straight, their mouths shut, and their eyes on Higher Things." With that, Miss Savage rose, excused herself, and left the family dumbstruck in the dining room, with only the constant thrump and throttle of the mine and the mill echoing gently through the open windows.

Beginning the very next day, the life of the entire Judd family underwent a resoundingly thorough reconstruction, a slow and painful process. The woman who had been hired to provide the niceties for the daughters, to refit them all to their prospects in life, summarily usurped power within the family, and assumed a superiority and authority not at all in keeping with her hired status. Miss Savage was critical, high handed, demanding, and unfailingly correct. Should Leona Judd be so bold as to object to the governess's plans, methods, goals, values, or assumptions, Miss Savage deferred immediately to Mrs. Judd's judgment. Then, within the course of the next few hours, a day at most, Miss Savage found occasion to refer (in passing) to miners, drovers, clerks, railroad men, farmers, to the lives they led and the lives their wives would lead, whereupon Leona inevitably took her aside and said in so many words that she had rethought whatever was under discussion, and clearly, clearly Miss Savage was right.

Ephraim was too tolerant and malleable to object to Miss Savage outright, but he resisted in his own way. As a result, within three months of her arrival, the Judd girls were appalled at their father's table manners. However, in keeping with the Savage motto, they kept their mouths shut.

The girls themselves never got the hang of Mamá and Papá and continued to address their parents as Ma and Pa, but on the whole they were obliging pupils and followed the Savage regime dutifully. They practiced their scales on the piano and worked over the sole piece of music in the house, "The Battle Hymn of the Republic." They practiced every day, each of the four girls in turn; "The Battle Hymn of the Republic" wafted through the house and out the open windows to the street, punctuated by the thrump and roar of the mine and the mill and the twice-weekly clank and rattle of the supply train. His Truth Went Marching On.

If the Judd girls had heretofore been innocent of music, they were equally innocent of literature, the only books in their home being the usual hoary tomes: the Bible, the Book of Mormon, the Doctrine and Covenants, and *Dr. Clapp's Remedies for the Home and Farm*. Early on, Miss Savage presented Mrs. Judd with a very long list of books to be ordered from a San Francisco bookstore and brought in by the supply train. (Brought to the house in the rig, requiring the Chinese servants and a couple of miners, heaving and perspiring, to hoist the heavy crates.)

To begin with, the girls did not read these books. They walked with them. They lined up and walked back and forth across the gold-tasseled parlor with books on their heads so as to perfect their posture, while, according to the metronomic drumbeat of Miss Savage's ruler, they recited English poetry, particularly Scott's "Young Lochinvar" and Shelley's "Ozymandias," which they learned by listening to Miss Savage recite. Young Lochinvar's story was fairly obvious, but the Judd girls had not the least idea what "Ozymandias" was about and only Mabel cared.

Even Miss Savage did not seem to care; to Mabel's repeated requests for illumination, Miss Savage finally stated emphatically that a lady need not always understand poems, only recite them. "The ability to pull a line of poetry quickly from a seemingly endless well of erudition is the mark of a lady. These lines can be used to soothe any sort of situation."

"Like what?" asked Mabel.

"Time enough for that," replied Miss Savage, reciting, "Remember your rhythm, remember your cues." Her ruler beat time against her hand and the girls continued to march up and down the room, the books upon their heads.

So from nine to one, and then again from two-thirty to five-thirty on any given day, one girl thumped out "The Battle Hymn of the Republic" at the piano while the other three chanted "Young Lochinvar" and "Ozymandias," sitting, rising, walking with books on their heads. The house had the air of a persistent dress rehearsal for some monumental production that never quite came to pass.

In art, Miss Savage pronounced her pupils hopeless. She curtailed instruction in watercolor after their first outdoor painting expedition when she fainted from heat prostration and the girls returned dehydrated and spent. Miss Savage had to be helped to her bed where the girls hovered around, wringing out wet cloths for her head. "The art of painting will have to wait till you have perfected other things," said Miss Savage still in the grip of a killing headache. "Besides, in this vile climate, this beastly desert, there are no colors. There's only white sand and white sky and gray mountains and pale dust. Everywhere. How can you paint what's not there? Where are your colors? I ask you?" (She always phrased her statements as questions.) "Where are your delphiniums? Where are your daffodils? Where are your tulips and peonies and primroses? Where are your poppies? Where are your lilacs and lilies? Where?"

The girls did not know where. The Judd girls would not have recognized these flowers, nor their colors, if whole bouquets had suddenly marched down the main street of Leona, California. The girls shrugged. Miss Savage, even lying heat-prostrated, flattened by the bloody heat and aridity, admonished them for shrugging. "A lady never shrugs. It's bourgeois."

The Judd parlor served for piano, posture, and recitation. The dining room served as schoolroom with Miss Savage usurping Ephraim's place at the head of the table and the girls lined up, the two oldest on one side, Mabel and Sarah on the other. Here they studied English literature (the only literature worth knowing) and the French language (the only language worth speaking). French, Miss Savage was fond of asserting, is the single accoutrement essential to anyone who would call herself a civilized being. She went on to catalog the many accomplishments of the French race, adding that they had managed to achieve all this despite their being Catholics.

"What's that got to do with it?" asked Sarah.

"It means they have no morals," Miss Savage declared. "They simply confess their sins to a priest. He forgives them. But what of God? I ask you, will God forgive them? Has God forgiven them?" she asked with more passion than was perhaps necessary. The girls' slack chins indicated dismay, or possibly only ignorance. "Sarah, the next time I see you put your hair to your lips, I shall call in the cook—with his cleaver—and instruct him to chop off your hair at the neck. Is that understood?"

Miss Savage used no text in her French instruction, but relied upon the same principles of memorization and recitation she brought to "Young Lochinvar." She began with polite greetings and had the girls address one another till they had got it down. Then she moved on to polite conversation, most of which (at first) consisted of observations on the weather and asking to be passed certain items present at the table. She gradually moved on to forms of address, directions, descriptions, and increasingly convoluted expressions of feeling and taste, pleasure and displeasure, affirmative and negative. She perpetually prefaced her French lessons with the injunction, "Inflection and conviction! Inflection and conviction are everything!" She kept the ruler always handy to snap at the girl who was deficient in one or both.

Only Mabel seemed to have the necessary ear and quickness of tongue to correctly inflect and convict. Miss Savage approved of Mabel. Her approval was worth having. Ruler in hand she instructed the other girls to emulate Mabel's pronunciation, "Toot Sweet, Agnes! Metnaw, Esther! Oh Contrare, Sarah. Form your R's gutturally."

At the end of one particularly dispiriting session, Agnes skulked away from the dining-room table muttering unflattering aspersions on Mabel, on the French people, on the learning of the French language.

Swiftly, as though galvanized by an electric current, Miss Savage (and her ruler) came between Agnes and the door. "You have forgotten the central tenet of my motto, Agnes. You have forgotten to keep your mouth shut. Whatever you may think," (she said this last word with a kind of mocking asperity), "silence is the better part of valor. Keep your own counsel. One's own thoughts, one's own words never enhance a lady. Are you blind, Agnes? Are you so dismally deficient, all of you, that you fail to understand *why* I have spent such efforts that you should know poetry? That you should recite? That you should have at your disposal any number of appropriate, oblique well-known phrases?" Abashed, the girls did not reply; by this time they knew Miss Savage did not expect replies, that she clad her wolf-like demands in the sheep's clothing of questions. "Never betray your feelings or your ignorance. Never allow your tongue to respond more quickly than your mind. Never speak your own words when someone else's will do. No one in society does that sort of thing," she added, cooling somewhat. "It's bourgeois."

November 1917

En route to Europe

Dearest Sarah, Roy and Family—

Last night I dreamed of Ozymandias. I recited it in my dream and I heard the mine and mill behind my voice, but I could not see them. I could not see Miss Savage either, but I am certain she was there, as we were all there, all four of us as we were in our precious youth. How strange it is that as I traverse these treacherous seas, I should be drawn back to our desert girlhood. Though, perhaps, not strange at all. At last I shall see Miss Savage's England. At last I shall see France, but not alas, the France of yore, but embattled France. Pray for France and Victory.

"Frogs," said Roy, his mouth full of fried potatoes.

"What?"

"Mabel's asking us to pray for Frogs, ain't she?"

"For victory, I think," said Dumpling, scrutinizing her sister's letter more carefully. Maybe there was something she had missed.

"Don't Aunt Mabel have anything to say about the boys on the ship? You know, the soldiers?" asked Cordelia, gnawing a piece of cornbread.

"I haven't finished the letter yet," her mother replied.

"Don't she even ask about us here at home?" asked Clarence.

"Mabel's going to the Western Front!" cried Dumpling. "How can St. Elmo compare to that?"

"Now, Dumpling," Roy said genially. "No need to get angry with Clarence. Just read on."

If the Hun has his way we shall all go down in the watery deep, but our cause is just and true and God will keep us safe from U boats. I trust I shall mail this letter from English soil, that green and glorious emerald isle we only imagined as we listened to Miss Savage read to us. I am billeted here on the ship with four young Red Cross volunteers from Michigan who think my enthusiasms unwarranted and faintly comic. How can I tell them they are too young, too callow, to know that we shall soon be walking on the very soil that nourished Shakespeare and Shelley, that the English earth is the very fabric of literature itself.

"You'd think Aunt Mabel's going on the stage, 'stead of going to War," Clarence observed.

"Mabel doesn't know anything about War," said Dumpling. "But she knows literature. We never had any history when we were growing up because our teacher said that what people did was vulgar. It was what they thought and imagined and wrote that was important," Dumpling added with a little grimace; she was unaccustomed to voicing her own thoughts.

"Pass me another one-a them chops, Clarence," said Roy. "If you ask me, all you Judd girls woulda been a lot better off if your pa and ma sent you to school like regular folks. 'Course in those days, you weren't regular folks, were you?"

Dumpling shrugged and glanced out the window, to the scrap of brown lawn and the squat oleander in her front yard. She paraphrased the rest of the letter for the family and slid it into her pocket, closing her eyes for a single moment, sharing with Mabel, the dream and memory of their precious youths, their desert girlhoods, saw her beloved parents, saw four sisters in the dining room, the lace curtains blowing back with the inferno breeze, the black-ash mountains in the white unbroken distance, the thump and throttle of the mill and mine, the sand blowing gold off the unpaved street, and Miss Savage transporting them far far from gold and brass and fire, from the smelter, and the squalor, carrying them on the tide of her declamatory voice, propelling the girls to lush England, moist England where meadows and moors rolled down to turgid, slow-moving rivers, green and thick with water lilies, heavy-boughed willows weeping into the waters. Dumpling remembered Miss Savage leading them to the swarming fetid streets of Dickens' London, leading them through brawny Scotland where Sir Walter Scott characters fought in glens, where they roved, loved, and died majestically. Oh, Miss Savage regaling them, the unquenchable vivacity of her ringing voice, fictionally instructing them in the ties of obligation and responsibility that bound king to subject, captain to clown, Miss Savage tearing her hair, smiting her breast as she recited Lear's speech on the wild heath.

"I shall assume you are literate," said Miss Savage, embarking on their first lesson in literature after the three crates of books had arrived from the San Francisco bookstore. "Am I correct?"

The girls nodded in unison. If the words weren't too big, it was a fair assumption that they were literate.

"Very well. We shall dispense with reading and begin enhancing your listening skills. All young ladies who wish to marry into good society must be accomplished listeners. The ability to listen well is concomitant to keeping one's mouth shut, is it not?" (The girls all nodded.) "Elbows off the table, Esther. In the vulgar parlance, one might be said to keep one's ears open and one's mouth shut. Agnes, would you like to listen with *Ivanhoe* on your head?"

"No."

"No?"

"No, Miss Savage."

"Then sit up straight or you certainly shall. Carriage. Courage. They go together. Now, listen."

They listened. Miss Savage did not simply read. Miss Savage enacted, declaimed, incited the girls to tears and laughter, sighs and exquisite, unbearable tension as she made her way through the works of Scott, the Brontës, Dickens, Thackeray, and Shakespeare. They were in thrall to the power of the governess's voice, to her flawless inflection and conviction. She never formally concluded these classes. She simply came to the close of an appropriately dramatic chapter and closed up the book, left it on the table. Tossing her skirt theatrically behind her, she exited the dining room as though gaslight flickered, as though applause and a descending curtain would certainly follow. Every time.

One afternoon, when Miss Savage had been in their employ for nearly a year, Ephraim Judd was considerably surprised to see Leona marching up the street of the town that bore her name, coming directly to his office adjacent to the thumping mine and throttling mill that likewise bore her name. She burst in, closed the door behind her, flung herself in a chair, and began to weep for a full five minutes before Ephraim could console her sufficiently to speak. "Please, Mother. What is it?"

"Unthinkable!" Leona gasped. "Horrible! With my own ears, Father! Our daughters' virtue, Father! She is—"

"What happened, Mother?"

"I was a-walking past the dining room and I heard her reading to the girls, some piece of—of filth! Something about a woman who had a son for her cradle before she had a husband for her bed! And I stepped right in and I said, Miss Savage, really! Girls shouldn't . . . I mean young girls . . . It ain't right, Miss Savage. And you know what she did, Father?"

Ephraim removed his glasses, and rubbed the bridge of his nose, said he couldn't guess.

"She gave me one of her awful looks. Her awful, awful looks. Oh, I hate that look, Father! You know how she raises one lip so you can see her horrible little white teeth? And she says to me: King Lear."

"King who?"

"Lear. Shakespeare. She said it was Shakespeare and I wasn't to interrupt till she got to the end of the first act and I was being rude and vulgar—I tell you, it's got to stop!"

"Well, you do what you think best, Mother."

"You tell her."

"Tell her what?" Ephraim sat down and his chair squealed in protest as he turned away from the rolltop desk cluttered with ledgers and oceans of papers, accounts due on emblazoned stationery bearing the names of faraway firms.

"You are the head of the family. You dismiss her."

"It's true, she ain't exactly a pleasure to have around the house."

"She's a—she makes me feel . . . she makes us look . . ."

"Well, she's done some good, Mother. Agnes don't chew her nails anymore."

"She dipped Agnes's fingers in ground pepper."

"And Sarah don't bite her hair."

"She called Wu Chan in with his cleaver to cut it off. She actually let that heathen lift his cleaver over the neck of our daughter!"

"Well, I'm sure you're right, Mother. I don't have too much experience with young ladies, 'cept for you, Mother, and you're just about perfect." He winked affectionately.

Leona gave him a wan smile. "Maybe it's time to see the proof of the pudding, Father. Maybe it's time to take the girls into society."

"Where would that be, Mother?"

"Well, somewhere. Somewhere where there's society. All that. The girls are accomplished. We have money. Maybe it's time for husbands."

"Mabel's mighty young for a husband, Mother. She's only thirteen."

"Agnes is eighteen."

"Well, you and me didn't marry till you was almost twenty-three."

"But I was *waiting* for you, Ephraim. Agnes has to *meet* someone before, well, before . . ." Leona sniffed. "Anyway, Mabel's the one I worry about most. Mabel adores Miss Savage. Just adores her."

"Well, she'll get over that. Mabel's a sensible girl. Now, I think if I was to worry, I'd worry about Sarah. I took Sarah to the dry goods t'other day and asked her to tally a few things and bless me if she couldn't add."

"Adding is bourgeois. It's not a refinement," said Leona, unthinkingly quoting Miss Savage.

"Well, that may be. Like I say, I don't know much

about what ladies do. What do they do, Mother?" he asked earnestly. "I mean, 'sides play 'The Battle Hymn of the Republic' and talk about Young Lochinvar coming out of the West. What do you reckon these girls are going to do with all this learning?"

"They're going to get married, of course. They're going into society and meet rich young men and marry them."

"Well, yes, but what then?"

"I don't know what you mean!" she replied so as to make it clear that she knew exactly what he meant and she refused to comment.

"I don't mean that." Ephraim's tanned face crinkled into a leathery blush. "I mean—why're we educating 'em up like this? What're they gonna do with French, Mother? Why don't they read them books 'stead of carrying 'em on their heads?"

"Well, I—they—" Leona's own background had not exactly fitted her for such a question. As the daughter of a St. Elmo livery-stable worker, Leona's education had not been graced with French and Young Lochinvar. Leona had gone to school for a while, but like most girls, her real education took place at home: canning fruit, kneading bread, mixing mush, boiling, stewing, baking, bluing, washing, starching, sweeping, mopping, scrubbing, all those undertakings guaranteed to make her dauntless in the war against dirt. Leona began to cry.

Ephraim patted her hand. "If these girls grow up to be half the woman their ma is, they'll be lucky. My hope for these girls is that they grow up to be like you, Mother."

"But I want them to have every advantage," Leona wailed.

"Having you for a mother why, that's all the advantage they need." The rolltop clattered down over the papers and letters, the past-due notices on the desk. Ephraim wiped the ink from his hands. "Let's go home now and have that heathen Wu Chan make us a lemonade afore supper."

She rose and took his arm and through the glaring heat, the dust motes glowing golden in the afternoon light, they ambled the length of Leona, California, to their high, white-galleried mansion. As they approached the front door, through the open windows of the dining room, they heard Miss Savage declaim, "How sharper than a serpent's tooth it is to have a thankless child!" They glanced in to see Miss Savage smite her breast and the girls weeping unabashedly.

en route to London!

Dearest Sarah and Roy and family—

I cannot begin to tell you of the joy that greeted our ship as we steamed into Liverpool. From the decks we could see the American colors flying and hear the people on shore singing American songs and welcoming us with such fervor as is beyond my poor pen to describe. We are the saviors of Europe and universally loved. I am proud to be an American and to be lending my small efforts on behalf of the War and civilization.

But Sarah, my dear, I digress because I originally took up my pen to tell you the most wonderful thing! England! England, Sarah. We traverse the sceptered isle and I am here! I feel like Cordelia returning to assume her battered birthright.

"My battered what?" asked Cordelia, spearing a chunk of potato from the meatless stew.

"That's a different Cordelia," Dumpling replied. "Someone you don't know."

"Well, go on, Ma."

I recognize this place, Sarah! Though I have never been here. Ah, but I have! You have. We have. On the tide of Miss Savage's voice we have visited this green isle, though we grew up in the white desert. We saw England's effulgent spring, though everywhere around us was the unrelenting desert. Miss Savage led us out of that desert, Sarah. Miss Savage led us to these greener pastures.

"I thought that was Jesus' job," snickered Roy. "Just like Mabel to be all confused, not knowing her Bible from her bootstraps. There she is in Limeyland and all she can talk about is Miss Savage." He shot an arch, conspiratorial look to his wife. "And we all know what she was."

"What was she, Pa?" asked Clarence.

"She was a governess," said Sarah quickly.

"Well, go on, Dumpling," Roy chuckled.

Green. Greener. Greenest. Such color, Sarah! My eye delights, revels in the color and life swirling everywhere. The very vineyard of color, Sarah. The evening dews and damps! The glowing lamps send their radiance into the softening fog. Oh, Sarah, it is not at all new and strange, but just as I imagined it. As good as memory. This is the country of the imagination, as the desert is the country of memory.

Is it possible, Sarah dearest, to be a free citizen of both?

Speaking of being free, I must also add that I have had my hair cut. Bobbed, as they say. Several of the young nurses have done so. At the Front we must be constantly prepared and alert; we cannot be fussing with vanity and long hair. So I went with the young nurses to a Liverpool barber and off it all came! I must tell you, Sarah, you ought to have let Wu Chan chop your hair off. It is so satisfying. So liberating.

"Aunt Mabel's cut her hair!" cried Cordelia with a shriek. "Oh, can you just imagine what she looks like with it around her ears!"

Clarence laughed out loud. "Who's Wu Chan, Ma? Were you really going to bob *your* hair?"

"Mabel has cut her hair as a sacrifice to the Allied Cause," said Sarah stoutly.

"Don't sound like no sacrifice to me," said Clarence, stifling another guffaw. "Sounds like she's having a great time."

Sarah gave her son a hard look. "Your aunt is going to the Front, Clarence. I don't see anything funny in that." She returned to Mabel's letter.

Shortly I shall leave for beleaguered France, for Picardy. I am to act as translator to American and British officers working in liaison with French officers. Oh, Sarah, here at the border between the country of memory and the country of imagination, I know it is all the more imperative that we bring down the hideous Hun or he will crush civilization's finest flowers. It's as though mine eyes have been the glory of Western Civilization, Sarah dear, nay, all mankind and it is just as Miss Savage always said, Lavee, Lagair, Lamore, Lamaird! Oh, let us pray for Lagair soon to end forever and for Lamore, Lavee, and Lamaird to reign forever supreme.

"What's all that mean?" asked Cordelia.

Sarah folded the letter and tucked it in the pocket of her green checked apron. "It means, Life, War, Love, and Peace."

"In Froggy," added Roy.

Sarah drew herself up with injured dignity. "I don't think any of you understand what Mabel is going through. This is War."

"And it was made for Mabel Judd, Dumpling," chuckled Roy. "She'll come back and we won't hear of nothing else till the day she dies. It'll be Limeyland-this and Froggy-that. She'll come back talking Froggy and 'spect us to understand her every word."

Of the Judd girls, only Mabel mastered Froggy. Early on there was no doubt: Mabel was the star pupil. Mabel could recite "Young Lochinvar" and "Ozymandias" without a slip or a hitch; Mabel could best thrum out the stirring chords of "The Battle Hymn of the Republic"; Mabel (after Miss Savage had closed the books and left them on the dining-room table) snatched those books and read them, savagely in fact. Mabel read as well as listened, ingested whole chunks of Shakespeare and Dickens and Scott and the terrible Brontës. Mabel alone could walk the entire length of Leona, California, with a book on her head. One day on a taunting dare from Agnes, Mabel did just that and not merely with one book, but three.

With a look of unconquerable disdain (which she had absorbed from Miss Savage), Mabel stepped out of the family mansion and raised her chin to the correct level. Acting unofficially as her second, Sarah handed her the three books and Mabel placed them, one at a time, atop her head. While her sisters gathered on the porch, Mabel Judd walked down Leona, California's single street, that sole navigable avenue of the country of memory, the metronomic thump and throttle of mill and mine beating time, waves of sound, cresting in the waves of heat. In the boardinghouse Mrs. Skaggs, her Chinese and Indian servants, stopped work in the middle of the afternoon to peer at Mabel from their windows. On the street itself, Indians gathered to gawk and the Chinese came out of the Golden Grotto and the Gold Camp Laundry. Drunken miners and hard-bitten whores tumbled from the swinging doors of the Golden Nugget and the Golden Floss to hiss and whistle. Mabel Judd did not heed them in the least. Fourteen years old, her brown hair curling down her back, her white blouse gleaming in the fiery heat, her narrow shoulders set, her chin erect with the books balanced, her eyes on Higher Things, Mabel Judd commanded herself to inflection, conviction, courage, carriage. As she passed, guffaws died on the lips of Leona's citizens, heathen, whore, and drunk alike, taunts blew away on the desert wind. They could not have been more silent and respectful if fair Ellen or Young Lochinvar strode the gold-dusted street, if Mabel's parade had been orchestrated with lutes and harps rather than mine and mill.

Mabel's prowess clearly endeared her to Miss Savage and, just as clearly, Esther and Agnes resented her. That Mabel should be so clever and adept, was unseemly, bad, as if Mabel had got married before they did. The last should not be first. Sarah, ever her younger sister's champion and confidante, did not share these ungenerous attitudes. Sarah remained happily in awe of Mabel. On those rare occasions when Mabel did not perform up to Miss Savage's standards, Esther and Agnes snickered audibly, downright enjoyed it when Miss Savage snapped at Mabel, reprimanded her, and then ordered the rest of them out of the room, closing the dining-room doors to upbraid Mabel in private.

"I expect perfection of you, Mabel," Miss Savage declared on one of these occasions. Mabel hung her head.

"The standards are higher for you than they are for your sisters. You may actually do something with your life, other than merely to get married. To get married and buried in the same breath."

Mabel looked up. "Is that why you never got married, Miss Savage?"

"It is very rude to ask personal questions." Miss Savage ran her hands over her abundant and still fiery red hair; two years in the desert had not dimmed that hair. She sat down across from Mabel and clasped her hands neatly before her, but the prim gesture could easily become wrought emotion with a turn of the wrist.

"Is yours a tragic story, Miss Savage?" asked the undaunted Mabel. "Was he very beautiful, your lover? Was he like Young Lochinvar—you know, 'so stately his form, so lovely her face?' Did you kiss the cup and let him drink?"

"You are too young to be thinking of lovers."

"Can I think of lovers when I'm as old as Agnes and Esther?"

"Agnes and Esther will never think of lovers, Mabel. Agnes and Esther will think of husbands. Husbands and lovers are mutually exclusive terms. Men are unreliable. At best. Higher Things. It is best to think of Higher Things. Men care not the sorrow they inflict. Men exonerate themselves and blame women."

Spurred on by Miss Savage's skirting so close to some brilliant, tragic, unimaginable truth, Mabel recklessly confessed, "But I'm dying to know what it's like to be kissed, Miss Savage. That's what I want. I want to be kissed. Can't I think of Higher Things after I get kissed?"

"After that," she replied tautly, "it is increasingly difficult to think of Higher Things."

Higher Things were continually under discussion

amongst the elder Judd girls. Not higher in the same sense that Miss Savage used the term, or as Mabel understood it, but in the more immediate sense of getting out of Leona, California, getting into high society, and getting husbands. There was talk of Leona and the girls moving to Pasadena. Leona had heard there was society in Pasadena worthy of the educated daughters of a wealthy man who owned a gold mine.

Miss Savage pooh-poohed the notion of Pasadena. She made casual, cavalier reference to New York and London. She added that rich American girls were all the rage in London, and indicated with a peculiar tilt of her chin that a title might not be wholly out of the question for the Judd girls. At the very least (as she explained the legal concept of primogeniture at supper one night), younger sons of the nobility were always eager for rich, accomplished American girls.

"London's impossible and out of the question," said Leona, effectively squashing the subject. (Agnes ran from the table in tears.) The announcement rather surprised Leona herself as never in her wildest dreams had she thought she might have occasion to say those words, or anything vaguely like them. She quickly put the memory of the livery stable from her mind and glanced at her beloved husband. "I wouldn't dream of going that far away from Father. Never. My place is with you, Father."

"Well, Mother," Ephraim scratched his nose in a contemplative fashion, "Maybe I can go with you and see what all this society is about. Maybe I can go and make sure my girls marry good men. I don't care so much about their titles. I'd like good Mormon men for my girls."

"Oh, Pa—" Esther cried. "How can you say that? I want to see England and marry a noble, just like, well—whoever it was in one of Miss Savage's books."

"I just need to get a few things settled here at the mine and then, well by golly, let's all go to London if you girls won't be too ashamed of your old pa."

"When, Pa! When?"

"Well, I got a man from an Eastern syndicate coming out here next month to have a little look over our operations, and if it all goes like I reckon it will, well I think he'll buy me out for a pretty good bunch of money. Yessir, a good chunk of money, so's I can come with you and make sure my girls get real men for husbands."

"Will you come too, Miss Savage?" asked Mabel. "Please say you'll come."

"Indeed I will not. I have done what I set out to do here." The flash of her sharp teeth lit a fleeting smile. "I have other offers. Quite good offers."

"How could you?" asked Esther. "You never get a speck of mail. All the time you been here, I reckon you haven't got but half a dozen letters and you said all those were from your sister in England."

"It is as rude to comment on other people's mail as it is to read it. Back straight, *mouth shut,* Esther. Eyes on Higher Things. Whatever I do when I leave this abominable desert, is none of your concern."

"I want to go with you, Miss Savage," Mabel cried.

"Mabel!" Leona remonstrated.

"But I do!" she wailed. "I don't want to go into society! I'm too young for a husband!"

Leona was about to further chastise her youngest when Ephraim cut in saying all this was just a lot of jawing till the man from the Eastern syndicate arrived and the few things with the mine got settled.

With the arrival, the following month, of the man from the Eastern syndicate, a good deal more than that got settled, when Mr. Charles Norby, representing Empire Mining and Milling, a cartel of Eastern bankers and industrialists, arrived on the supply train, bringing with him, to Ephraim's surprise, a fair young man named Pilch. Abner Pilch. A recent graduate of the Colorado School of Mines.

Abner Pilch was about twenty-five, six feet tall, and weighed in at about 180 pounds of muscle and fur (the latter easily imaginable given the luxurious blond hair atop his head and the thatch of hair on the backs of his big, capable hands). He was—as the girls managed to discover by inquiring after Mrs. Pilch—unmarried. And so, for Abner Pilch, the girls' education came to its finest fruition; they burst into gilded flower, befitting the children of a man who owned a gold mine. On Abner Pilch was bestowed two years of sweating and straining and reciting and piano-pounding and posturing, two years of having their manners retooled and their language enhanced. Lavished on Abner Pilch were two years of mottos and admonitions and injunctions, their eyes continually on Higher Things as they endured the sharp sting of the ruler on their wrists, the pain of gnawed nails thrust in ground pepper, the wink of Wu Chan's cleaver blinking over the mane of hair. The finest flower of young womanhood bloomed forth in the desert, in the Judd parlor after dinner as Agnes rendered "The Battle Hymn of the Republic" and Esther recited "Young Lochinvar" (with special loving emphasis donated to the maidens more lovely by far "who would gladly be bride to young Lochinvar"). Sarah rose to bring that traveler from that antique land, and to recite deathless lines about the shattered visage of "Ozymandias," king of kings, to extoll the heartbreak of "that colossal wreck, boundless and bare" right into the Judd parlor. So entranced was Mr. Pilch, he did not even clap till Ephraim grinned and gave an enthusiastic round of applause.

Mabel was called upon to recite from Shakespeare and

chose Lear's speech on the heath, beating her young breast in the manner of Miss Savage. The girls shone brilliantly for Abner Pilch while Ephraim and Leona looked on proudly. While Miss Savage eyed Mr. Norby.

Mr. Norby was about forty years old. By the same subtle means used on Mr. Pilch, the girls discovered there was a Mrs. Norby, but this was not of any enduring interest. Compared to the beautiful Mr. Pilch, Mr. Norby was of small concern, though he was attractive in a florid, well-fed way, his manner both affable and crisp. Mr. Norby had indicated during dinner that he foresaw a great future with Empire Mining and Milling, that he would not long be traversing these antique lands, these boundless, barren deserts, doing business in the killing heat. He wore a real suit and a massive gold watch on a chain draped across his torso and he occasionally patted the watch as though to reassure himself his time in boundless bareness, these desert dumps, was finite.

The windows in the parlor were open to admit such breeze as there was, though the breeze was unkind, bringing in with it the smelting odor of the mill and the grit and sand and unlit dust from the street. It was intolerably hot and Miss Savage got out her hanky, daubed the moisture beading her lip. The hanky slipped from her hand, and Mr. Norby, with the gallantry Young Lochinvar himself might have envied, reached to retrieve it. Their fingers brushed momentarily, and they both excused themselves.

The gala evening ended with everyone singing "The Battle Hymn of the Republic," though the Judd girls alone knew all the verses, and then Ephraim said that he and Mr. Norby and Mr. Pilch had a long day before them tomorrow and everyone had best get some sleep. But then Ephraim's brow furrowed: the boardinghouse could not accommodate two men, not when they had been expecting Mr. Norby alone. Of course, there were the rooms above the saloon, but prudently Ephraim did not mention these. He said Mrs. Skaggs's boardinghouse was pretty primitive for men from the East.

"It don't matter to me," said Mr. Pilch genially, "I'm from Idaho. I slept with mice and I slept with lice. I can sleep any old where."

The girls thought this wonderfully witty, and Esther suggested why didn't the family put both men up, that she and Agnes could double up with Sarah and Mabel. Mr. Pilch and Mr. Norby could have their bed. "I mean," Esther flushed, "our room."

"Yes," Agnes chimed in, positioning herself strategically behind Mabel. "Mr. Pilch can sleep in our room just fine. Mabel is glad to sleep on the floor." And then, swiftly, before Mabel's objections could spring to her lips, Agnes dealt her an emphatic kick.

"Perhaps Miss Savage might be kind enough to give up her room for the night," Leona said sweetly. "She could have Wu Chan's bed. I'm sure Wu Chan can go, well, somewhere for the night. He's Chinese," she added as though this explained everything. "Miss Savage could sleep with Li Chun in their quarters outside."

"Preposterous. Out of the question," said Miss Savage, biting down sharply on the *not bloody likely* that fluttered just under her tongue.

A good many offers and counteroffers and objections and proposals flew around for at least twenty minutes till at last it was decided that all the girls would sleep in Sarah and Mabel's room, that the three older girls would share the big bed and a pallet on the floor would be laid for Mabel. Mr. Norby and Mr. Pilch could have Agnes and

Esther's room. Miss Savage would keep her own quarters, as would Wu Chan and Li Chun.

It was a restless night. Leona lay awake wondering if Abner Pilch were good enough for her daughters and if so, whether Agnes or Esther ought to get him. Ephraim lay awake worrying that he had not reckoned on Mr. Pilch at all. He had reckoned on dealing with an Easterner, a man who would content himself with talk of money and tonnage and contracts. Talk only. Not a mining engineer. Not a graduate of the Colorado School of Mines. Not a man who could probably sniff out the declining quality of the ore with his nose, much less detect it with a trained professional eye. Ephraim lay awake wondering how he could gracefully alert his foreman, Skaggs, before the morning light. He decided it could not be done gracefully, but it must indeed be done, that he must rise before dawn and go to Skaggs, warn him, instruct him as to what could be said—and what could not.

Mabel lay awake twisting and turning on her blanket laid over the hard floor, thinking it patently unfair that she should be assigned the floor simply because she was the youngest, wishing she could have traded quarters with the Chinese. At least they had beds. She tossed, slept fitfully, waking often, wondering finally if she might not be more comfortable on the red velvet settee in the parlor, knowing that if she took her blanket and pillow in there, she would have to wake before dawn and be back in her room before the rest of the house was up and about. Ma would die of shame to find her in the parlor in her nightdress when men were present.

The very idea of men present kept the other girls awake, giggling over the muffled question of which side of Agnes and Esther's bed would Mr. Pilch lay his fair head, and if, in the morning, they might find some token of his esteem lying beneath that pillow.

Mr. Pilch slept like the dead.

Mr. Norby decided to have a cigarette, got out of bed, pulled on his pants and suspenders, buttoned his shirt halfway up, took his papers, tobacco and some matches, and stepped quietly out the door of the room, tiptoed down the long hall till he found the kitchen. He crossed the kitchen and stepped out on the back porch, rolled a cigarette, and lit up, listened to the nocturnal desert creatures scurry about the godforsaken brush. He inhaled and looked to the star-spangled sky, chips of light grated unevenly over the unrelenting blackness.

Miss Savage put on her nightdress and took down her savage red hair. She took her candle to the cracked mirror on the wardrobe where she met her reflection, skewered and oddly angled, as though the two sides of her face would forever disagree. She touched the knobs of her collarbone gingerly. At the sound of footsteps, she blew out the candle and made her way across the tiny room, parting the thin curtain, looked out to the back, to the endless desert and the outbuildings clustered close in like uncertain moths snuggling up to the white flame of the house. Her gaze lingered on the shack where the Chinese slept and she muttered something deprecating about the very bloody idea of Leona Judd's offering her the Chinaman's bed. She was about to drop the curtain when a glow caught her eye from the porch, a tiny fiery gleam piercing the darkness, moving swiftly upward. To a man's lips.

A few minutes later, Mr. Norby wheeled about. "Miss Savage! You startled me!"

"I saw you smoking from my window," she said, clutching her shabby calico wrapper against her white nightdress. "I wondered if I might trouble you for a cigarette."

Mr. Norby's eyes lit with surprise. Even in the darkness she could see the surprise. He said by all means. He rolled her a cigarette.

"A cigarette now and then is civilized," she declared defensively.

"I'm not like some men," he assured her. "I say if men can smoke, why not women?"

"Why not indeed?"

He lit the match and cupped his hands protectively around the thin flame; Miss Savage bent into the light which, for that moment illuminated her sharp face, her wild red hair. Mr. Norby held the match till it burnt his fingers. "There ain't much civilized out here. A lady like you, I don't know how you bear it."

"One must eat, Mr. Norby. One must live."

"Here?" He gestured to the desert beyond the puny, clustered buildings.

"We are villains by necessity, fools by heavenly compulsion."

"What?"

"Shakespeare."

"Oh." They continued to smoke silently, standing side by side till Miss Savage shivered slightly. "Now if I'd known you was to join me, Miss Savage, I'd have worn my coat and I could offer it to you. Hot by day and cold by night, this godforsaken hell. Excuse me, I mean—"

"Do not excuse yourself, Mr. Norby. I am not Agnes Judd, a green girl. God was right to forsake this country. God showed more sense than men."

Mr. Norby flicked the butt of his cigarette into the brush.

"You mustn't do that," she cautioned him. "You must be sure to put it out completely. It's very dry here. Things burn here. They burn."

He stepped off the porch and retrieved the glowing butt, ground it under his heel. He turned back to look at her, her nightdress gleaming white where the shabby wrapper was undone, her bright hair illuminated by starlight, the veil of night itself kind to the hard planes of her taut face. Miss Savage finished her cigarette, watching Mr. Norby who moved closer, and remarked that her feet were bare. "Let me put that out for you."

"Please."

He took the butt from her fingers and stomped it out in the dust. Mounting the porch steps, he stood close by her. "It's a hard life out here for a lady beautiful as you."

"A woman, Mr. Norby," she replied, her husky voice reverberating in her narrow chest.

He touched her hair, took her in his arms, astonished to feel her fragility, astonished that such a tiny woman could answer his hands and lips with such fire and vivacity; as his hands sought the rounded tips of her breasts, the calico wrapper gave way under his eagerness. Miss Savage thrust herself against his eagerness, knowing exactly where and how to thrust so that she might enjoy and exacerbate the throbbing impact of his body. Mr. Norby groaned against her hair, laced his arms across her back, and pulled her high to meet his lips again and again.

"Not here," she said at last, whispering harshly, "not here."

"Where then?"

"My room. Let me go first. I'll open the window for you. Can you come through the window?"

"I'll do anything. Anything you ask."

Miss Savage slid down his body, splaying her hands across his torso. "What is your name?" she murmured, placing her forehead against his ample chest, "your Christian name."

"Charles. What's yours?"
"Flora."

December 1917

Darling Sarah—

I have seen the fearful lightning of His terrible swift sword. I have seen such things as my pen refuses to describe. Such carnage. Such putrefaction. Such horror, Sarah darling, but not, alas, wholly the horrors of War. You cannot know, nor guess the degradation I have endured. The disgrace. The humiliation. The shame. Oh Sarah, I burn to think of it. And shame visited not simply on my head, but implicating you, dear sister, implicating Esther and Agnes and our dear dear parents whom death hath mercifully spared this revelation.

"What's your parents got to do with the War? Shut that baby up!" Roy barked. "Can't a man come home without hearing a baby wail? Shut him up."

"Her, Roy. The baby is a her."

"I don't care what it is! A man's entitled to some peace at home. You took care of your children, Dumpling. Why can't your daughter look after hers? She's a married woman. Why don't she keep them at home?"

"Cordelia, you go in and soothe your niece."

"I want to hear Aunt Mabel's letter. I want to hear about disgrace and degradation."

"Keep your back straight and your mouth shut, Cordelia and do as I ask."

"Yes, Ma."

"That's better," said Roy, unlacing his boots as the baby's wails softened in the other room. "Now go on. What's Mabel talking about? I swear, Dumpling, I never could understand a word that woman says."

"Mabel means well."

"I'm not saying she don't. Now, go on, what's all this about disgrace?"

But Sarah's eyes had already quickly traversed the page as best she could, given her limited literacy skills, and for her husband she paraphrased Mabel, saying that the conduct of the War was a disgrace to all right-thinking Americans, which would have included herself, Esther and Agnes and their late parents.

She tucked the letter in her apron pocket, not pulling it out until Roy was asleep in the living room with the St. Elmo *Herald-Gazette* spread across his chest, not until Clarence and Cordelia had gone off to the church young people's Mutual Improvement Association, not until the restless granddaughter fell asleep with oil of camphor on the teething gums. Even then Sarah took the letter into the bathroom, locked the door before continuing.

I have been relieved of my post as interpreter working in liaison with the French. I have been, in a word, sacked, and under such circumstances as no decent woman should have to endure. The truth of it, Sarah darling, is that I cannot speak French. You cannot speak French. We cannot speak French. We never have. We never will. Miss Savage (O thou aptest of names) cruelly abused our innocence and the trust of our parents. In the guise of the French language she taught us merely a collection of nasal intonations, throaty-R's and strings of sounds correctly inflected, but signifying nothing. Would that were the worst of it, my dear sister. Would that I could will my pen to halt here, but you must, you shall know the excruciating truth.

Not everything she taught us was a jumbled lump of

sounds. There were words. Words such as you and I, our sisters, our parents, would never have dreamed of speaking, not if devils sloshed our bodies with burning oil would we have uttered such phrases. But utter them we did. Utter them we have. Filthy beyond belief. In our dewy innocence we thought we were conducting polite intercourse. Nay. We referred unblushingly to the parts, the bodies of men and women and animals, those secret parts of women, the male member, that part common to men and women and animals for the use of defecation. Defecation itself. Excrement, Sarah, those lumps of ordure issued from the body. In the most vulgar parlance of all, Sarah, and described in French as Lamaird. Peace? We were taught Lamaird, peace? Peace! We exhorted to Life, War, Love, and Shit. My pen cannot spare you further. Shit. Lamaird is the word for shit.

Sarah wept audibly, stuffing her apron into her mouth to stifle the sobs as she continued reading.

When I spoke French, as I knew it, the French officers at first paled and then blushed and then burst out at me with a volley of abuse recognizable in any tongue. I stood by, confused, appalled, asking, as best I could to be informed of the problem, and with each word I spoke, their anger mounted and their arms flailed and their shouts deafened me till the American colonel demanded to know what I had said, why the French were screaming at me, why they ordered one of their own to come drag me from the room, to lock me up, while I cried out at the injustice, while I was marched, nay, dragged from the room protesting my innocence, shouting Lavee! Lagair! Lamore! Lamaird!

The French locked me in a tiny room with a single table, a candle, and a cot. I stayed there, fearful and uncomprehending for hours, knowing not how I had offended. Not until one of the French translators came in to question me was I given full, brutal knowledge of my transgression. Our transgression.

In our unspoilt innocence, Sarah, we greeted people as the dirty rumps of dogs and sheep. We said to men that they committed unspeakable acts with animals. We said to women that they committed unspeakable acts with everyone for pay. We asked not to be passed condiments of the table, but the smelly effluvia of old women, the procreative juices of men. We believed we were expressing pleasure in someone's company, but in fact, we were commenting approvingly on the length of the male [scratched out] *and when we believed we were complimenting someone on a job well done, we were telling them that they had passed gas with fire. I cannot continue. This is but a portion of the French that tripped daily from our virginal lips under the instruction of that viper. That serpent. That devil, Miss Savage. When the French translator told me these things I endured as much as I could before begging him to stop. Next the British and Americans questioned me. Satisfied finally that I was but the victim of a cruel, cruel hoax and not an agent of the Hun, they released me from incarceration and ordered me to return home.*

I refused. I cried, I begged, I demanded, I vowed to do whatever was required of me, whatever the War might ask. I volunteered to go into the trenches if need be, but please, please do not send me home to St. Elmo, to allow this story, this mockery of everything my parents believed in, this folly and disgrace to follow after me.

At last they relented. As I have no training as a nurse, I will do the low work assigned me. I receive no pay. I want none. I carry bedpans of bloody urine and I wash bloody rags and burn bloodied bandages and boil bloodied scalpels. I beat down beds that men have died in. I throw disinfectant on the floors where they have vomited. I pull soiled pants from their blasted legs.

Can you imagine how the story of my disgrace has spread all through the lines? The Americans, the French, the British all know of it and laugh at me. Perhaps the Hun is laughing too. Perhaps even heaven laughs at me. My dearest darling sister, I may tell you that I am mocked, yes, but I am not beaten. I shall redeem my honor. I shall keep my own counsel. But at night, Sarah dearest, in the privacy of sleep, the only privacy vouchsafed us at the hospital stations, I toss on my pallet and dream of Miss Savage. I see her in my dream as I saw her that one terrible, terrible dawn, that fleeting glimpse of the woman sitting naked at the edge of the bed, her hands folded in her lap, her small white teeth bared in

Sarah could read no further. She crumpled the letter tightly in her hand while her breath came hard and sharp, stabbing swiftly through her breast to remember that infamous dawn when their home was split asunder by screams. Shrieks, blast after blast, shot through the house, resounding from the hall when her father had collided with Mabel, clutching her blanket, standing face-to-face with the naked Mr. Norby carrying his clothes, coming into the hall. And visible across the expanse of the kitchen, Miss Savage's door flung open and the woman herself seated, smiling, naked on the edge of the bed.

Sarah glanced once again at the cruel words peering up

from the crumpled sheet, and she suffered yet another pang when she imagined Esther and Agnes's reaction to the hideous cruelty perpetrated against their innocence and the innocence of their parents. The blood descended rapidly from her head, leaving her woozy, slightly nauseous, but then, Sarah collected herself. She forcefully, physically commanded her body to obey while she sorted through her thoughts. Why should Esther and Agnes know? Why? She asked herself again and again, psychically shaking off the name Dumpling and all its implications. Why indeed?

Sarah acted in haste, took the fetid letter to the kitchen sink where she struck a lucifer and lit it afire, pushing open the kitchen window so the smoke should not waft into the living room and disturb her sleeping, unsuspecting husband. Trembling, but filled with the conviction of her own correctness, she watched the letter burn, hoping that the flame that consumed the paper would likewise consume the soul of Miss Savage for time and all eternity. And even at that, Sarah could not imagine her repentant.

The baleful task fell to Ephraim. After the terrible events of that dawn, Leona was bedridden. Mabel was sentenced to the dining room, and the doors closed sharply. She was ordered not to come forth till Ephraim himself should release her. The other girls, sobbing, were ordered back in the bedroom. Mr. Norby and Mr. Pilch (for he was implicated—somehow) had been dispatched from the house by the dawn's early light, angrily ordered into the streets of Leona, California.

Ephraim gulped as the two men stepped into the desert dawn, walking toward the Golden Grotto, knowing that word of their abrupt departure from his house would percolate quickly from the Golden Grotto through every Indian nook and Chinese cranny, amongst the miners and the whores alike. Knowing, too, that he now had not the slightest chance of conferring with Skaggs. But he closed the door on their retreating backs and it was done. Worse lay in store. Much worse. But now, more immediately, Ephraim must confront the terrible matter of the infamous Miss Savage. Should he—

His dilemma was cut short by the appearance of Miss Savage herself. Her hair done up, her collar neatly bound about the neck, the jacket of her suit buttoned, her movements brisk as ever, she strode into the foyer in complete possession of herself, in complete possession of the situation. At the very sight of her, the ghosts of Ephraim Judd's Mormon ancestors rose up in fury, screaming at him to assume the patriarchal stance, accost the evildoer with the full weight of her transgression against God, humanity, and the family that had taken her unto their very bosom. But Ephraim could only glare at her.

"You shall have to do better than gawk at me, Mr. Judd," she said lightly, placing her carpetbag on the floor and brushing the feather on her hat.

"You're no better than a common . . . a common . . ."

"Whore? I beg to differ. I am not a whore and I am certainly not common. Oh Contrare. You are common. You and your family are insufferably common. Bourgeois," she added the stinging epithet remorselessly, "vulgar, and I despise you. I have always despised you. You and your common wife and your foolish virgin daughters—"

"Do not mention my daughters!" cried Ephraim. "Get out of this house!"

"Oh, I am leaving, Mr. Judd. But not in disgrace. Call it what you like, but not disgrace. I am a woman of the world. I have seen and done and endured what a man as common and limited as you cannot even guess at."

"Of course you have! You . . . you bawd!" he shouted, retrieving the word from the long-ago days at Ma Grant's Saloon and Pleasure Palace.

She jabbed her hatpin through the crown of her hat. "I have given your daughters the only moments of illumination their sorry lives will ever know."

"Out! Get out!"

"When they are married, when your daughters are drudges to drovers, chattels to farmers, sex slaves to nasty-minded little clerks and hulking railroad brutes, they will remember me! I have spent my life revenging myself on people like you, Mr. Judd, on your smugness, and certainties, on your pretensions and your assumptions and your pious, untested values."

"No decent woman—"

"Ha! I despise decency, Mr. Judd. Loathe it. Decency and complacency and stupidity, they are inseparable. I have nothing but contempt for them, for you." She laughed, baring her small, white teeth, and cried out, "Lavee! Lagair! Lamore! Lamaird!"

And with that, she picked up her bag, the same bag she had come with two years before and marched through the door, retrieving her coat from the hook, and stepped out to the porch and into the pale, relentless glare of morning, leaving the door ajar behind her. She walked, looking neither right nor left, down the single yellow ribbon-road of Leona, California, to the dock to await the supply train due that morning.

From the window of Golden Grotto Café, Mr. Norby watched her tiny figure retreat, the sun brazenly lighting her red hair. "What a woman," he murmured.

"You must have been out of your goddamned mind,"

said Abner Pilch (proving himself once and for all, unworthy of the Judd girls). "You are a goddamned fool."

"What a woman," Mr. Norby sighed and returned to his hash, grits, eggs, and coffee.

March 1918

Beaumetz-les-Cambrai

My dear sister—

They sing a song here, Sarah, "The Bells of Hell Go Ting-a-ling-a-ling," but no hell created by Satan could equal this creation of man's. Mine eyes have seen the coming of the end. How can the world survive this? This mire of blood and squalor and Lamaird. Truly those words, Lagair, Lamaird were meant to be spoken in the same breath. Did Miss Savage know?

I wear a Red Cross emblem on my sleeve, but the emblem itself is splattered with blood. I cannot keep it clean. I have not slept in 24 hours. I dare not sleep now. If I did, I would sleep like the dead and there are too many of them. Besides, the near-dead need me. I have held down boys no older than Clarence while their legs and arms were amputated to save their lives, though many will die of infection. Some have had their limbs shot off. I think of Clarence constantly, though I must in all candor tell you I never much liked him, but he is in my thoughts constantly when I see fair-haired youngsters, their lips twisted in the unmistakable grimace of death. Boys, all of them are boys. The soldiers have all died. The French and English and Germans alike are sending young boys to be slaughtered. Boys like Clarence. The waves of the dead are inexorable and still there is no peace. No life. No love. Only blood and slaughter, Lagair,

Lamaird, only those obscenities and shelling and gas and bombs and rockets screaming, artillery and mortar fire exploding. Rain. It is endless. It never stops. Like the sound of the mill and the mine, that constant rumble and thump beaten into the very furrows of your brain, that

"Open up, Ma." Cordelia rapped at the bathroom door. "I need help with my costume, Ma. I can't find my torch."

Sarah flushed the toilet, turned on the taps in the sink, and quickly washed her face, bringing it, dripping, out of her hands to meet her gray reflection. She folded her sister's letter and put it in her pocket and opened the door to behold Cordelia dressed as the Statue of Liberty for the Liberty Bond Drive parade in downtown St. Elmo.

"Ma? You look awful, Ma. You seen a ghost? You look—"

"Your torch is in the kitchen. I will get it." Sarah clenched her teeth and went into the kitchen for the papier-mâché torch. She found Clarence practicing his salute in front of the tiny mirror by the back door. "What are you doing?" She demanded.

"Practicing," he replied with a grin.

"What for?"

"For when I join up, Ma. Soon's I'm eighteen, I'm going to join up and hinky dinky parley voo."

Sarah walked up to her son who towered over her. She stared into his youthful face, his empty blue eyes, his unfurrowed brow, and unwillingly she saw the twisted grimace of death, the obscenity of his ignorance. Sarah slapped his face.

Clarence winced; tears and shock struggled over his features. "You shouldn'ta done that, Ma. I'm a man now. Shouldn'ta done that to a man, Ma."

"Shut up, you little fool."

Clarence bolted from the kitchen, the screen door squealing, slamming in protest. Chest heaving, Sarah stared out to the laundry flapping on the lines and from the center of town she could hear the high school band futilely warming up to the opening accolades of "The Battle Hymn of the Republic."

"Close that piano this instant! I never want to hear that song again!" Leona barked as Mabel fingered out the tune. "Never, never again."

"Yes, Ma."

"Are you packed?"

"Yes, Ma."

"Then go get your coat. We're leaving."

"Yes, Ma."

"And don't walk like that!"

"Like what, Ma?"

"Like that. With your shoulders straight and as though . . . as though . . ."

"I'm never going to be a tall woman, Ma."

"Just do as I say. I can't bear it."

"Can't bear what?"

"And don't answer me with a question!"

Leona Judd adjusted her hat and looked around the home she was leaving forever. For once, it was quiet. Only the desert wind could be heard, its little yellow claws scratching at the windows, gnawing at the doorframe, snapping at the gold tassels festooning the room. No more thump and throttle of the mine and mill. The mine and mill were closed till further notice from Empire Mining and Milling. Abner Pilch had found what he was not supposed to have found, what a graduate of the Colorado School of Mines would probably have found even if

Ephraim had briefed Mr. Skaggs. And news of what Abner Pilch found rippled through Leona, California, even more quickly than (and right on the heels of) the story of Miss Savage, the (ha ha) governess and Mr. Norby, the (ha ha) man from the Eastern syndicate who bought the gold mine at a fraction of what he'd originally been willing to pay. Moreover, the Judds saw only a penny of that pittance, because aside from the shattering discoveries in the mine itself, there were equally shattering discoveries to be made in the books and ledgers, papers in the rolltop desk, shrill demands for payment long, long overdue from firms far, far away.

In 1889, the Judds closed the door of the white wedding cake of a house for the last time and walked down the gold-dusted single street carrying their few bags to the dock to await the supply train from St. Elmo. On the day they left, the town already seemed forlorn, deserted, vanquished: the miners had been given drafts drawn on Empire Mining and Milling instead of their last month's pay and many of them, predictably, got drunk and looted businesses, most of which had already been closed down anyway. Certainly the industrious Chinese seemed to have vanished overnight and as the Judds walked down the street, the doors on their empty shacks squealed and banged in the wind. Broken windows of the Golden Grotto, the Gold Camp Laundry, and the dry goods store gaped at them like open maws. A can of peaches rolled lazily down the step and seemed to shine and wink and beckon, pawing at Mabel's skirt like a lost cur. Dust blew into her eyes and she rubbed them against the gilded glare. When they reached the dock, the wind picked up; sepia sand blew over the narrow-gauge tracks and a hard knot of fear congealed inside Mabel as she prayed for the train to get there. Soon. Fast. Now. Before the sand swallowed the track altogether and snatched away their every hope of escape.

The Judds limped back into St. Elmo with their suitcases, a few hatboxes, and a trunk of household goods, in short with nothing to show for the glory days of their gold-mine grandeur. Empire Mining and Milling took over Leona, California, and stripped their great white house of all its furniture and accoutrements. Indians moved into the shell, some two dozen of them, whole families, toothless grandmothers and squalling babes hunkered down in the high, airy, splendid rooms. The house was rendered all the more ghostly when a fire started in the Golden Floss and leveled everything between there and the Judds' home, the flames licking out, reaching the lacy balustrades just before the wind reversed. The blaze went in the other direction and finally died, burnt out, exhausted. After that, the Indians left Leona, California.

Perhaps their financial and social disgrace ought to have destroyed Leona and Ephraim as well, but it did not. Almost immediately Ephraim found work at the St. Elmo Feed and Seed; he spent the rest of his days measuring out oats and alfalfa to leather-palmed ranchers. He died in 1912. Bereft without him, Leona died in 1913. She was a loyal wife first and foremost, so the reversal of their fortunes did not fundamentally alter her intrinsic self. If she shed tears for her daughters' shattered prospects, she did so privately and without a word to any of them.

The family stayed in St. Elmo where the girls' ability to play "The Battle Hymn of the Republic" went untested. No one noticed or gave a good goddamn that the Judd girls could walk with books on their heads: chin up, back straight, mouth shut, and eyes on Higher Things. That they were poor and plain did not stop Agnes, Esther, or

Sarah from marrying, from marrying young. Nothing stops a Mormon girl from marrying. Their husbands resembled Young Lochinvar only insofar as they came out of the West: Latter-day Saint men, farmers, and clerks and railroad men. As married women, Agnes and Esther and Sarah cursed their rudimentary math skills when they tried to balance narrow household budgets and saved the rag ends of soap and bone and bits of gristle; they denounced their limited literacy when they struggled with recipes for eggless cakes and red-eyed beans, as they skimmed grease off stews and saved it, as they covered up the holes in their stockings with boot blacking, as they burnt their fingers on hot, heavy irons and rose before dawn on inferno-summer days to build washday fires, to bake cornbread they would eat without butter. They cursed "Ozymandias" that they could not sew a patch on a pair of workingman's pants, or dye a rusty skirt to make it look like new, or put up a jar of peaches without the rot seeping in, curdling the peaches to a sickish bronze. Among them, Agnes and Esther and Sarah bore twenty-one children; they nursed, and dispensed, sat by the sickbeds, buttoned the hand-me-down shoes and shirts and dresses of those twenty-one children while they cursed King Lear and Sir Walter Scott and Shelley and Dickens and the Brontës, while they cursed the French language.

All except Mabel. Suitors came and went, but Mabel Judd kept her eyes on Higher Things, wore her specs to see those Higher Things more clearly, went to work at the library, and kept her back straight and her chin up and her mouth shut. When she did open her mouth, she was blunt to a fault. At first her sisters bore her carping presence, bore her intolerance of their shortcomings with Christian forbearance, pitying her for her unmarried state. Then, increasingly they grew bitter and snappish.

"Zeke swore if she told him not to eat with his knife again, he'd walk out and never come back," Agnes complained to Esther and Sarah as the three gathered in Sarah's kitchen Christmas Eve, 1907.

"Mabel means well," said Sarah, flouring her rolling pin.

"Oh, you always say that, Dumpling. She's out there right now with the men in the living room. Your husband don't think she means well, Dumpling, I can tell you that. She's always telling Roy he can't say ain't, correcting his grammar, and criticizing his clothes." Agnes plunged another clove into the thick white rind of fat enveloping a scrawny ham. "Why isn't Mabel in here with us, helping? She eats, don't she? She can just get in here and help the women."

"Mabel doesn't cook, Agnes. You know that."

"That's 'cuz she lives with Ma and Pa. I told Ma, Christmas Eve, Ma, you don't need to cook. We'll do it. I said it right in front of Mabel and she just stayed sitting where she was, looking at me like . . . like . . . looking right through me. Like I wasn't even there."

"Just like Miss Savage," said Esther, peeling parsnips into a newspaper spread across her lap. "Mabel's getting more like Miss Savage every year."

"Oh, Esther, how can you even say that woman's name in the same breath with Mabel's?" Dumpling cried.

"Why not?" Agnes demanded. "Mabel says it enough. And don't you think she don't. My Becky comes home t'other day and asks me to tell her all about Miss Savage. That's right! By name. That whore-of-Babylon's very name. Becky says she heard it from a friend of hers, a girl who's at the library, talking to Mabel. Mabel's going on and on about learning Shakespeare and poetry and literature and French from our governess, Miss Savage, and how Miss Savage gave us all these wonderful refinements." Agnes bit down hard on the last word, like the end of a line of thread. "I set Becky straight. Right there. Right then. I can tell you that."

"Well, when all that happened, Mabel was just too young to understand what . . ." Esther frowned and parsnip skins flew from her fingers. "You know what I mean. Maybe Mabel didn't understand what she saw that night. Maybe she still doesn't. She isn't married, you know."

To her sisters' surprise, Dumpling laughed out loud. "How can you *not* understand when you're face-to-face with a naked man? When your own Pa comes out and finds you, screaming, face-to-face with a naked man?"

"I'm only saying . . ." Esther intervened.

"And on top of that—" Dumpling went on, determined to be done with evasion, "from that naked man, Mabel had only to look across the kitchen and the door to Miss Savage's room was wide open and Miss Savage was sitting on the bed, stark naked, too. Married or unmarried, you understand that! It don't take marriage to make you understand that!"

The parsnips fell from Esther's hand and Agnes dropped her clove. They said, more or less in unison, *she saw that?*

"Yes." Dumpling deflated a bit; her sisters could always cow her.

"And even after *that,* Mabel went down to the dock to wait for the train with her?"

"Yes. She went to the dock to wait for the train with Miss Savage. Miss Savage just sat there without even speaking for a long time, without even looking at Mabel till she took her hand."

"We never heard this, Dumpling! What happened then?"

"You want to know past that, you'll have to ask Mabel

yourself." Sarah wiped her hands fiercely on her apron. "But I won't hear anything more said against Mabel. Not in my house. You do what you want in your own place, but not here."

"I hope I have not done you a great disservice." Miss Savage clutched Mabel's hand, but kept her gaze riveted to the narrow-gauge tracks before her, the distant desert beyond. "I came here never thinking I would grow to care for you. For anyone. Thinking I was beyond caring for anyone. But you—you are different, Mabel." She squeezed the girl's hand tightly and then released it. "You are special."

"Thank you, Miss Savage."

"The train should be here soon."

"Yes, Miss Savage."

"You have a mind, Mabel. That is more important than a gold mine. Twenty years ago I might not have said such a thing, but it is true. Gold, beauty, your very health, your ideals, your family and friends, they may all be snatched from you, but your mind is your own. If you have your mind and courage, you can do a great many things in this world. People will always tell you that you can't. People will always be telling you what you can't do, but you mustn't heed them."

"Just like I didn't heed Pa when he told me I couldn't come wait for the train with you?"

"Yes. Like that. You have courage, Mabel. You will need courage in this world. The world will punish you for having your own mind, for speaking it, just as your father no doubt will punish you for waiting with me."

"I s'pose, but . . ." Mabel began to sniff. "I just couldn't . . ."

"Don't blubber. Say what you have to say."

"Oh, Miss Savage—what will I do without you?"

"Exactly what you would have done with me. Grow up. All girls grow up. The graveyards are full of grown-up girls. Ladies," she added disdainfully. "Ladies are nothing but grown-up girls."

"And boys? Boys grow up too, don't they?"

"Yes. But they grow up to be men."

Mabel twisted her hands in her lap, bit her lip against the question she longed to ask, knowing if she did not ask it now, she would never have it answered. "Do men and . . . and ladies grow up to do what you and Mr. Norby were doing, Miss Savage?"

"Women. Men and women do that."

Together they looked down the tracks, molten and annealing in the inferno waves of heat. Mabel swallowed hard, longing to ask more particularly what Mr. Norby and Miss Savage were doing, but so paltry was her vocabulary, so devoid of anything but Lochinvarish gesture that she could not frame the question and it dissolved on her tongue for want of words. Instead, she asked, "You want to move into the shade, Miss Savage?"

"No. It would be like retreat. Never retreat. Courage and carriage, Mabel."

"Inflection and conviction?"

"Exactly. Inflection and conviction are everything. Strike your own path, Mabel. Use your mind and your courage and scorn piety and custom. They are nothing but fetters. Break those fetters and strike your own path. It is difficult. But rewarding. Sometimes."

"Not always?"

"Nothing is always. Don't you remember 'Ozymandias'?"

"'Nothing beside remains / round the decay,'" Mabel chanted, "'of that colossal wreck, boundless and bare.'"

"'The lone and level sands stretch far away,'" continued Miss Savage with a wistfulness altogether foreign to her. "Just like this bloody desert."

Mabel looked out across the boundless barrenness, out to the bruise-colored mountains ashen in the morning light, and then to Miss Savage, equally ashen.

"I hope you will not have occasion to hate me, Mabel. I doubt the occasion will rise for you to—to know the extent of what I have taught you, but if you do—no, don't interrupt, it's vulgar—please remember, remember, please that I never meant you personally any harm. I have great faith in you." Awkwardly, Miss Savage put her arm around Mabel's shoulders as the train whistle shrilly split the distance. Mabel began to cry. "Don't cry. I can't bear it. Run along home now."

"But the train's not here."

"All the better. I despise farewells. I shan't say goodbye."

"Orv-wa, Miss Savage?"

"Yes, something like that. Now, off you go. Go, I tell you. Cry at home. Please, Mabel, I beg of you. Go." Miss Savage rose, and as the tears spilled down her cheeks, she bustled Mabel off the dock as the supply train clacked and clattered along the narrow-gauge tracks.

August 1918

Amiens

Dear Sarah—

In all this carnage, this colossal wreck of humanity, this boundless decay, amidst these rats and annihilations, this daily death, a miracle has unfolded. The old persis-

tent miracle rendered fresh each time. The old persistent miracle of the flesh. I have met a man.

Sarah stifled a little cry and flushed the toilet to further mask her reaction to these words. She always read Mabel's letters in the bathroom. She always collected the mail as soon as it arrived, before anyone else could see there was a letter from Mabel. She now kept them completely to herself. This day there was a letter from Clarence as well, from Plattsburgh, New York, where he was training with the army. That letter she tossed to Roy. Sarah knew well what Clarence's letter would say: the usual litany of woe, how he hated the food and sleeping quarters, the weather, and having to mix on equal terms with unconverted Jews and Catholics and people with weird accents. Nothing Clarence could say would surprise her, so she gave that letter to Roy and retreated to the bathroom with Mabel's letter, locked the door, and sat on the commode.

"Dumpling!" Roy cried, banging on the bathroom door. "Dumpling! What's Clarence mean?"

"What, dear?"

"What's Clarence mean, 'Oh, Ma, you were right to slap my face.' When did you slap his face? Dumpling! Open up."

"I can't just now dear, I'm on the toilet," she lied cheerfully.

"Get out here where I can talk to you. What's this about your slapping Clarence? Dumpling!"

"Quit calling me that, Roy."

"What? What! I'm talking about Clarence!"

"I'm talking about me, Roy. Quit calling me Dumpling. My name is Sarah."

"What's got into you? Get out of that bathroom."

"Not till you quit calling me Dumpling, Roy. I'm never coming out till then."

"What?"

"You heard me, dear. I mean it. I'm not coming out. I'll never be Dumpling again. I am Sarah." She heard his heavy footsteps stomping away from the bathroom door. She heard the screen door slam. From the backyard she heard the ring of the ax; Roy always chopped wood when he was upset. She unraveled her sister's letter.

A man, English by birth, gentle by nature, who has lost his arm, but not his soul. Not his heart. He was my patient and now he is my lover. I write you this, my dearest sister, not to shock or horrify you, but so that you will know that if I die, I have lived. I have lived, Sarah, and loved and been loved. Love, Sarah, not all those vainglorious Lochinvar gestures, not all that simpering, posturing piety. But love between a man and a woman. Bert and I have our love and we have this moment and it may be all we have and all we'll ever have. Lagair has taught me that much of Lavee. Lagair has taught me Lamore may flourish in the midst of Lamaird. I use the word without a blush. Lamaird, after all is part of the price mortals pay for being gifted with flesh, just as love is the reward for being cursed with flesh, the certainty of death. Everything perishes. The body you are loving tonight may, on the morrow, be a blasted bit of blackened rag impaled on barbed wire, left to lie rotting. But love such as ours is not fragile as flesh. It is an expression of the flesh, but transcends it and once your heart and spirit and flesh have been imbued with such love, you are never quite the same, are you?

"Are you?" Sarah wiped away her tears and listened to the steady thwack, thwack, thwack of the ax. She stepped to the bathroom window, parted the curtain, and looked at Roy standing over the woodpile, his shirt off, the sun gleaming on the blade of the ax, his white shoulders, on the graying hair matting his chest. Could Roy ever be a blasted bit of blackened flesh? A surge of love, hard and visceral, shot through Sarah, compounded, annealed with the fear of loss, the need to have her flesh imbued with love. She tucked her sister's letter in her pocket and went outside to her husband. Roy continued to thwack at the wood until he saw her. Then he put his ax down; a look of infinite sadness crossed his face. Sarah put her arms around him, her head against his chest, and breathed in the warmth of his familiar scent.

The Great War ended before Uncle Sam could send Clarence Over There. Spared Lagair, Clarence had nonetheless seen something of Lavee beyond St. Elmo, California. He had tasted the sweetness of salt-sweat lingering at the neck of a Plattsburgh lass and this was closer than he'd ever come to Lamore. Certainly, he had broadened his acquaintance with Lamaird in its many guises, though he said nothing of any of this to the admiring girls in the bunting-draped St. Elmo station who welcomed him home when he was de-mobbed. He was treated as a returning hero, though he well knew he was only returning. Along with his parents, Clarence was greeted by his Aunt Agnes and her feckless husband, his Aunt Esther and her dour husband, his cousins, his sister Cordelia, his married sisters and brother and their toddling broods. His Aunt Mabel was not there.

Mabel Judd never returned to St. Elmo. Her name, however, was not listed on any sort of glorious plaque commemorating the supreme sacrifices of St. Elmo's youth in the Great War. Of course, she was not one of the St. Elmo youth. She was forty-two, stout, bespectacled, and wistful when she went to France to interpret, when she discovered she possessed the vulgar tongue alone, when she sacrificed every scrap of piety and custom she'd been taught to revere, cast all this off in the name of love.

Her lover, although one-armed, was a man of good humor, good instincts, and incredible luck. He had been amongst the first to join in August 1914 and though he had been badly wounded more than once, he survived: of his original battalion, only seven other men could say the same. After the War he returned to London where his family owned a pub in a district much frequented by music-hall types. Even lacking his right arm, he went back to work with the jocular observation that it only took one arm to pull a tap or pinch a girl. He was a married man, but his wife had left him early in the War.

All but this last bit of information, Sarah shared with Esther and Agnes when she informed them that Mabel was not coming home. (Sarah tidied up the pub, referring to it as a small family business. No Mormon could work in a pub.) Moreover, Sarah informed her sisters Mabel had reason for not coming home; in the summer of 1919 she had been delivered of a daughter she had named Sarah. *A child?* said Esther and Agnes more-or-less in unison. *At her age?* To which Sarah replied that she saw no reason to think that Mabel was lying. *Well, is she married?* And Sarah, with appropriate carriage and courage, inflection and conviction, said, *No, she is not*. At that, Esther and Agnes concurred that the family should just declare Mabel Judd dead, dead in France, a victim of the Hun and the War. Sarah objected: *Say that and I shall call you liars,* she told her sisters. *Mabel did not die. Mabel lived.*

She lived till 1940. She remained as loyal a wife to Bert as Leona had been to Ephraim, though she was not able to marry him legally till 1920 when Bert got word that his first wife had died of the Spanish influenza, which took up the task of global death and destruction after Armistice ended the War. With courage, carriage, inflection, and conviction, Mabel survived all, everything but the Blitz, so she was, after all, a victim of the War. A different war. In love, in marriage, Mabel prospered, and though her means were modest, her heart was large. Mabel even forgave the aptly named Miss Savage her cruel joke. She delighted her regulars at the pub with her funny story, mimicking the French officer's expressions when she had first offered him her expertise.

Perhaps it was the Great War itself that taught her forgiveness, forbearance; certainly it taught her not to put her faith in Higher Things. Mabel put her faith in love and was rewarded with a one-armed man who remained forever smitten with her, and a daughter who adored her. Mabel's daughter was very likely the only child in England to be sung to sleep with "The Battle Hymn of the Republic." When she sat on her daughter's bed and sang those stately lyrics, behind the cadence of her own voice, Mabel invariably heard the counterpointing thump and throttle of the mill and mine, the clank and rattle of the supply train; she saw the neutral empty sands stretching far away, the indifferent bleached-blue sky blazing down, the boundless bare desert shrouding narrow-gauge tracks, the dust still blowing golden in a vanished street, the wind alone left to rattle the broken panes of that colossal wreck of a house, to testify to its departed grandeur, to whistle and moan through that airy, aching splendor, those empty rooms, that antique land.

How Maxwell Perkins Learned to Edit

OF COURSE HE WAS A GREAT EDITOR, but Maxwell Perkins did not spend his whole life, pencil in hand, a paragon of self-effacing good taste and nobility. It is a little known fact that Max served in 1916 under General Pershing when the American cavalry went down into Mexico to find Pancho Villa. (In this, Pershing failed, but later, in 1918, he vanquished the German army.) For Max, however, Mexico was crucial. Here he met the *jalapeño* of destiny.

Lieutenant Perkins rode with the cavalry into Chihuahua, fruitlessly searching for the elusive Pancho Villa. Max was saddle sore, hot, cross, thirsty, and bored. At least until he met Maria Concepcion, with whom he had a torrid, hot-tamale love affair. She taught him about sex, salsa, and everything he would need to be an editor.

Maria Concepcion is ubiquitous in American Literature (she also appears in the Katherine Anne Porter story of the same name). However, before she bedded Max Perkins, she had an affair with Pancho Villa. This should not surprise anyone as all Mexican women born between 1855 and 1908 claim to have slept with Pancho Villa. Many American women, too. For all I know, Katherine Anne Porter slept with Pancho Villa. Certainly Pancho graced many a bed and he was always gallant, *muy hombre,* and never mistreated a horse.

During those short, hot nights in the summer of 1916, Max and Maria lay naked and—oh well, we can only follow this story as it applies to literature. Anyway, Maria Concepcion sometimes talked about Pancho Villa. She said Pancho could make love, yes, but what he really made was salsa! Holy frijole, Max! I tell you! Here in Chihuahua, virgins are not allowed to taste Pancho's salsa. In Chihuahua, Pancho's salsa is considered a sin of the flesh and the devout confess it to the priests. I don't know who the priests confess to. Pancho's salsa will win *la revolución,* even if Pancho does not.

Max begged Maria to taste Pancho's salsa, having already adored Pancho's woman. And, on his last night in Mexico, so *muy hombre* was Max to Maria, at dawn she rose. She brought to him a couple of tortillas, a cold beer, and a bowl of Pancho Villa's salsa. Maria nodded. The tortilla swathed in salsa, Max ate fearlessly. His eyes opened wide, tears streamed down his face while he groaned, salivated, shuddered, and his breath went *oof oof oof,* as the blood drained from his face on its way down to fight the fire in his belly; the agony was equaled only by the joy radiating out from his taste buds to his every extremity. He collapsed, breathless, ecstatic, and satisfied.

OK, *gringo*—Maria said, kissing Max—Now you know. Never forget this: great literature is like great salsa. It must evoke a gut reaction, it must take your breath away, it must make your eyes water, you must weep and laugh, maybe at the same moment. And Max, you can always tell the great writers because they can do this to you more than once, in book after book. For great writers, the work—like Pancho's salsa—is always satisfying and yet, each time, a little different. Say what you want, *amigo,* no two *jalapeños* are exactly alike, so the salsa is never the same. Only the effect, that is the same.

And with that, she sent Maxwell Perkins off to meet his destiny.

Right-Hand Man

IT'S ONE OF THOSE AFTERNOONS, cold and so damn dull you can only shit and shiver, and all four of us guys, we're hunkering in a square of sunlight in front of Dewitt's filling station, flicking our smoking butts out toward the pumps. No one cares how close they roll either. Dewitt would care. Plenty. But Dewitt ain't here. He's at the funeral of his wife's aunt, holding the wife's hand, moaning in the Methodist graveyard, laying on the Methodist smarm. "And don't I know it," says Eddie. "I got Methodists crawling all over my family! 'Course I ain't been in the church since before the Great War."

We all wish he hadn't said that last. That's the whole trouble, see? We were all too young for the War when it started. Now it's a couple of months over and the soldiers are coming home with their uniforms and their canes and crutches, their arms in slings, and the girls just swoon into little honey puddles at their feet. Who'd want an eyepatched cripple when she could have a whole man? That's what we want to know. Who'd want to hire an eyepatched cripple?

Duke quick wipes his nose with his oil rag and says, "So, how much you think Dewitt'll get from the aunt?"

"It was the wife's aunt croaked," says Lew.

Duke gives Lew a look like he don't have buckshot for brains (and poor Lew, he don't) and Duke says slow and patient, so Lew can take it all in. "When-the-wife-gets-money-the-husband-gets-money. It'll be Dewitt's money even if it's her aunt died." Duke rolls a quick fag and licks it. "Hell's bells, Dewitt don't even need the money. He's got the only two filling stations in St. Elmo and now that Stetler's selling Fords downtown, don't tell me Dewitt ain't raking in the straw. And plenty of it."

"Too bad Dewitt don't love you like a son, Duke," I say with a little snicker and the others snicker, too, because Dewitt's got a son named Richard and a daughter named Frances and so we always laugh 'mongst ourselves because the Dewitts got a Dick and a Fanny all in the same family. The same rich family. I flick the last of my butt. It rolls, smoking, real close to the first pump. Too close, but don't no one go after it. Don't no one want to look like he has chicken giblets where his balls oughta be.

Just then a gas buggy rumbles up and Duke hauls out his oil rag and jaws with Hec, the driver, while he puts the stick down the tank, brings it out, and reads it. Same time, he's stepping neatly on my still-smoking fag. Duke's smooth like that.

Hec Fleagle, he says Hey Boys to all of us, but who's going to pass the time of day with a man who's got grease stuck to his hands and his hair stuck out all over his head? But Duke, he's got to listen to old Hec's old Whizz Bang jokes and laugh. I guess that's part of Duke's job, too, same as pumping gas. At least Duke's got work. More'n the rest of us have. Finally Hec's flivver is out of there and Duke comes back, squats in the sunshine with us, and says pretty soon everyone in this whole town is gonna have a car.

"Ever'one 'cept us," sulks Eddie.

"It's cold," I say, buttoning up my coat. "We live in the goddamned desert and we're cold."

"It's the wind!" says Lew, his big round face shining.

"Shut up, Lew," says Eddie.

It is cold though. The wind, in January, that cold snaking wind blows down Jesuit Pass, and way out here at Dewitt's filling station on the eastern road, well out of town, there's nothing to stand 'tween you and that wind. Out here, worse'n the cold is the stink. City dump's half-mile away and you can smell it all right, even in January. In summer that dump-smell's a killer. Duke always says the trenches couldn't have smelled no worse than the St. Elmo dump. We call it No-Man's-Land out here. It's a goddamned shame Dewitt put his filling station so close by the dump. Dewitt's other filling station, the one in town, his son Dick gets to work that one. Dick even gets tips when he steps lively. Out here all Duke gets is yahoos like Hec Fleagle that just come through. Well, you could say Duke was lucky to have the work and you'd be right. All the rest of us ('cept for Lew, he didn't make it that far), we all graduated from St. Elmo High last June, class of 1918. I wanted to quit school and join the army 'fore that, wanted to join up just soon as I knew America was in the fight against the Hun. But, oh no, my old ma says no, I got to graduate or I'll break her heart. Then she tells me I got to fix the roof afore I join up because who knows if I'll come back from Over There and the roof would still need fixing if I died in battle. So I miss the War. I finished that roof the day before the War ended. Months ago. And still I can't find no work fit for a white man. What work there is goes to de-mobbed soldiers. They get the girls and the work, and the money. Me and Eddie and Lew, we got nothing, no work, no girls, and dick for money.

Duke gets up off his haunches and looks to where the sky is getting gray and faint, sun starting to set, and he says, "The aunt's funeral will be over pretty soon and Dewitt'll be back out here to close up. Bastard still don't trust me to close the till. Afraid I'll nick him."

"He'd deserve it," says Eddie.

"So I better crack on the delivery truck Mason Douglass brung in this morning. It's his mother's truck for the Pilgrim Restaurant, and he lets me know she needs it in a jiffy. That's why he brung it out here, so I'd better look smart about it. Lousy bastard."

"Didn't he just get back from—" asks Eddie.

"Didn't he?" snarls Duke. "The Mademoiselle from Armentières, Parly Voo." Duke peels a piece of tobacco from his tongue. "Mason Douglass was prick-proud all right, and I had to listen to all of it. All his battles. All the jobs he's been offered. All the girls." Hands cupped against the wind, Duke lights his fag. "The thought of Mason Douglass makes me wanna puke. So maybe I'll just leave that truck go till tomorrow."

"Yeah, but Duke—" Lew's jaw goes slack and worried-looking, "when Dewitt comes back to close up, he'll know, Duke, he'll see you ain't touched the Pilgrim truck and he's gonna peel your dick right down to the bone."

I'm all ready to laugh because I know Duke's going to say something funny about dicks, and I got my papers and tobacco out, ready to roll one, but when Duke don't say nothing funny, nothing at all, I look up. Duke's face has gone sort of greeny white, the color of pigeon shit and he's looking out way beyond the pumps. I look and I see it too: coming out of the dusk, wrapped in that chalky blue and milky winter light comes something staggering, stumbling, gray hair, gray face, and blue gray lips, right hand wrapped round the left wrist, holding out the left hand or what's left of the left because hanging down are red bloody strings and bloody stumps, staggering toward us, arm out, it's braying, bawling. No one moves. Lew starts to cry.

"Help," lurching toward us, dripping blood, *"Help."*

We four stand up together, slow, not scrambling to

our feet, but slow and wishing we *was* Methodists or Mormons or mackerel snappers or even Chinks, all of us praying this ain't bloody Death come for us at Dewitt's filling station. "It's Mr. Forrest," whispers Eddie at last.

"He'd be in town, running the newspaper. He wouldn't be out here."

"He would if he was dead," I say, quiet like. "If he was dead and a ghost, he could be anywheres he wanted. He could be here. He could look like that." Good clothes, coat, vest, pressed shirt and pants, collar and tie in place, but his arm's nearly red to the elbow. Flapping untied at the thigh there hangs a mutilated holster.

"Help me, boys. Help me. Help me before I die of the pain." So he wasn't dead, but slumped now against a pump. Just fell down beside the pump still clutching his own wrist. His face was gray as his hair, though Jake Forrest ain't that old. Forty maybe, but out here in No-Man's-Land he looks like Death itself. He brings his blue eyes up to rest on us and says, "I've bitched it, boys. I've done it this time."

I hotfoot in and get clean rags. (Duke had his oil rag out, but thought better of it.) We start to wrap the left hand while Mr. Forrest keeps pressure on the wrist, but it's hard because the ends of the two middle fingers are still hanging by long bloody threads. Right then, one drops, the bloody thread spindles, and the stump drops into Mr. Forrest's lap, and with another clean rag (and a quick breath) I pick it up, wrap it, and put it in my coat pocket.

"Where's your flivver, Mr. Forrest?" Duke shouts like he's deaf.

Mr. Forrest sputters out somehow that his Ford wouldn't start or crank over or something. He somehow scratches up enough words so we get the meaning. He'd left his Ford. At the dump.

"Dump's a half-mile from here," says Eddie.

"Longest walk of my life. Get me to the doc, boys." He grinds his teeth so hard we can hear them breaking down. "Any doc. I got to save my fingers. I'm a printer. I got to have my fingers."

Well, his fingers was long past saving, but didn't none of us say so. Along with the blood you could see little white dangly nerves and white bone sticking up jagged. The top knuckle of his ring finger was clean shot away and gone altogether, but his wedding ring clung there, twinkling wet and gold though it was all bloody, too.

"I'll run to the dump and get his car," says Eddie.

"No time," I say. "He'll bleed to death. We need to—" I don't even know what we need, saving for a chariot to get us into town. "There's the truck," I say, "the Pilgrim delivery truck. It runs, don't it?"

Says Duke, "Dewitt would flay me alive. I can't take that. He'd have my hide on a—"

Mr. Forrest starts shivering and his breath comes rough, in long streaks, like the sound of something being ripped out of his chest. Duke looks once at me and we nod. What else can we do?

Eddie sprints into the garage and opens up the back doors of the truck. It's sort of like an ambulance already, and there are shelves on the sides, but the floor is dry, only a few burlap bags there. Eddie jumps in the back and me and Duke hoist Mr. Forrest between us, up to Eddie who pulls him in and makes a pillow of the burlap. Duke tells Lew to stay here and mind Dewitt's station, but Lew don't heed or hear and and he climbs in the back with Eddie and Mr. Forrest. I close the doors.

Duke gets in behind the wheel and tells me to give her a crank up and I do, but the truck don't start. Again and again. Duke calls that truck a motherless, fatherless piece of flyspecked dog shit.

"Hurry," Eddie cries from the back.

Duke gets out and I get in behind the wheel. Duke gives that truck a kick, I mean right where it hurts. Duke is big and he's smart. Duke can fix anything that don't bite back, but I know (and so does he) that when Dewitt comes to close up and finds the truck and Duke gone, it won't matter if Duke had ferried Adam and Eve back to the Garden. Dewitt'll fire him sure. That'll be tough on Duke because his old man don't work regular, though he drinks regular, and Duke's got a mother and three sorry sisters, and a mule tethered out in their front yard. In fact, Duke was just last week cursing Jake Forrest because the *Herald-Gazette* was having a paper rage about cleaning up St. Elmo and going after people who kept illegal livestock inside the city limits, picking on Duke's family's mule in particular, saying it (and they) was a disgrace. Duke was ragging all over Mr. Forrest then. Here he is now, saving his life. That Duke is a good man.

Duke has a long peer around the truck's innards and still cursing, he fumbles this and that and next time he gives her a crank, she starts. She don't purr, but knows to start and I move over and Duke jumps in and drives us west, back into town. We rattle and shake all over, raise up a lot of dust to mix up with the smoke coming from the back of the truck. Smoke's so powerful up here in the cab, I wonder if they're dying of it in the back. If they're all three dying and not just Mr. Forrest.

We drive west into the dusk that has got itself down to a hard, blue line in the sky, like it does in winter and there's a single star hanging there. I kick myself and say inside, *damnit, Emmett, damnit, you forget that stuff, there's a man bleeding to death in the back,* but every time I look up to that fool goddamned star, there comes rolling back through my head that verse that Helen McComb wrote me in Geography class that one day last spring:

For Emmett Wells:

When evening drops her curtain down
And pins it with a star,
Remember that you have a friend
Though you may travel far.

And I seize up, just like I did that day she sent the note back to me, got it passed under desks, right under the teacher's nose as she stood there with her pointer going over the War in Europe. What did I care about the Western Front? I read Helen McComb's poem and I got this queer, deep ache, right down there where you live, and my face got hot and my own pointer spronged up and it wasn't aiming for no map of France either. I stare over at Helen and saw only the back of her golden head till she turned around, slow. Till she all but rested her chin on her shoulder and give me a look. Not quite a smile. It was all in her blue eyes, that look, and suddenly I knew I was close to her—my body even was close—I could smell the soap and talc on her arms and the lavender-water at her throat, could touch the buttons down her blouse, ease them loose between her breasts, free them, free her, free us both, even though my body was stuck there in the pint-sized desk where my knees scrape. When she gave me that look, her eyes were blue and level, open as the sea, and I knew she knew, too, how it was my hand touched her golden hair, her shoulder, what it felt like, what it would feel like, what it will feel like, if I can only get a job and some money and marry her.

"There it is! The lights are on!" cried Duke, "Doctor's in. Damn! Thank you, God! Thank you!" He pulls the Pilgrim delivery truck in behind Dr. Tipton's house, out back of the house so no one'll see us. He turns it off and says, "Trouble's in the pistons." (Duke's smart like that.)

We're out of the cab and round the back and the doors fly open and there's Lew and Eddie and Mr. Forrest. Lew and Eddie, they were looking pretty gray, too. "I th-think he's d-dead," says Lew.

Maybe he was. His grip had slacked on the left wrist (Eddie's holding it now) and there was blood on the floor. We tug Mr. Forrest's legs and pull him out, and he ain't dead yet because he twitches and winces all over. Two of us carry him to the back door, already open, the light shining up behind Lucius Tipton, lighting his wiry hair as he fills the doorway, his hazel eyes taking everything in. He says for us to follow into the surgery where Doctor flips on the electric lights and then he's washing his hands in the sink. Whew! The smell of some powerful antiseptic he pours over his hands just about knocks us out while he's asking us what happened.

We don't have any damned idea whatever and we say so. Doctor don't look like he believes us, but he takes Mr. Forrest's left wrist from Eddie and binds it fast with something, and right then, Mr. Forrest's eyes pop open and he reaches out with his right hand. He grabs hold of my wrist, clutches like he is trying to keep *me* from bleeding to death. His lips curl back from his clenched-tight teeth, his eyeballs roll into his head, and Mr. Forrest says to me: "Don't let him cut my fingers off."

I look over to Dr. Tipton and I say, "Tell him yourself, Mr. Forrest. Tell him. Doctor's right here."

"It's me, Jake," says Doctor. "Lucius Tipton."

But it's me, Emmett Wells, who Mr. Forrest clutches, all

the tighter and says again, fierce, "Don't let him cut off my fingers. I need my fingers. I have to have—"

"Jake," says Doctor, "I'll do what I can, but I got to tell you now, Jake, it looks bad. It looks real bad."

Then I remember the wrapped-up fingertip in my coat pocket. With my other hand, I find it. The rag is all bloodied up and soaked through. Doctor takes it. I try to get my wrist from Mr. Forrest's grip, but he don't let go. Won't. My fingers tingle.

Doctor tells the other guys to go into the study and in the bottom desk drawer they'll find a bottle of Burning Bush and they all look like they could use a drink. They close the door. Doctor's hazel eyes come up and meet mine. "It looks like you have been drafted for this one, Emmett. I need your help. I need someone to hold the fingertip in place. Go wash your hands over there at the sink. Use the disinfectant. You ready?"

"I'm ready, sir."

But I wasn't. I done what he told me to do, everything he said and I didn't vomit or scream or pass out, even with the blood and Doctor's needle stitching in and out of flesh and Mr. Forrest's screams about bitching it and saving his hand and the pain. The snort of chloroform Doctor gave him was merciful for Mr. Forrest, but it did not do me a damn bit of good.

When it was over, I had to go outside and have the dry heaves, fight off the shakes and chills, walking around out back, smoking, kicking clods, flapping my arms at my sides, and hooting a few times. Dr. Tipton saved Mr. Forrest's fingers, or saved what was left of them. What I mean is, he sewed the one still hanging down and he even sewed up the one I gave him from my pocket. The top of the ring finger was gone for good and the mended ones would never look or work right. They were whole, but broken and would always be so. It was some job, and even Dr. Tipton said it woulda been so much easier just to cut them off and be done with it.

Finally I come back inside, stop at the kitchen tap, put my face under the water. My own hands still smelled like Doctor's disinfectant. I can hear their voices from the study as I dry off and go in there. Doctor's behind his desk and Mr. Forrest, I am surprised to see, is propped up on the settee, white bandages glowing in the electric light, his left hand splinted and the arm in a sling. The sleeves of his coat and shirt have been cut away and you can see he has a small tattoo. A rose and anchor. The pain must be a killer, but you got to admire Mr. Forrest, he's keeping it all in his clenched jaw. He's pale, but Lew looks worse than he does. In fact, they all look pretty grim, 'cept for Doctor and Blanche, Doctor's skeleton, hanging there behind his chair. Blanche is grinning like she just heard the one about the traveling salesman.

Doctor Tipton has a glass all ready for me, pours me a quick shot of Burning Bush (and he don't have to ask!), and then he says to Mr. Forrest that he hates to have to be so specific, but he must. "I didn't say—*were you alone?* I didn't ask if you were alone, Jake. I asked what happened, and how you happened to have your gun at the dump."

Jake Forrest takes a little sip of Burning Bush like he don't really need it. His right hand trembles and he slowly lowers it back on the arm of the couch. Finally he says he was out at the city dump shooting rats. Target practice on the rats. Quick draw on the rats. And funniest damn thing, he forgot to tie his holster to his thigh (and he points to the holster still buckled round his hips and shot to hell), "And I quick-drew and the gun went off, still stuck in the holster, and since it wasn't tied, it twisted and I had my hand out and—" He raises his right hand again, sips slow on the Burning Bush.

"Careless, Jake," says Doctor. "You were careless."

"That's the worst of it. I did it carelessly."

"You're an experienced man with a gun. How could you forget something like that?"

The pain must be eating Mr. Forrest alive by now, but he answers the question, slow and studied-like. "I didn't know how important it was. I bitched it bad all right. Careless."

"Well, Jake, you own the newspaper, and you probably wrote more words about this town than any living mortal, so I don't need to tell you what the law is. When a doctor tends a patient and there's firearms involved—accident or not—the doctor's got to tell the Sheriff."

"Well, sure I know that, Doctor. Everyone knows that," says Jake, like Doctor has asked after the tune of the "Rock of Ages." "Why every man in St. Elmo—" he looks at each of us, "knows that." He holds up his mummified left hand and I can almost see the pain throbbing in front of my eyes, beating through his hand, but it don't show on his face. Mr. Forrest grins. I never seen anything braver. He grins and he says, "Gentlemen, you see before you, walking testimony to the kind of accident you do not want to have. Careless." He laughs.

Lew laughs. Only Lew sounds like the mule in Duke's front yard. HaWHaWHaW.

Doctor don't laugh. He pours himself another shot of the Burning Bush and digs around the desk till he finds a cigar and a safety match. He don't light the cigar. He's thinking on lighting it. He's thinking. He shakes his head. "Jake, I can't—"

"Listen," Jake says fast, "no one else was involved. It

was an accident. A damned, stupid accident. I forgot to tie the damned holster down, that's all. It was a target-practice accident. Shooting rats." He takes another drink and you can see him fighting pain back into a corner, dueling with it. "Can't we just forget it?" The blood is starting to beat back into his face and his blue eyes are focusing hard.

Doctor Tipton, he thumbles around with the cigar and the unlit match. He finally strikes that match and then another and another, but he don't ever light the cigar, though he keeps his eyes there. He don't look at us.

But Jake Forrest does. The pain is killing him off, but he looks at us, each one. And I think: *Yes, of course.* And it's like my mind can see the banner runs atop the front page of every issue of the *Herald-Gazette.*

WE SERVE THE TRUTH.
NO SECRETS. NO LIES. NO FAVORITES.

In fact it was that very same line, the one about serving the truth, Mr. Forrest used when he gave the speech at our graduation. To the St. Elmo High class of 1918, he said, In print as in life, to Serve the Truth, that was his motto. It made your blood quicken, his speech about growing up and keeping yourself clean and proud so's you could serve your family, your native St. Elmo, the great state of California, and this great nation America, too, his talking about how you could serve God, boys and girls, by serving the truth, always. No lies. No secrets. No favorites. That's the kind of man Jake Forrest is. Though he don't hold public office and never has, he lives a public life. There's no one in this town who don't know—or know of—Mr. Jake Forrest. Seems he has time for everyone. He can talk with working men who wear boots and braces, with growers in overalls. He knows the citrus and alfalfa crop, understands railroads and irrigation. He charms the old ladies who get their health asked after, and dazzles the young matrons who get listened to (like they never do at home—you can bet). Schoolchildren who graduate at the top of their classes, they get their names in a special column in the newspaper and a silver dollar if they come by the front counter of the *Herald-Gazette* which believes in education. Hell, right there at the front counter of the newspaper you can see why the *Herald-Gazette* supports education. There's Mr. Forrest's framed degree from Central Methodist College in Kansas, hanging up on the wall. Jake Forrest is the only man in St. Elmo, 'cept maybe for Doctor Tipton himself, who can walk from the railyard roundhouse, down where the old town once washed away, all the way up to New Town, and know everyone in between. Mr. Forrest ain't rich, but everyone courts him up anyway. Anyone who hates him is afraid to say so. (Usually. Duke's old man said so after the mule business, all right, said plenty, but he didn't *do* nothing.) NO SECRETS, NO LIES, NO FAVORITES. In its columns, since Jake Forrest took over the *Herald-Gazette,* the newspaper's always throttling on about making St. Elmo safe for democracy, about water rights and community spirit, sanctity of the public trust, and the civil rights of Chinks. Mr. Forrest is in the Methodist pew every Sunday alongside his wife and daughters, and you need only ask Jake Forrest for a favor to find that he is ever-obliging and wise. People always say, *That's the kind of man Jake Forrest is.* You got to admire a man who's good as his word and no hypocrite. Mr. Forrest don't try to hide it that he's also the kind of man plays five-card stud. A couple of nights a week you can find him in the poker game at the Alexandria, which was a pretty nice saloon before the Women's Christian Temperance Union smashed it up last summer. Jake Forrest's been known to drop a hundred dollars on a pair of black queens. (Imagine, that kind of money, running on a simple pair.) When he loses, he folds up his hand and leaves with only a nod and a single word in farewell, *Gentlemen*. But when he wins, why everyone from the dealer right down to Lew's old man (who used to clean spittoons there), Jake Forrest strews money on them like they all done him a personal favor by drawing breath. Everyone likes to see him win.

And me, right now, I'd like to see him win. I know (like humming the tune when you only hear the song-words spoke) that it ain't the dump, or the gun, or the untied holster, or what's left of the left hand. He bitched something else. He has a secret. He has a lie. He is not now serving the truth. Say it, Mr. Forrest. I think, Say the words. I can smell the words. And the greenbacks. Say it. Say: *I'll make it worth your while.*

Then I look over at Lucius Tipton, and I know Jake Forrest would be a damned fool to say those words to Doctor. There couldn't be two more different men. Lucius Tipton has kept secrets for hundreds of people, for folks who live on Silk Stocking Row, just like he's kept them for Chinks who smoke opium in the cribs out back of their laundries, for the Mex's who can't even ask him in English. Dr. Tipton plays favorites and if his silence is what's needed, well, he'll favor you with it. But you couldn't buy his silence. He'd never be bought. If it wasn't a gift, it wouldn't be at all.

But I am not Lucius Tipton. I am Emmett Wells and I think: *Say it, Mr. Forrest, you can buy my silence if you'll only just say it.* And I look to the others ('cept for Lew. He don't know what's happening) and I know they're thinking too. *Make it worth my while.*

So, I can see the words and smell them, but I don't

hear nothing except the tick of the clock and the snap of Doctor's match when he (finally) lights that goddamned cigar and the squeal of his chair and the clatter of Blanche's bones when he accidentally bumps into her. "Jake, it can't work this way. Even if I want it to. Even if you want it to. Every soul in this town—including the Sheriff—is going to come up to you and say, what did you do to your left hand? Everyone's going to ask after that hand, Jake, and wonder how it was these men brought you into town from way out there at Dewitt's and—"

"Then we'll have to think of some other story. Let's make up a story."

Doctor shakes his head. "Let's tell the truth. Some of it anyway. Enough. All we got to do is satisfy the law."

"It can't be—I can't say—It would—" Mr. Forrest finishes off his Burning Bush, studies the empty glass in his right hand. "There is a woman involved. A married woman who is not married to me." He swallows hard, so hard we hear it. "I was at the dump because—she . . ." He paused and Doctor poured him some more Burning Bush. "I was alone at the dump. Shooting. But not at rats. It was not target practice. I did not care what I hit or hurt. I just wanted something else destroyed. Something besides me. It was the old destruction," Jake looks at Lucius Tipton alone. "You know what I mean. It was the old destruction incumbent on love." Then he raises his gaze to Blanche, behind Doctor, studies the skeleton, and I think he's going to cry. But instead, he lifts his glass, like a sort of toast to Blanche and as he does, it's like he pulls another trigger, a trigger inside of him. BANG! The man who was heartbroke and near to tears vanishes. Jake Forrest puts on the cheer and the charm like they was hat, coat, and collar stud, all snapping into place. He laughs. "Well, boys, you can't change the past, can you?"

Dr. Tipton says: "You get one chance at the past. And that's when it's still the present. That's the only chance you ever get to change it."

Then it was all quiet. And it stayed that way while Eddie rolls a fag and rolls me one too. Mr. Forrest don't smoke, but Duke and Lew are smoking, and with Doctor's cigar, the smoke in here is like a nice gray curtain so's we don't have to look at one another.

Finally, Doctor's arm cuts a big swath through all the smoke, waves it away and he says, "Well men, shooting rats in the city dump, that's a public service by my standard. I can't go calling the Sheriff every time a citizen renders a public service. Why that would mean—" He puzzles over what it would mean.

"You'd have to call the Sheriff when someone fell out of a tree chasing a cat," says Lew, his round empty face glowing.

"Good work, Lew," says Doctor.

"Or a dog or maybe a baby bird. Or a chicken. Chickens can get into trees. I seen one once."

Well, then Eddie has to jump into it. Eddie offers up how the four of us might just have sort of happened on Mr. Forrest there with his hand hurt and needing a ride into town. Eddie rattles off a tale sounds like we're all on our way to a Methodist picnic.

But Duke don't jump on this wagon. Duke says, "I'm glad Mr. Forrest done us all a public service, but there's still the matter of the Pilgrim delivery truck. Dewitt's closed up by now. He's found me gone, and the truck gone. He'll have my hide and he won't buy no cock and bull story. I'll be outta work in a snap."

"The Pilgrim restaurant?" Doctor says thoughtfully. Duke nods. "Then don't worry about that, Duke. I can right that easy with the Widow Douglass and she'll right it with Dewitt."

"Then we can say it happened in town," Mr. Forrest offers. "At the paper. In the press room. Press room's deserted in the late afternoon and that's where it happened. I mangled my hand in the press and I ran out back just as Duke was driving by."

He went on and on, swinging this story around like it was a sackful of kittens. About how Duke had brought the Pilgrim truck into town, had drove it all the way into St. Elmo from out there at Dewitt's just so he could figure what was wrong with it. Lew and Eddie, even Duke, their heads are bobbing up and down, oh yes. Only Doctor looks real doubtful. Then Mr. Forrest stands up, weaving a bit on his feet. With his good hand, his right hand, he unbuckles the empty holster and it falls to the floor. He kicks it from him. He says again the accident happened in town. Blood on the floor of the truck? That's because Duke was driving by, says Mr. Forrest, and stopped when he seen there was trouble.

Me, I'd heard enough.

"There's blood on the ground by the pump at Dewitt's filling station," I say. "And there's blood at the dump where you shot your own fingers off." *Make it worth my while, Mr. Forrest. Buy my silence.* "And your Ford's at the dump, too." *Make it worth my while,* "along with the top of your ring finger." I don't say wedding-ring finger, but he knows. We all know now.

Mr. Forrest eyeballs Doctor who puffs away, interested maybe, but he's not white-knuckled. Not Doctor. He done his job. He smokes away as if to say, well, it's up to Mr. Forrest and to us.

Mr. Forrest gives a laugh, a warm, low chuckle, and a great big smile, the grin of a man who has never bitched a thing. I move forward in my seat because I 'spect he's going to make it worth my while. But instead he says something about the headlamps on his T, they work just fine. He says it's dark now and who would notice if when Duke returns the Widow Douglass's truck to Dewitt's, Duke—and someone else, another guy—could also drive by the dump. Duke could start up Mr. Forrest's T and he and this other guy could drive it back to town, leave it out behind the *Herald-Gazette* building, "where the accident happened," he adds. "Someone could do that."

"Me!" cries Lew, just joyful for the opportunity to serve the truth.

"Like Eddie," says Mr. Forrest, knowing that for the truth, Lew might serve. But for a lie, you gotta have someone steady. Like Eddie. Eddie nods and Mr. Forrest beams at him like he beamed at the class of 1918 on graduation day. Then he offers up some tripe, the sort of warm-flannel well-worn phrase you'd 'spect from your mother. "Least said, soonest mended," Mr. Forrest advises us all. Then he turns to me, holds out his right hand for me to shake. "Thank you, Emmett. Thank you for letting me hold on to you in my hour of need. It was a real service. I guess you are my right-hand man."

"It's nothing," I say. And I know that's true now. It is nothing and whoever she was, the married woman not married to him, the woman who drove him to the old destruction, she's part of the past because he has jiggered the present. He has jiggered the present and jiggered us out of money we coulda had even if we wasn't entitled to it really. We still coulda had it. It shoulda been worth my while.

We leave Doctor's and go out to the truck (she starts, first crank). Lew and Eddie get in the back. Me and Duke with Mr. Forrest between us, in the cab.

It's full dark now and that single evening star that

made me think of Helen McComb is lost in a hundred thousand stars all looking like each other, spilled across the cold black sky. Duke drives without even asking where Mr. Forrest lives because everyone knows where he lives. Everyone in this burg knows everything. Hell, in St. Elmo you know which dogs are summer homes to which fleas. But I would give my own right hand to know who was the woman, once the present, now the past, the married woman who is the reason that a man like Jake Forrest was out at the city dump trying to destroy something besides his own self.

Just then we pull slowly behind a man in uniform walking with his arm around a girl, his lips against her ear. Duke snorts out, "Another goddamn returning hero."

"Yes," says Mr. Forrest, like we might not know this, "the War is over."

I don't know the soldier, but my heart comes up and beats in my throat because I know that girl, that golden hair, those hips and shoulders. I know, or would have known them, and I push the window down quick and look out into the cold to see *when evening drops her curtain down* who Helen McComb is with *and pins it with a star.* "Can you beat that?" My breath hard and hurtful in my chest. "Mason Douglass. Mason Damn Douglass."

"Hope he don't notice his mother's truck," Duke mutters, speeding up.

He won't notice anything, I think, but what Helen McComb must feel like, close up, near to his body, so close he can smell her soap and talc and lavender-water.

We stop in front of Mr. Forrest's house, the windows spilling yellow light on the porch and the porch swing, which they had not yet took down, even if it was January. In the cold, it rocked a steady squeal like the ghosts of summer lovers. You could hear one of his daughters playing piano. Trying to. I get out and I ask Mr. Forrest if he wants some help up the porch steps.

He says he is fine as he is. And, he seems to be—the old Jake Forrest back in place, his graduation-day smile promising you Principles and Interest in whatever you was about to say. He says he hopes his wife has kept his supper warm. He gives us a kind of salute. "Good night, men." Then he walks slowly up the stairs. He don't look back.

It turned out Dr. Tipton couldn't right it about the delivery truck, even though Mrs. Douglass did just as he asked. She wrote a note to Mr. Dewitt to say how very pleased she was that Duke had driven her truck into town to try to find out what was wrong with it. She wrote how Duke was a fine, responsible, clever young man and Mr. Dewitt was lucky to have him as an employee. Wasn't it even more lucky, she writes, that Duke happened to be driving past the *Herald-Gazette* when Mr. Forrest had had his accident? Also, Mr. Dewitt should not give a thought to the blood on the floor as she would have it painted over.

Dewitt still sacked Duke, turned round and hired one of Our Boys Come Back From Over There.

Dog vomit. That's what Duke calls Dewitt. But he stayed home after that, sulking, stuck with his drunk father and his sorry sisters and the mule tethered in the front yard.

For me, I might go out afternoons, maybe even look for work, but mornings I'd always hang around home till the mail come. (Even though my mother gives me this sneer she's been practicing for nineteen years that I know of.) I hang around the mailbox hoping Mr. Forrest would still make it worth my while, reward me for having been his right-hand man, buy my silence. But time passes and I know I have given my silence for free. Seems everyone buys the story how he'd smashed his hand up in the press, an awful accident right there in the pressroom of the *Herald-Gazette* and Duke just happened to be driving by in the Pilgrim truck. Oh, I think Lew mighta said something else, but no one pays him any mind because Lew means well, but he don't have biscuits for brains.

Then, mid-February or so, Duke turns up behind the counter at the *Herald-Gazette*. He tells us Mr. Forrest really wanted to hire someone experienced in setting type because his hand is so busted up now and won't ever be the same, but he hires Duke anyway. Duke's fast and mechanical. Days, Duke's on the counter, nights he's learning the presses. And then, why looky here, Lew's delivering papers along with boys half his age. He's working, ain't he? And if you give Lew a set task and tell him how, he's a good man for it. And well, next thing you know, Eddie's up, well before dawn, doing a man's work, getting paid for loading newspapers off the dock and driving the *Herald-Gazette* truck, supervising Lew and the others. Eddie's doing real good. He's still living with his mother, but he is busy days and I am not. They are, all of them, my friends, busy during the day. And I am not.

So, one of them un-busy days, I'm looking for work or something like it, I hitch me a ride with some cowboys going east to Arizona, but I thank them and jump off the back of their rig out there in No-Man's-Land, way the hell out by Dewitt's. I walk on by the filling station where the new man is jawing up a yahoo. I just keep walking till I come to the dirt road that leads to the city dump and walk on, a half-mile up there. The smell—whew! How many cat and kitten corpses are rotting out here? I walk round the edges of the dump, paper blowing past me, kicking a few cans and bottles, piles of dusty rags, keeping my eyes peeled for rats. Mr. Forrest couldn't have shot them all. And looking too for his pistol. It must still be here somewheres, but not on the edges, more likely somewheres in the middle of dump where I stumble over buggy wheels and wagon tongues and singletrees because everyone's got Fords now and don't need to hitch horses. I kick candlesticks and headless lanterns because the whole town's electrified. Don't no one need this junk. Sun squints off broken glass and warms up rusted cans and broken scales, a toothless rake, a busted bucket, a stove up-ended to look like a fat lady kicking her feet, iron skirt over head. The sun shines off a broken bedstead and heats up, simmering the killer-death stench. The flies wink at me and rub their legs and chuckle over all these things that have been thrown out of people's lives. Like me.

I'm ankle-, sometimes knee-deep in this trash, kicking and looking for Mr. Forrest's ring finger. Lost the finger. Saved the ring. That's the kind of man Jake Forrest is. Everyone likes to see him win, but for a man whose life is open and shut, public as a clothespin, you long to know who was the woman before that present became past, and what it was he bitched so bad. However old Mr. Forrest lives to be, his left hand will always be crooked and broken and cut off. He'll die with his left hand all warped and busted up. Me, my hands are fine. Look at 'em. My hands are strong. *Remember that you have a friend.* Hell, my hands are big and strong and my fingers ain't wrecked. My fingers could have laced through Helen McComb's golden hair, cupped her chin, and brought her lips to mine. My hands are strong enough to wrap round Helen McComb's bare shoulders, that's how strong my hands are, gentle enough to stroke her bare back, strong enough to pull her body up against me, tight, and hold her there forever in my arms. My arms are so goddamned strong I can fling this goddamned topless food mill so it strikes an old bureau, hits, splinters the bureau, and the bottles I throw, they break and splinter too, one after the other—shatter, splatter, sing through the air, burst, empty cans ricochet off my boots as I kick what I can't crunch. The old destruction comes on me, *Though you may travel far,* because I'm not going anywhere, am I? With my strong hands I fling a busted-up sewing machine, cabinet and all, high over my head, throw, and it bounces twice, before the wood cracks open on a broken soapstone drainboard. And the ash-sifter I hurl, it hits a rusted washtub full of paper and rags and when I kick that over, the paper and rags all fly before I trip on a skillet with a hole in it, curse it, hoist it, heave it. Destroy it. I want to destroy something that isn't me, like that kettle that's got no bottom and all this crockery. Crash that, smash the rest, throw whatever was warped, whatever was worthless, like this dirty goddamn clock lying on its wooden side, its hand sprung off, but its giblets don't splinter when I kick it. *All right. All right,* and kick again and again. My boot goes through this time, but the clock's dirty goddamn face is still grinning at me and I pick it up and throw, not aiming or caring what I hit or hurt, just wanting it destroyed, but it bounces off an unstuffed mattress, goddamnit and don't break. Paper flying from my feet, I run. I find that goddamn clock and this time my boot catches its handless face and splits it off and it goes sailing, high, falls, lands in a goddamned one-wheeled baby carriage that creaks and squeals and falls over. Damned if it don't! I laugh out loud. Laugh. Because that's what Mr. Forrest did, isn't it? You don't catch Jake Forrest crying. He shot his fingers off and screamed all right, but he didn't cry. And when it was over, he laughed.

By mid-May I was working the front desk at the *Herald-Gazette*. Duke had took over the pressroom, so I am on the counter days. Nights, Duke's teaching me to set type. I'm not smart or quick as Duke, but I am doing all right. I am working anyway. None of us ever talks about that day at Dewitt's, nor mentions how Mr. Forrest has learned to keep his left hand half-hid, just like it was comfortable that way, half-hid, and not like he'd bitched anything at all. So, maybe, even with the busted-up fingers, he forgot the woman who drove him to the old destruction incumbent on love. I didn't. You only get one chance at the past and that's when it's still the present. Helen McComb married someone else.

A Brief Inquiry into the Origins of St. Elmo, California

IN THE BEGINNING was the Pass. As though God's massive knuckle curled up at the white desert, and bore down, scraped up the foothills, the track rises high into the mountains and from there, careens downhill, a long natural pass, Jesuit Pass, spilling into a sea of sagebrush. The Pass might even have reached the Pacific, except God seemed to lose interest in it, in the St. Elmo Valley for that matter. Of course He did. If His aesthetic attention had not been so clearly called elsewhere in California, surely God would have carved out a genuine riverbed here, instead of the broad invisible channel, locally known as Dogsback Ditch, which floods, cruelly, every decade or so. No, face it, instead of a real river, God's forefinger punched holes in the earth's crust, artesian wells, like the St. Elmo Valley was just a geological pie and the steam needed to escape. It's certainly true that beneath the earth's crust, this unstable pie continues to cook in thermal fires, the bubble and boil resulting in frequent earthquakes. Grand quakes send people rushing into the street or crouching under tables, clutching their robes and children. But more often, the quakes are ticklers. That's what the locals call them, ticklers, not simply for their having juggled passions long dormant in the earth, but stirring other, long-dormant urges, rousing long-dormant spouses, lying in dry connubial beds. Many's the St. Elmo child who owes his life to an aftershock.

But one day, they say, the Big One will come. The fires

inside will erupt, explode along the San Andreas Fault. This fault is one of the staples of imagery in the work of California poets. They wax on as though the fault line reflects the flawed thread of human nature. Or, for some, the fault functions as a retribution pageant, Cecil B. DeMillian in scope, that would otherwise be too corny for words. Here, in St. Elmo, it's less cosmic. The city has the dubious honor of sitting squarely atop the San Andreas Fault. When the Big One comes, everything west of Jesuit Pass will split, rip, tear off, and—with the rest of Western California—become its own island republic. O say can you see the breakers crash and foam on the St. Elmo foothills? The long coppery ropes of seaweed lapping obscenely in the mouth of Jesuit Pass?

If that Big One comes to pass, then the name, Jesuit Pass, will not seem so strange, and the Jesuit's story perhaps plausible. People won't ask: What was a crazy Jesuit doing here? Perhaps California's inland reaches always provided a sort of open-air lunatic asylum—placid, flaccid, lots of climate, no weather—where indifference passes for tolerance. But when this valley was named, there were only Indians here. So why would a valley this far inland be named for St. Elmo's fire, a phenomenon associated with sailors and storms at sea, balls of green fire streaking across the heavens, striking ships, masts, and bowsprits? St. Elmo, California, is—was then, anyway—a sea of sagebrush, rabbitbrush, tough grasses, cottonwood, mesquite, an ocean of wind and light. Nonetheless, here's the story: a shipwrecked Jesuit woke on this valley floor, built a tiny chapel of thanksgiving to the patron saint of sailors, named the pass and valley and moved on. From time to time and in various places, people claim to have found the remains of this chapel. That people believe remains of this chapel might even exist testifies that the Jesuit's story (while it cannot be held unmelting in history's crucible) has nevertheless accumulated a furry mantle of truth, the sort of thick, obscuring mold that crusts those bits of bone and hair in jeweled reliquaries, dust that decently veils what would otherwise be merely dismal or repulsive.

Anyway, more likely he would have been a Franciscan and not a Jesuit. Franciscan padres accompanied the armies of Spain into California—yoking together Crown and Cowl along the axis of the spear, the musket and the whip, establishing the mission system, converting the Indians, giving them, for their pains, Christian burials when they died under the spear, the musket, and the whip. The Jesuits were not a presence in early California. The Jesuits were active elsewhere in North America where they died really grim deaths, rivaling those of early Christian martyrs. After their deaths at the hands of the Iroquois (and other tribes of exquisite torturers, people whose relish for unthinkable pain was unexcelled) Jesuit fathers like St. Jean de Brébeuf and others were canonized, the church acknowledging that their faith had been tested beyond mere human endurance, as they were staked out spread-eagle and disemboweled before their own eyes.

The Indian tribes of the St. Elmo Valley, by contrast, had no such sophistication. They were by all accounts, a peaceful, even Edenic lot. In summer they slept under cottonwoods, in the shade of rocks; in winter they hunkered under thatched-brush shelters. They poked about for food, caught jackrabbits, held them by their ears and clubbed their brains out on rocks, skinned, cooked them on open fires, and used the skins for shoes. These Indians wove baskets of surpassing beauty, but by Iroquois standards, there was not a warrior amongst them.

However, after the Spanish arrived this far inland, these Indians became known as horse thieves, their knowledge of the Pass and its many rivulet-like canyons essential to their astonishing success. These natives substantially harassed, in turn, the Spanish military, the missions, the Mexican rancheros, Mormon wagon trains, freight convoys, the U. S. Army, and assorted other travelers. The Indians attacked and then vanished with the livestock, occasionally taking the women, sometimes taking people's lives, but leaving their bowels intact.

But by 1866 the Indians of the greater St. Elmo area had been dissuaded from horse thievery, forcibly stashed on reservations scattered throughout the county's most uninviting reaches. St. Elmo's first historian, Herschel Petrey (1859–1928), tirelessly visited these reservations in the course of his research. He was, however, a historian over-reverent of the written word and not especially gifted with imagination. For these reasons Herschel Petrey gave little thought or inquiry to the Indians' lives before the Spanish came. The Spanish brought into California the whole notion of recorded history; this was the only sort of history that Herschel Petrey truly understood. So the questions he asked of the Indians elicited little more than the memoirs of horse thieves. Still, his book, *History, Heritage and Legacy of St. Elmo* (1916) is the first of its kind, a landmark, and remains a collector's item.

The volume's slightly redundant title reflects Mr. Petrey's grand conception of his work. At the same time, it suggests a fundamental confusion of intent. *History, Heritage and Legacy* absorbed Herschel Petrey's life, his fortune, his sacred honor, and his entire family. It was co-authored with his wife, Edith Brewster Petrey (1863–1931), and both of their daughters, Helena and Eleanor, served as amanuenses for the project. Helena compiled the index. After the deaths of Herschel and

Edith, their daughters donated tons of their papers to St. Elmo City College, of which Herschel had been an original trustee and founding father. (These papers had survived St. Elmo's many disastrous floods because the Petreys were originally Midwesterners and their homes—like their lives—had both foundations and attics.) After earning degrees from the Corinthian Methodist College in Nebraska, the Petreys came to St. Elmo at the urging of Methodist friends. Over their long careers, the Petreys served St. Elmo's youth as teachers, Edith in the elementary grades, Herschel as a high school history teacher, principal, and eventually President of the Board of Education. A fit, florid man, active in the Temperance movement and an avowed teetotaler, Mr. Petrey and his family were devout members of the Methodist church where Edith taught Sunday School and Herschel served on the lay board of deacons. Herschel was also a founder of the Sons of St. Elmo, a beneficent organization of like-minded white men, lampooned by the less lofty as Sonsofbitches of St. Elmo. In addition to all this civic, educational, and church service, Petrey toiled for nearly a quarter of a century in history's vineyard. He was obsessed by time and hated clocks.

In *History, Heritage and Legacy of St. Elmo* (hereinafter *HH&L*) Petrey attacked the legend of the shipwrecked Jesuit. He noted that the first recorded mention of this valley was in 1775 when Spanish soldiers, searching out deserters, had stumbled on it. The valley's next appearance on record was circa 1806 by which time the names *St. Elmo* and *Jesuit Pass* seemed already to be in common usage and legal parlance (judging from the earliest court records involving land disputes).

In a particularly astute passage, Mr. Petrey points out

In 1773 Pope Clement XIV abolished and dissolved the Society of Jesus altogether.[1] *They were not formally reconstituted by the church until 1814. Thus we can see that there could not possibly have been a Jesuit in California between 1775 and 1806. There could not have been a Jesuit at all. How could a man be a part of something already dissolved?*

(HH&L, page 20)

In Herschel Petrey's view, these names, *St. Elmo* and *Jesuit Pass,* were but corruptions of Indian languages and he had intended to say just that, to call it the Corruption Theory, but his wife demurred. Edith intimated that *corruption* was rather a strong and slightly briny word, trailing a whiff of well, wickedness, a taint of unwholesome miasma, a word redolent of the grave, the odor of decay, reeking somehow, too, of moral rot and the implied corruption of young people.

So in the book, *HH&L,* his theory appears as Semantic Mishap. Herschel concludes Chapter One thus:

Sober inquiry must lead us away from the fanciful tale of the mad, shipwrecked Jesuit naming an inland area after the patron saint of sailors. Semantic Mishap better explains these names. It is my hope that subsequent scholars with time, resources, and talents far exceeding my own will uncover the truth, but in all likelihood, that truth will substantiate my conclusions that the simple fact is, the Spanish incorrectly understood the Indians and turned these sounds on the lathe of their own language.

Then, in about 1830 when Mexican sovereignty replaced the Spanish in California, the missionized Indians

[1] Pope Clement died the next year. Unrelated. (*HH&L,* footnote, page 20).

were dispersed and any possibility of documenting this Semantic Mishap went with them.

There was said to be recorded testimony of the early Indians' alleged encounter with the mad Jesuit (even that, mere stories passed down orally, then written down, but not substantiated). The Catholic church in the St. Elmo area kept a Book of Asistencias, *a sort of hodgepodge of parish activity from 1806 to 1829. Early priests were said to have recorded in these pages several similar accounts of this legend and other fantastic stories that came to them. Unfortunately, none of this can be verified, or even investigated as the book has vanished.*

No one has seen it since the death of Father Nuñez. His successor, Father Callahan, could not read Spanish and offered only hearsay as to the actual contents of the Book of Asistencias.[2]

As this history goes to press (1915), the present Catholic pastor of St. Elmo, Father Stoddard, concurs with me that the origins of these names lie in Semantic Mishap, the obscurities of the Indian tongue and ill-tuned Spanish ear.

(HH&L, page 23)

For Herbert Petrey to so much as mention the alleged *Book of Asistencias* was a generous gesture, considering his disastrous interview with Father Callahan, who was drunk, ranting and absolutely incoherent by the time Petrey left him.

To witness and record Father Callahan's interview, Herschel had planned to take his usual amanuensis, his

[2] Father Callahan died, drowned in a boating accident off the California coast in 1902. Unrelated. (*HH&L*, footnote, page 23).

eldest daughter, the fair Eleanor, with him. Edith quietly vetoed this plan, pointing out that Father Callahan (never minding he was a man of God) had a reputation for, well—let us be candid—drink and the occasional salty expression. Edith added that she herself preferred not to go with him to interview Father Callahan for those reasons.

This alarmed Herschel as Edith was equal to anything. Edith had gone with him into the despair, the lightless hovels of Indian homes on all but un-navigable reservations interviewing aged natives. Later, years later, in 1909, Edith stood with him, watching while St. Elmo's Chinatown burned; she brought her notebook and pencil and she dutifully, as befits the historian's helpmeet, recorded the event, though her hand shook and tears ran down her smoke-streaked face. And then, it was Edith who told him not to include this event in his history. Herschel argued that he must, that he was time's servant, history's footman, truth's advocate. Edith said, *If you once record what the people of St. Elmo did to the Chinese, allowed to happen to the Chinese, you will tarnish this town forever. Forever, Herschel. Forever.* (This is why *HH&L,* published in 1916, concludes with events in 1908, before the burning of Chinatown.)

However, to interview Father Callahan, the Petreys agreed Herschel must have a recording witness, preferably a teetotaler, a like-minded Methodist unimpeachably reliable. Someone like Wilbur Frett, because naturally, Father Callahan would lie until his teeth fell out. He was a Catholic, wasn't he? Catholics drank and smoked with impunity. Catholics thought they could simply slough off their sins, just slide out of them like a dirty shirt before a Saturday-night bath. Catholics never felt called upon to struggle with sin as Protestants must. Methodists especially. Moreover, as a priest, Callahan was absolutely sworn to the triumph of Rome, which would include making a hero out of a mythical Jesuit.

When Seamus Callahan had first arrived in the parish as assistant to the aged and infirm Father Nuñez, the local girls had giggled, whispered amongst themselves it was a great pity to waste a man that good looking on the priesthood. Such talk quickly faded however. He had a sallow face, intense gaze, and coarse, curly dark hair, sprinkled eventually with gray. He seemed always uncomfortable, as though some thorn in his clerical robes perpetually nettled. He seemed moreover, unsuited to the clergy, or at least to what St. Elmo expected of clergymen. He was neither cheerful and forthcoming like the Methodist pastor, nor bland and efficient like the Mormon elders, nor confident, fiery, and energetic like the Baptists. Callahan was moody, emotional, and taciturn; drink intensified these qualities into an indelible melancholy, indigo blue. He had been known to break down and weep, so moved was he at the penultimate moment of the Eucharist. But at funerals he conducted the dead out of this world without feeling or tenderness. He baptized babies without so much as a chuck under their fat chins. He was not sociable, refused invitations, preferred to deal with people singly in the confessional rather than in the aggregate. He made it clear he had no use for Protestants. So it's surprising he should have agreed to discuss *The Book of Asistencias* with Herschel Petrey, and one can only wonder what Callahan thought when he saw Wilbur Frett in tow, Wilbur weighted with ink bottles, pens, and sheaves of paper.

What Wilbur thought is easier to surmise. Wilbur was honored to play caboose to Petrey's mighty engine. Petrey was President of the Board of Education. Wilbur taught shorthand and typing at the city's new Blakely School of Business. Wilbur's features were knotted around his nose and such hair as he had combed from ear to ear over his freckled dome. Wilbur's record of this interview is still extant, both the original shorthand transcriptions and the fair copy made from that. Under "witness" is his own signature, a no-nonsense W. F. FRETT.

"Know ye by these men present that we, the undersigned, do set our signatures below, and hereby sweareth and deposeth to the truth of this testimony taken in the city of St. Elmo, County of St. Elmo, State of California, on this 30th day of August, 1898."

FR. C: Hot, isn't it?
HP: Don't write that down, Wilbur!

The above exchange is then crossed out, but not inked over. (Wilbur's shorthand was as lucid and uncomplicated as his mind.)

There were a lot of preliminaries where Father Callahan acknowledges that he is indeed Seamus Callahan, born Sydney, Australia, that he is thirty-one years of age, that his occupation is Catholic priest. The three sat in Father Callahan's study where the curtains were closed against the searing afternoon heat. The study (like the Church of the Assumption itself) had a brick red, impenetrable solidity to it, lest anyone should doubt its permanence or its purpose. Father Callahan sat behind his capacious desk, his visitors in deep armchairs set on a Turkey carpet. There were Catholic icons and images on the wall that made Herschel rather uncomfortable, but not nearly so uncomfortable as the doleful ticking of the grandfather clock in the corner. Herschel began to pop sweat before they even began.

Seamus Callahan saw himself as God's servant, and

Herschel Petrey saw himself as Time's servant. Neither man was comfortable with his master. Perhaps a servant never is. And never should be.

HP: Would you please describe the Book of Asistencias?

FR. C: I have held it in my hand. Often. It was kept right here in this desk. Father Nuñez used to read from it.

HP: But you have not seen it since his death?

FR. C: No.

HP: What became of the book? Please don't gesture in reply.

FR. C: What difference does it make?

HP: Wilbur can't write down gestures. This is a written record. The book vanished, yes?

FR. C: Lost. Gone.

HP: How?

FR. C: I don't know.

HP: Well—what do you think? Fair means or foul?

FR. C: Nothing that disappears is fair. It's all foul.

HP: So, Father Callahan, you suspect foul play with this book?

FR. C: I suspect nothing. I am a believer.

HP: You BELIEVE it disappeared by foul play?

FR. C: I believe it disappeared.

HP: Are you having a Jesuitical joke with me?

I am not a Jesuit.

Well. Well. The purpose of this inquiry is to discuss the origins of the names of our valley and our historic pass. That's pass, Wilbur, not past.

Right. P-a-s-s.

People have often wondered, Father Callahan, how this beautiful inland valley came by its odd nautical name.

I don't think we can get sentimental over the St. Elmo

Valley, Mr. Petrey. It's not a place that has ever created anything, nor produced very much. It owes its existence and prosperity to Jesuit Pass. It lies sprawled across the mouth of that pass in a ramshackle, an obscene sort of way. The heat in summer is hellish and the wind—winter and summer—is merciless. Drought is endemic, relieved only by flood. The people are slothful and bigoted. Those who are not slothful are smug, complacent and stultifying and bigoted. Ugliness and squalor are rampant. Do you mind if I smoke? Can I offer you a cigar?

No. No. No.

I admit, there are certain spring mornings when you can ride up into the foothills and look at the sheltering mountains and across the valley floor, smell the new grass, the dew drying on the sage, breathe deep, feel whole, even rooted, but hardly sentimental. Would you be wanting a walk in the church garden? It's walled, but there might be a breeze there, some shade. The heat's a killer. A killer, it is.

Wilbur can't record if we're walking. Let us go on. I, that is, my, the—read me my last question, please, Wilbur.

'Are you having a Jesuitical joke with—' That's not what you wanted, Mr. Petrey? Oh. Here? Odd nautical name.

Yes. Let's go back to the Book of Asistencias. Can you describe it?

It was a large volume, folio-size, calf-bound, the leather shiny from its having been passed through so many hands. The pages were sewn in, probably by Indian women, and the paper was thick and of good quality.

I mean the contents. Describe the contents. Please.

It was an informal record, parish record, comings and goings, baptisms, marriages, deaths, repairs, accounts, and crops. This parish was never so large or grand as the missions along the coast, but there was always a church here, and fields were cultivated. The Indians built the first irrigation flumes that white men later

I have all that elsewhere, Father Callahan. Here, it's the beginnings we wish to inquire after, the origin of the name.

The book was also used as a commonplace book, that's what Father Nuñez called it. Some of the earliest priests collected stories that seemed to them miraculous or apocryphal, or even simply worth noting.

Like the legend of the shipwrecked Jesuit.

Call it what you like. Contented people have no need of legends.

I have come here today on behalf of history, which also has no need of legends. History requires truth. I am on Time's errand. I am looking for the truth. Why do you scoff, Father Callahan? Surely you believe in the truth.

The truth is like the human body, being always subject to growth and decay. Corruption.

What?

Think of it this way, Mr. Petrey. The truth is the body and history is a suit of clothes. It can be a fine, full silken suit, or tattered rags cobbled together, clutched against nakedness because truth never goes about naked. It can't. The truth, unlike the human body, can't be seen in the nude.

What!

The truth is too terrible. It must always be clothed, and one man's doublet is another man's cowl.

What?

To the man who prefers his truth in a toga, the frock coat of our enlightened nineteenth century will look preposterous, but it will nonetheless cover nakedness.

[Wilbur Frett has here inked out several exchanges on the original transcript, inked them out fully. His record continues:]

FR.C: Very well, then, I'll be sticking to the point of your coming here, Mr. Petrey. And the truth of it is, one day the Indians came upon a white man lying on the valley floor. He had no name, but he was from the Society of Jesus. He was alone. He had come from a foreign country far across the sea. He had made a long and dangerous voyage and on that voyage he endured a terrible storm. No, not endured, he welcomed that storm, opened his arms to the wind and waves and lightning that battered the ship, tore at the shrouds and sails, lashed at the riggings, and beat the halyards mercilessly against the masts. He did not crouch in his cabin, but stalked the deck, praying—not to be delivered from the storm, but to be delivered to the grave. He prayed for a swift, watery death so that his soul would never again want or hunger, but bask in eternal glory. For his body, he cared nothing. Release, that was all he was wanting for his body, deliverance from the unendurable loneliness that had battered his heart and mind for years, the aloneness, the anguish. And then, when it seemed that God was about to grant his wish to die, fire streaked from Heaven and struck the ship. Light blazed round the tops of the masts, mad halos, terrible upright torches illuminating the rain, blinding balls of light, light in the midst of darkness, fire in the midst of rain! The belly of the ship split asunder, ripped open by the storm, all hands went down, and the ocean's rough blanket wrapped round the wreck.

[Wilbur's pen here stayed too long on the page and there is a big pool of ink that sogged and mottled, softened the paper of

the original shorthand transcript. A few drops then hastened to catch up with the account that continues with:]

HP: That was St. Elmo's fire he saw, correct?

FR. C: There is no St. Elmo. Surely you know that. It's a corruption.

Corruption?

Of St. Erasmus. St. Elmo is a corruption of language, a bit of bright phosphorescence shining out of decay. St. Erasmus is the patron saint of sailors. One of them.

You mean—are you saying, telling me—there's no St. Elmo?

Ah, but if there were, Mr. Petrey, if there were, such a saint would have a halo, a crown of flames round his head, and perhaps green flames to lick round his feet and he would hold, with impunity—no, more aggressively, he would hold like a weapon—his hand clutched round lightning bolts tied up in sheaves, tied with ribbons of smoke. Yes, that would be it, smoke. His symbols would be light and fire and water. He would be the patron saint of illusion. Which, when you think of it, makes him equally, just as much the patron saint of delusion, of disillusion, of dissolution, the dissolute, for all those dissolving in—shipwrecked in their own—Can I—let me ring for Marta to bring us something to drink?

No. No. Thank you. What, Wilbur? Very well then. Yes. Fine. Ring. Fine. Well, this is all rather discouraging and confusing, ha ha ha. It seems to me ha ha, that we Protestants have been sadly misled!

That you have, Mr. Petrey, that you have.

I was speaking metaphorically, humorously suggesting that we, all of us, assumed there was a real St. Elmo.

There is. We're here. This is the church in the real St. Elmo, California. Ah, Marta—lemonade for these gentlemen. Whiskey for me. No soda, but ice. Now, don't be giving me that look, Marta. Ice. Do you think you could find us a bit of ice? I'd be forever in your debt, Marta. Truly. But if you can't, just bring the whiskey. And the bottle, Marta. The bottle.

Getting back then, Father Callahan, this Book of Asistencias. Did you read it?

Ah, well, Mr. Petrey, my sainted mother, God rest her, taught me to read English. My granny taught me to read tea leaves. The priests at seminary taught me to read Latin, but I cannot read Spanish.

If you don't know Spanish, you could hardly vouch for, or testify to the contents of this book.

Father Nuñez could read Spanish. He was a Mexican priest. He read to me. He was a humble man, a fine priest. He served God. He served the people of this benighted parish and I am not his equal.

I am here to discuss history, Father Callahan, trying to save the book, the alleged book.

The book is gone. It can't be saved. To be saved you must believe. Now, isn't that so? Even the Methodists— Thank you, Marta. Ah, you found some ice. Bless you. Ice. Lemonade, Wilbur? Mr. Petrey?

[Wilbur's account is smudged here, presumably from long rivulets of sweat dripping off his icy glass in the breezeless August heat caged in the priest's study. Wilbur continues with:]

FR. C: To be saved you must believe and so the book is beyond redemption because you don't believe. You don't believe me, Mr. Petrey. You don't believe Father Nuñez. Perhaps you do not believe that such a book existed, or that it told varying accounts of the same impossible tale, a nameless Jesuit beached here in this valley, a man still dazed and blinded by the fires, the lights at sea, dashed and blown by the storm, all order dissolved, the chaos complete. Think of him, facedown on the earth, his clothes wet, caked with mud, seaweed strangled round his wrists and ankles, his skin torn, his beard matted with salt water, shipwrecked, alone, beached, cast upon these shores.

But we don't have any shores.

Shut up, Wilbur! Please. I'm sure Father Callahan was speaking metaphorically.

Cast here upon this valley floor, a man who had longed for death, his eyes slowly opening, expecting that he will see the briny lightless ocean floor, the cradle of earth, expecting his bones to be forever rocked in those long long currents, expecting that schools of spangled fish will strip him of his clothes, his very flesh, but now, he raises himself up slowly on his arms, blinks as his gaze falls upon an ocean of stubble and sagebrush. He would shake his head, spit salt water, and realize he'd misunderstood God's will. He would look into the broad leathery faces of Indians. More lemonade? The Indians also had no names.

When? No lemonade, thank you. When did all this occur?

These people had no names. How can you expect them to have dates?

No names! No dates! Isn't that, really, finally the same thing as saying they did not exist! This is all fanciful! A tale, not history!

I'll have some lemonade, please, Father Callahan.

[Again the original transcript is splotched and swollen where beads of water have dropped from Wilbur's icy glass. Wilbur continues with:]

HP: Here, sir, is the history. In 1775 a party of Spanish soldiers searching for deserters came upon this valley and this Pass. Their passage through it was merely incidental, and though they recorded its existence, they did not name it. In 1775 it had no name. We know this from the military records of the garrison in San Diego. There is nothing else until 1806. In 1806 the church and the military began keeping records here and we also had the rudiments of a legal system, which requires that things be written down. By then, 1806, these names, Jesuit Pass and St. Elmo were already in use. They were used in legal descriptions! How did this happen? Please! Do not merely shrug, drink, smoke your cigar and gesture! Speak, Father Callahan, speak! Who wrote these stories down? Where did they come from? Speak! Who had access to this book?

Everyone.

Who?

Many people.

Who?

The dead, Mr. Petrey, the equally nameless, dateless dead. The book was kept here in this office. In this desk, or over there in that bureau. It was not a sacred text.

So it could have been falsified at any time! Many times! Any number of people could have altered the records.

Why are you here?

Because I am trying to separate fact from fiction! That strikes you as funny, Father Callahan? Funny! I suppose after you drink yet ANOTHER of those, you'll tell me that the Church of the Assumption, this very church, was built on the sacred remains of the Jesuit's chapel to Our Lady of St. Elmo.

There was no chapel.

What? What? You contradict yourself, Father Callahan.

No. The chapel's just a misunderstanding.

A semantic misunderstanding perhaps?

Perhaps. In the Book of Asistencias, the word is capeeya. That's c-a-p-i-l-l-a. Capilla could be a chapel in the usual sense, a structure with walls and a roof and some permanence and solidity, but more likely by the eighteenth century, the church in California, the Catholic church, had discovered what the Jews have long known. You cannot be carrying Chartres on your back.

What?

If you rely on stones and stained glass, on flying buttresses, high towers, and brass bells, your religion will not travel well. You cannot carry vaults and cloysters.

Is that right, Father Callahan? C-l-o-y . . .

Spell it later, Wilbur!

If you intend to explore the undiscovered, your religion must be free of stones and buttresses, permanent structures. You must keep it to words, which are portable and impermanent. You must believe—absolutely—in your power to make holy any place you endow with words and spirit. Like the Jews do with their weddings. They . . .

Please! Father Callahan! We are not here to discuss the Jews!

Capilla might have been a chapel, but not a structure. Perhaps it was a three-sided thatched-brush shelter. Perhaps it was a tumbleweed palace, a towering tumbleweed palace erected over a rabbitskin reliquary, shrouding a flimsy crucifix of spars splintered off from the ship that went down, spars yoked together with seaweed, tied with

Very funny, Father Callahan.

A tumbleweed palace. That all blew away.

In short, you're willing to concede there was no chapel. No Our Lady of St. Elmo. Why do you laugh?

St. Elmo is just a name corrupted into light and fire and

all the things you cannot hold or keep. A name of light and fire, a miraculous occurrence now bestowed upon this squalid town full of toadies and humbugs.

Why do you hate St. Elmo so much, Father?

Wilbur—stay out of this!

It is not my country. I have been shipwrecked here. Beached.

Where is your country, Father?

Wilbur! Please!

I have no country. Oh, I am tired, tired, and it's all useless.

You are drunk, Father Callahan!

Useless and wasted on you, you, and everyone like you, Mr. Petrey. You think I lied, that Father Nuñez lied, that the nameless Indians lied, and the anonymous Jesuit lied, that the will of God might not have triumphed over a mere man's killing loneliness, his wish to die, that the will of God might not have triumphed over nature, and a storm rise up that would swell those mighty breakers so that they escaped the bondage of the beach and crashed up here, on land, inland, receded, left salt and foam drying on this valley floor along with the Jesuit priest. You do not believe that he pulled barnacles from his beard, spit salt water from his lungs, that he tore at the seaweed binding his wrists and ankles. You don't believe he could have found splintered spars yet clutched in his hand, that he made from them a crucifix, an emblem so that he might never forget God's will. You do not believe that he could have named this pass after his order and this valley after God's certain sign—not that he should live or die, but that he should cease quarreling! That he should do God's bidding and not ask for release. Not ask for freedom, not ask for death. No, it's wasted on all of you! You will never understand. How can you? You travel in packs! Protestant packs and Masonic processions, Sons of St. Elmo parades, temperance crusades, teams of mule drivers, and regiments of railroad men, and those long, dauntless wagon trains full of Mormons. Mobs of Mormons! Oh God! Hordes of Protestants always, who distrust solitude of any sort, who cannot even breathe in and out unless there's multitudes all around them! How could you understand? How can any of you? You all live in swarms—in that knit of swarmed, connected flesh, flesh like blankets, all tight-woven, warm, stultifying. Children come into the world with pain, out of the loins of people who have coupled without pleasure. People who touch without feeling! How can you understand the passion—the madness! Call it what you wish!—the illusion, delusion of one who lives celibate and alone and unconnected to humanity, swearing himself to some greater, invisible good? How can you understand what it is to pluck yourself from the sweet mire of flesh so you can enter God's service, be His servant, and find that God hath shipwrecked you on this foreign shore? How can you guess—what it would be to open your eyes thinking sure your eyes must roll from their sockets untethered to your head, like pearls, your eyes must roll across the ocean floor, in the black and briny deep—but, no! No. Light blinds you, and the wind is merciless, and God will not let you delude yourself longer. What to do, but call this place after a saint that never was? After an order dissolved, suppressed, abolished. And then—what became of him, that priest? Where did he go? Where did he go after that? Where did he die? Who buried him? To die on land, you must, you need someone to bury you. To die at sea, the shroud is already there, cold before you're ever cold—empty. The bottle is empty. Ah well, you, Mr. Petrey, you are an unbeliever. You don't believe this Jesuit ever drew breath, of course, so how can you believe he died or care who buried him?

I'll tell you what I believe, Father Callahan, and my religion—thank you—teaches me to venerate the truth. My profession teaches me to venerate the truth. While yours—in your religion and your profession—you practice sophistry. You traffic in superstition. You venerate idols and relics. And you are drunk! That's what I believe! At best, the kindest that could be said of you is that you are an unreliable witness! At worst, I believe you destroyed that book. Yes, I do. After Father Nuñez died. Perhaps before his death. Perhaps the two of you conspired to destroy it. But I am sure that it did not simply vanish. You burnt it. Didn't you?

Petrey, you are a Pharisee, and Wilbur, you are a scribe. You are the very people that Christ—in His infinite wisdom—threw out of the temple! You pray in the streets, you slaver after the opinions of men, and you care nothing for God! You serve two masters!

Save your invective, Father Callahan. We are leaving. You are an insult to your vocation.

I am human. Do you know what that means? In the singular?

Come on, Wilbur. This is fruitless. Finished.

But, Mr. Petrey. We . . . uh, he has to . . . it won't be . . . I mean, if he doesn't sign . . .

Very well. Father Callahan, you must sign this. Such as it is. Father Callahan! Pay attention to me!

Please, Father. Would you sign? Yes. Here's the pen. Sign, please.

Where?

He finished off the ice in their glasses as their footsteps diminished hastily down the passage. The clock ticked slowly in its muffled tenor, chimed the hour in a contralto, and the pigeons, protesting the heat, softly counterpointed under the roof tiles. Seamus Callahan moved slowly across the room to the water pitcher on the bureau and disturbed the flies. He poured himself a glass of water, then another. The third he poured upon his head, heedless of the Turkey carpet.

Suddenly his eyes lit, as though clearheaded and refreshed, and he shambled back over to the massive desk and rummaged about the drawers, pulling them out, dumping them on the floor, and scavenging through their miscellaneous contents, working swiftly, glancing up now and then, to be certain no one was watching (at least that no one he could see was watching).

He must have found what he wanted because he stood unsteadily and went to the door, abashed to see Marta there, tray in hand. Her broad, leathery Indian face wrinkled with pity and contempt, which he wordlessly ignored. He left her, reeled down the passageway and into the old church garden maintained by Marta's husband, Manuel.

It was an unimpressive garden, walled once with adobe, now red-bricked like the rest of the Church of the Assumption and set about with young crepe myrtle trees, their dry lavender tears scattered on the balding grass. The best-tended part was the kitchen garden, the domestic garden of Manuel and Marta. Neatly staked peppers and tomatoes shone in bright necklaces of red and yellow.

At Manuel's shed, he pulled open the rickety door and stepped inside. He blinked in the dimness and the smell, oddly, richly rank. He got hold of a shovel and dragged it over to a crumbling corner, near what was left of the old adobe wall and he began to dig, and dig and dig. Sweat ran down his sides and arms and dripped from his upper lip, caught along his eyebrows and clerical collar; his robes grew damp and he panted, but when he was done, it was a deep hole, a fine hole, or at least it would serve its purpose.

He squatted and pulled from his pocket what he had taken from the desk drawer—a moth-eaten bag of what might once have been fur, but it had fallen out in clumps and now looked only balding and mangy. He opened the bag and threw it in the hole, holding before him what he'd managed to extract, a small, crude crucifix. It was no bigger than his hand, shards, sharp sticks, hastily tied together with rust-colored material, thicker than yarn, but fragile as paper. Bits of it flaked off in his fingers and drifted, copper-colored motes, into the hole. Tenderly he reached down and placed the crucifix atop the bag. He stared. He sought some words appropriate to the occasion, but only rutted conventional phrases came to mind, learned phrases. They would not do. So he just muttered, *So be it*. That's what Marta and Manuel thought they heard as they stood at the gate watching him shovel, filling the hole. Their broad Indian faces were painted with surprise. He finished, coughed, choked as the dust blew in his face and stirred the crepe myrtle blossoms at his feet. He wiped the sweat from his brow and turned, shocked to meet their gaze, amazed as though they were great spangled fish swimming toward him over the briny lightless ocean floor.

Little Women

LIKE I WAS SAYING, we knew. You do, living on an island. In Arcadia's case, we knew what and we could guess at when. Where is easy on an island. But who? Still, like the girls here at Island Title and Trust say: you'd have to be blind, deaf, dumb, and a virgin to miss or mistake what Arcadia Pruitt was up to.

About April we notice that Arcadia, who is as plain as unbuttered toast, suddenly, her brown hair's curling and sort of sun-streaked (*out of a bottle,* says Phyllis) and her glasses are gone and her eyes a brightened-up blue (*contacts,* says Darlene). Her skin seems to glow (*Max Factor,* says Cyndee) and even though she still wears a brown raincoat that looks like a padded book mailer, she seems sort of, well, radiant. In the typing pool, we all know what that means. But Arcadia Pruitt? She wouldn't even think of sex unless she was playing Scrabble and got stuck with the X tile.

She was always too smart for her own good and too good for Isadora Island. Valedictorian for Island High (same year as Phyllis, Darlene, Cyndee, and I graduated). Arcadia's old father, Luther, he was all over Isadora Island on his motorcycle telling everyone who'd listen—and a lot who wouldn't—that Arcadia's got a full scholarship to Stanford and she's going to study Literature.

That summer after graduation, Phyl and Cyndee and Darlene and I, we all stood up at each other's weddings. (Yes, and when the time came, we all stood up at each other's divorces, too.) And what with all the excitement in our lives, who gave a thought to Arcadia Pruitt off at Stanford? Once she left Isadora Island, she didn't come back even at Christmas, and she wrote to no one except her old dad, Luther. He read her literary letters to the tellers in the bank and the clerks in stores. Everyone, from the gang at the Oar House Tavern in Dough Bay, to the ladies at the Crystal Kettle Tea Shoppe here in Massacre, they all knew Arcadia won an award for Literature, that she was studying in literary England. One payday, we're celebrating Cyndee's divorce with a couple of hot pastramis at Rand's Café, when Luther comes in with picture postcards from literary Boston and we have to hear all about her graduate work at Radcliffe and the great Harvard Library where she had a job.

Then, one day, a couple of years later, old Luther—who had no business on a motorcycle, not at his age—he spins out on a wet road and slams into a tree, had to be airlifted off the island, he was so banged up. Everyone was sorry for Luther, but he didn't have any family left here to send so much as a card to. Too tough to die, Luther was left with one leg shorter than the other, and when he finally limped back to Isadora, who brings him home but Arcadia. And she stayed.

One morning, here at Island Title and Trust, Phyl looks up from her computer and she nudges me and Darlene and Cyndee, asks, "Who is that Chuck Reynolds is leading through the office like it's the Sea of Galilee?" Chuck Reynolds is the Personnel Officer and we hear him saying, oh, just ask if she wants a new chair or lamp, anything at all.

"That's Arcadia Pruitt," Darlene whispers.

I'm not so sure. Small, narrow-shouldered, she looks like nobody and anybody, wearing a brown skirt, brown shoes, a beige sweater, brown hair tied at the back of her neck, little pearl earrings, and glasses.

But we can tell it *is* Arcadia Pruitt because of the way Reynolds is sucking up to her. He graduated the same year we did. He has a wife and three snotty kids, and like us, he's never lived off the island, so Chuck Reynolds is joyed-over, proud to have Arcadia Pruitt and her Stanford degree and her Radcliffe background working here.

She says hello to us. She smiles and says, "Well, you have to start somewhere, don't you?"

That was six years ago. She's Chuck's executive assistant now and like the other officers' assistants, her desk fronts the typing pool in a big semicircle. She's efficient, pleasant enough, but you wouldn't call Arcadia friendly. We kept waiting (hoping) for some hanky-panky with her and Chuck Reynolds, but no, not a bit of it. Arcadia Pruitt isn't even good for gossip.

She had moved back in with her dad. She still fixes his meals, keeps house, and looks after him. (We all wonder if she even knows when old Luther stays out all night, because that bearded duffer is always good for gossip.) Arcadia pruned the apple trees in front of their place, which is set just off the road and down from the Useless Post Office on Useless Point. Her first year back she put up a hammock between the apple trees and every summer evening, if you drove down to Useless, you could see her there, feet up, reading novels. She read novels in the lunchroom on her every break, no matter how noisy the rest of us were. She carried the books in a bag with her lunch. Library books mostly. She volunteered her time after work and on weekends at the Island Library, a two-room building at the junction of School Lane and Cutlass. There was just the one librarian, a woman who's been there since the glaciers melted, and nothing's changed for eons till Arcadia went in and volunteered. Arcadia redid the card catalog, set up a kids' corner, started a Wednesday-night book club for the island's old folks. Then she gets this idea to raise money—for more books, a new roof, new front steps, maybe a whole new building one day—and she starts up this group called Friends of the Island Library. On her lunch hour, Arcadia comes round to each of us and asks if we'll join. For ten dollars we can be Charter Members. Well, we joined. We had to. She took your IOU if you didn't have the ten bucks.

Can you believe it? In a couple of years, the Friends of the Island Library is just The Thing to belong to on Isadora. Even members of rival book clubs all belong to the Friends. Pretty soon, there's so many Friends, they can't even meet in the Library anymore, and the Massacre Bay Yacht Club is falling all over itself to lend them space. And their fund-raisers! All the doctors' wives want their homes used for the Friends of the Island Library Christmas Auction, where people come for wine and cheese and holiday cookies and a look at million-dollar views while they bid silently on donated goods and services. But by far the greatest event was their annual summer Garden Party. You had to come dressed as a character in a book or a poem and you had to recite lines from that book. (And pay, of course.) This was all Arcadia Pruitt's idea and she organized the whole thing.

The Garden Party started out in someone's backyard and then, the next summer, we're reading about it in the Seattle paper. The year after that it gets written up in *Pacific Northwest Magazine,* then *Sunset* and *Victoria.* Now on that June weekend Isadora Island is absolutely flooded with people who can't wait to put on funny costumes and spout a bunch of goofy lines. The Friends of the Island Library Garden Party brings as many tourists as the

Fourth of July, Labor Day, and Opening Day of yachting season. Well, no one on this island is about to say, *Tourist, go home,* of course, but it was pretty hard to hack when Mr. Reynolds gave Arcadia the afternoon off so she could go to the Isadora Tourist Board annual luncheon and accept her plaque for being Woman of the Year.

They put Arcadia's picture, front page, in the Isadora *Courier-Enterprise* and Cyndee was painting her nails over it in the lunchroom. Cyndee says: *If I was Arcadia, I'd rather see my picture in the wedding section, or even the engagement*. But Arcadia's never even had a boyfriend, and it's a local joke that old Luther Pruitt (who's been through three wives already), that Luther would get married before his daughter did. Arcadia is his youngest, the only child of his third wife, born when Luther was pushing fifty.

It wasn't too long after the Tourist Board luncheon that Darlene remarks to us that some Fridays Arcadia doesn't read novels in the lunchroom anymore. Cyndee's noticed on Mondays Arcadia often comes in late, dark circles under her eyes and a radiant smile on her face. Chuck Reynolds says nothing to her. Not so much as a frown. You can just imagine what he would have said to one of us. Of course, we don't lead the Friends of the Island Library on to greatness. We're just sitting here in the lunchroom at Island Title and Trust peeling Styrofoam coffee cups on a rainy May afternoon (sky's the color of pillow ticking) when Phyllis comments Arcadia's changed completely. She looks different. She acts different. *She's sleeping with someone,* says Cyndee. The question is who? There just aren't that many available men on Isadora. We know this for a fact. We've all been married and divorced. We've dated every available man (and a few who weren't).

Then, in June, rain vanishes and Isadora seems to stretch its island arms out into the Puget Sound. The sun drips down on us, yellow like just-cracked yolk, and everything lies in sunny splendor, light braiding gold through the green leaves. Mildew, moss, rot, and damp all dry up, and on one of these glorious days, a Friday, we come back from the lunchroom and put our purses in the bottom desk drawers, roll out the trust deeds and reconveyances, go into the hearts of our computers to pull up the legal language and property descriptions. Phyllis whispers over to me: *Where's Arcadia?*

An hour later, in she walks. She's wearing a man's denim jacket, salt water stains the cuffs of her beige pants, and her feet are sandy, thrust into wet shoes. Panty hose hangs out of her purse along with a bit of sea-lettuce. In one hand she holds tight a fistful of wild daisies and behind her ear there's a spray of dog roses with the pink blossoms falling off, catching in her streaked hair and on her shoulders. In her other hand she has a can of Diet Pepsi. Ribboned around her is the smell of wind and rocks and salt off the ocean, the scent of yarrow and petals crushed, creased in fingertips, and you can all but see the sunshine and wild grass still on her back and in her hair. All our keyboards fall silent, but Arcadia just sails in, not looking at us, not like she's not-looking, but like she's not seeing. She gets to her desk and pops the Diet Pepsi, sips it, then thrusts the daisies in the can. She takes off the denim jacket and puts it over the back of her chair. Her starched blue blouse is buttoned wrong. She checks her messages, peers at her computer, then she puts her head down on the desk and falls asleep. Mouth open.

Chuck Reynolds comes out to ask Arcadia something, but finds her asleep, hair spilled over the desk, computer humming, phone lights flashing. He glances round at the rest of us and we quick, look away. He goes back into his office and closes the door.

A few of us took bets, nothing serious, on who would have the guts to go over and drop a volume of Washington Estate Law near her desk, but no one collected. At four she woke, put on the denim jacket, and left the office without another word.

Right after work the four of us are out in the parking lot. It's time to get serious. We walk down to Pancho's Mexican Restaurant, where Sally takes our order for nachos and a round of Margaritas. We ask ourselves: Who is Arcadia sleeping with? We start with the Regulars. On an island you got three kinds of people: Regulars, Tourists, and Sojourners. They never mix. To be a Regular, you're born here or been here twenty years. We try to think of Regular single men, but there's hardly any, unless you count duffers old as Luther Pruitt, and a handful of gay men. Of the married Regulars, we go through the names of every man who plays around. Arcadia's not the play-around type. So it's not a Regular. And not a Tourist either. Tourists come, stay three days, drop a lot of money, leave. Isadora is a boater's island, an artist's island, it's a sailing, sleeping, and walking island. Honeymooners might come here, but not single men looking for fun. Besides, anyone looking for fun would not look at Arcadia Pruitt.

That leaves Sojourners. They come for a few weeks or a few years. They live on boats, or in houses you got to be an eagle to get to. Sojourners have money, so they're not wandering the island searching for work (not that there is any work here, unless you bar-tend, table-tend, till-tend, pump-tend, or fish). Anyway most Sojourners bring their own women, wives, girlfriends, live-ins, and those who don't are weird as gull poop. We just can't figure out who'd sleep with Arcadia Pruitt. We tell Sally we'd like the bill when . . . in walks these four men. Old enough to be interesting and young enough to be—well, young enough.

They look clean and athletic, like they've just jumped over tennis nets or come off a sailboat. They're wearing deck shoes and shorts and T-shirts with faded logos of Mexican beer. They're tanned and clean-shaven except for a mustache here and there. They have nice smiles, good teeth, and they're fair, but for one dark-haired, intense-looking guy. They sit nearby and relax in their chairs. You can see the muscles in their shoulders and their legs. They take their shades off, catch Sally's attention, and joke with her while they order nachos and Margaritas.

Sally brings us our tab. We decide to have another round of nachos and Margaritas.

If you didn't crack your nachos too loud, you could put it together like this: three of them took the ferry just this afternoon, and from the ferry landing at Dog Bay, they'd driven to Massacre to meet the dark-haired, intense-looking guy, Austin. He had sailed over yesterday. He asked Sally for some hotter salsa and you could see his five o'clock shadow beneath his tan. His boat was tied up now at the Massacre Visitors' dock, but he couldn't stay overnight because the Massacre Marina was full up. He'd tried the dock at Useless too, but it was already filled. He didn't want to anchor offshore because *Lone Star* didn't have a dinghy. He said he'd heard there might be space at Dough Bay.

That's when Cyndee scoots her chair over toward them, clears her throat, and says she couldn't help but hear their conversation. She feels it is her civic duty to say that Dough Bay just isn't a good place. It got its name from, well, low tide.

"Where else can I moor?" asks Austin. "This entire island is full. It's the Friends of the Island Library Garden Party weekend."

Right! Of course! We knew that! Then we suggest Ditch

Nelson. It's on the other side of the island, but never crowded because only locals know about it. The four guys move their table closer to ours while we tell them how, in the thirties, a guy named Nelson tried to dig a canal out there. He got about a mile dug before they made him stop. But there's a nice little marina there now. We could show them. We certainly could. Someone went for a map.

There was more nachos and salsa and we are all thinking about ordering dinner and it turns out these guys are all tennis friends (and not married!). Cliff and Stuart were actually working this weekend, Cliff's a writer and Stuart's a photographer for the *Seattle Weekly,* sent to Isadora to cover the famous Friends of the Island Library Garden Party. "Nice work if you can get it," says Neil, a Microsoft engineer who took a couple of days off to sail with Austin and his friends on the *Lone Star.* Austin doesn't work summers because he teaches Spanish at Edmonds Community College. Well, that made everything easy, speaking of Spanish, right here in Pancho's Mexican Restaurant with big blow-up pictures of Pancho Villa stuck all over the walls. Austin says he grew up in El Paso, Texas, Pancho Villa's old stomping grounds. Austin had a nice low voice with a comfortable sort of drawl that added to his funny stories about the grief he'd taken for having a name like Austin and living in El Paso. He said his great-granddad actually rode with Pershing when the U.S. Army went down into Mexico looking for Villa in 1916. He told a story about how his great-granddad could have shot Pancho. And didn't.

Neil winks at us and says: "They expelled Austin from El Paso for slinging bull."

Austin laughs and says no, he left El Paso because there he couldn't sail.

"Well," says Phyllis, "you can sail on Isadora all right. That's about all you can do here. Sail, walk, talk, eat, drink."

"And read," Austin says. "You must have a lot of readers on this island."

"Oh, lots. We're all great readers," I said.

"We're Charter Members of the Friends of the Island Library. We wouldn't miss the Garden Party for anything," says Darlene.

"Who are you going to be?" Cliff asks Cyndee with a smile to slay her.

Cyndee bites into a great big nacho full of cheese and salsa, chews slowly, and raises her eyes to me.

"*Little Women,*" I say. And the guys thought that was great.

The Friends of the Island Library charged admission even if you were a Charter Member. We had to park our cars about half a mile away, and walk up to the gate at Cross's Meadow where a couple of girls I recognize from the Safeway were sitting at a table taking your money and making you recite your lines. One had her hair in braids and a little stuffed Toto under her arm. The other was dressed in tatters and a bonnet. They would let you in without the lines, but not without the money. We sort of dawdled, giving neither. We were supposed to meet Neil and Stuart and Austin and Cliff here at the entrance, at least that's what we'd informally agreed upon at Pancho's. We were all going together, you might say, though not Going Together. We were worried maybe the guys had already got there, and we waited at the gate a long time. As all these people came to the Garden Party, I was embarrassed really. Here we were, native to this island and

Charter Members, but we looked pretty dull compared to everyone else. We'd just flung our costumes on, and none of us knew a line from *Little Women*. I could barely remember the story, only that there were four of them and they wore long skirts. There were four of us, and we wore long skirts. We had belted up T-shirts and shoved our feet into sandals, without a thought to the book. We didn't know it was such a big deal. Our costumes weren't—well, we could have done better. Tom Sawyer, Huck Finn, even Nancy Drew would have been a cinch.

Finally we see the four guys coming down the path toward Cross's Meadow. The Safeway girls see them, too. I mean, these guys lit up the whole island, and I don't think they even knew it. Neil is wearing a paper chain around his neck and tells the girls he's *Lord of the Rings*. Austin, he's pinned a bunch of candy wrappers to his shirt and says he's *The Three Musketeers* and recites his lines in French, no less! Cliff and Stuart were wearing polka-dotted ties and passed themselves off as the Bobbsey Twins. Stuart took Dorothy's picture with Toto and asked the other girl who she was. With a dazzling smile she says, *Little Dorrit*.

We walked up Cross's Meadow that June day, and sunshine floated like a scarf over the poppies and buttercups and dandelions crushed under hundreds of pairs of feet, and the green smell rose from the grass, the air so clear. Sunlight cut like a silver knife across the dark distant waters of Useless Bay. There were tents and canopies everywhere, and Friends of the Island Library sold beer, lemonade, hot dogs, sandwiches, homemade jam and applesauce, cookies, ice cream, popcorn (a feast for the seagulls). There were tables of donated books for sale, and local authors autographing and local artists selling watercolors and ceramics, and the Island High School Chamber Orchestra playing off-key Mozart. Later on, the high school jazz band would play.

The meadow was broiling with color and heat and it was like everyone here—Tourists, Regulars, Sojourners—shook themselves out and upside down and became what they'd always intended to be. There's Chuck Reynolds's wife wearing nothing but a black silk slip and calling herself Maggie, *The Cat on a Hot Tin Roof.* Chuck Reynolds—tight T-shirt, tight pants—calls himself *Studs Lonigan.*

We counted twelve Scarletts and four *Scarlet Letters,* a few Rhetts, and couples calling each other *Pride* and *Prejudice* and *Sense* and *Sensibility.* There's a guy in a hula skirt and his girlfriend in a sailorsuit calling themselves *Hawaii* and *Tales of the South Pacific.* There's about three *Shoguns,* one in authentic costume, and a few men in World War I uniforms, with their arms in slings, *Farewell to Arms.* Mr. Tubbs, the island's only accountant, is Sherlock Holmes and his old wife is Watson. Even a bunch of fishermen from Dough Bay, they're here just wearing their work clothes, and telling everyone, *Call me Ishmael.* Angie, from Duncan Donuts, barefoot and distraught, cries out, *Heathcliff! Heathcliff!* And I about died when Luther Pruitt heaves himself up behind me, gooses me, and shouts, *Avast ye mateys!* He scratches the gray hairs peeking out of his shirt, tells us he's Long John Silver. Then he limps off, leaning on his crutch, looking for other bottoms to pinch.

We moved through the crowd to see a few *Alices* and more than one Mad Hatter. Ernton Hapgood is wearing an old plaid bathrobe and introduces himself as Boo Radley. All the little girls look like *Heidi* or *Pippi Longstocking.* Little boys in caps and rags beg pennies off you, or try to pick your pocket, *Please sir, can I have some more?* Phyllis near-died to meet her ex; he's in raingear, his hair all floured up white to make him look old, carrying a stuffed marlin under his arm and chatting up *Lolita*. And all around us people would just whoop and holler when they found others from the same book or author: *Lady Chatterley* reunited with her *Lover,* Tigger found Pooh. Stephen King and Daphne Du Maurier characters met themselves coming and going. The waiters from the Chowder House were *The Last of the Mohicans*. Celia Henry, and everyone who worked for her, were the cast of *The Wind in the Willows*. Bill from Island Cycles was (what else) *Zen and the Art of Motorcycle Maintenance*. Under a beach umbrella *Mrs. Dalloway* ate ice cream with *The Lion* and *The Witch,* while *The Wardrobe* drank beer with *The Great Gatsby*.

Strangest of all were those reunions of characters from books no one ever heard of, unsung novels, unremembered poems. These characters would spy each other, laugh, exclaim to discover another passionate reader, embrace, even weep to recite lines, or relive scenes by obscure authors. The gathering in Cross's Meadow was like a big family reunion. Walking through the throng, I wished I really did love *Little Women*. I wished there was a book I cared that much about. I wished there was some character who had moved into my life forever, some author whose lines I would never forget, some poem I could recite by heart and from the heart. I felt a pang of loss and wondered what I'd missed by not being a reader.

Suddenly Austin stops walking. He stares, gape-mouthed at an Island County Commissioner, a paunchy man in natty duds, wearing a huge white fang on a chain around his neck and talking to a woman in white. She turns, smiles at Austin, not a big joyful smile, but veiled and only for him. She leaves the Commissioner with his lips still flapping, and ignores the rest of us. She says hello to Austin.

I didn't even recognize Arcadia Pruitt. She wore a simple white dress of fine, gauzy material, so flimsy you can almost see her tan line under her blouse, cinched round the waist with a coarse cottonweave belt of hot pink. Draped over her brown arms she carries a tasseled shawl of parrot blues and tropical greens. Except for wisps that curl round her face, her hair's pinned up with weird-looking flowers of a throbbing, unreal pink, their hearts a wicked magenta.

Austin says, "You look beautiful, Arcadia. You look . . . well, scrumptious."

"Thank you." She says that with her lips, but with her eyes she is saying something the rest of us couldn't hear.

"You still have my denim jacket?"

Arcadia nods and laughs and her eyes shine at him.

Austin reaches up and touches the flowers in her hair. "Where did you get the hibiscus? I haven't seen hibiscus since I left Texas."

"Anything is possible in books."

"Which book are you?"

"This book hasn't been written yet," she says slowly, carefully. "This book ought to be written. It's about lovers on a sailboat, lovers sailing to Mexico this summer. This book will take a long time to write."

Austin seems to sway toward her, like gravity is pulling him. "A whole summer?"

"A whole lifetime."

She really said it. Just like that. I'm standing there with the sunlight dappling all around me and I can smell the bleach from Arcadia's cotton dress and somewhere just behind it a splash of citrus, like a lime slice hitting the salted rim of a fresh Margarita, and even this far north, here in the Puget Sound, I could sense Mexico, as surely as if my toes curled into hot, golden sand.

Austin reaches out and touches the base of Arcadia's throat, brushes some powder caught there, moves his hand slowly up to her cheek. Arcadia turns to graze his fingertips with her lips, but one of those impossible pink flowers falls to the grass. He picks it up and puts it behind his own ear. He asks if she would like to dance.

I look around. No one is dancing. But the high school jazz band is playing now, some old standard, "Cheek to Cheek" maybe, and Arcadia says she would love to dance. She doesn't actually speak, not with words. She says she would love to dance with him forever, says so with her hands and shoulders, her eyes, says *yes,* and the voltage, the current that electrifies between them is so intense it could run the spin cycle on your washer. Then, they're gone. It all took about thirty seconds.

We're kind of dry mouthed and slack jawed after that. Neil asks if it's the heat or something. Something, we say.

So we all drift off to get Cokes and overpriced sandwiches and Neil tells us how Austin got invited to a party here on the island last February, an afternoon party at some artist's house, a Sojourner, who had a friend visiting from Mexico. In February it's dark early, dank and wintery. Austin got lost, and he stopped at the little library at the junction of School and Cutlass. That's where he met Arcadia Pruitt. She was struggling with a ladder, trying to fix the shelving in Biography. Austin never did get to the party. Neil laughs. We smile, sort of.

Then Neil sees a guy he knows from Microsoft, wearing a hat of rubber rats. *"Of Mice and Men!"* Neil calls out, splits, leaves us here, marooned.

Lots of people are dancing now. We can see Arcadia Pruitt and Austin. Her hair has tumbled down, but her chin is tilted to his lips, and her arms around his shoulders. I gasp because I get goosed by Luther Pruitt. He nudges the others with his crutch and says, "Well, girls, what do you think?"

Phyl might have muttered something, but the rest of us were just struck dumb.

Luther gives his horny laugh. "Don't underestimate Arcadia. They'll always surprise you, people like that. Arcadia's been surprising me for thirty years."

"How?" says Darlene at last, "how did she do it?"

Luther leans on his crutch. He frowns and scratches. "She wanted to love a man who appealed to her imagination, I guess, and she wasn't going to waste her time with anyone less. Why bother? But when she found him, well, it was love, girls and—you'll forgive me calling you girls, I hope, young as you are."

"Get on with it, Luther," snaps Cyndee.

"Well, once she's in love, Arcadia's not going to mess around. She's going to get it right. She had those tropical flowers FedEx'd in from somewhere. She bleached that dress within an inch of its life, starched it, too. It's like Arcadia, in her own imagination, could see what Austin knew. When Austin came up to her, he would see the sunlight beating down on his childhood, the shade underneath the backyard pepper tree, and the hibiscus all dusty and wilting by the porch. He would feel the wind rattling the sheets hanging on his mama's clothesline, all bleached and blinding white." Luther breathes deep and grins. "Now, you girls, when you look at Arcadia, all you see is a woman with talcum powder dimming her tan and a shawl splashed tropical across her shoulders. But you know what he sees? He's gazing at the Mexican girls, arm in arm, crossing the square in noon light, turning, giving him one last serious look and a flash of smile before they go into the cool Catholic church for confession—oh, and him, nothing but a slavering Baptist boy. All over again, he feels it, the old thump of longing. You know what I'm talking about, girls?"

"Lust?" asks Phyl.

"No," Luther lifts his eye patch. "Lust is simple. Longing is complicated."

"Memory?" asks Cyndee.

"No, not what you remember, but what you mix out of memory and imagination. Memory is everything you leave behind, not knowing you'll miss it. Longing is what you always carry with you because you've never quite got hold of it. You mix 'em up, see?"

"Has Arcadia ever been to Texas?" Darlene asks, drily.

Luther laughed and shook his head. "She don't need to go to Texas, girls. She reads books."

He snapped his eye patch down and gave his old low chuckle. He says, "Avast ye mateys," and limped, disappeared into the costumed crowd where Arcadia and Austin had already vanished, into the music, the voices, the restless colors, melted into memory, possibility, and longing.

Cromwell's Castle

THE BLUFFS WERE HIGH and wild and long banners of nasturtiums hung from them, colorful ropes waving to the sea and the narrow beach below. Dotting these cliffs were a few old junipers that the wind had shaved and flattened. Their roots, gnarled as arthritic fingers, roiled above ground. Patchwork grass and motley-colored ice plants straggled from the uncurbed street to the ragged edge where the sandstone frayed and tattered, where the cliff dropped finally, two-hundred feet to the beach. For us, the locals in this sleepy California beach town, these bluffs provided a sort of open-air church. Paths threaded through the rough grass, beaten out by our feet. You could come with a friend and a six-pack, or only your own thoughts and troubles, stay as long as you liked, and look out over the Pacific, an unparalleled view to the horizon. Behind you, to the east on Fourth Street, there were a few clapboard houses weighed down with bougainvillea, and some ramshackle apartments, beach towels hanging from their railings like faded battle pennants. But here, on the west side of Fourth, the ocean side, the only building was a concrete castle, imposing but unglamourous, stark, solitary, utilitarian with a heavy door and long uncurtained windows. The property line was marked by a low wall made of stones, even and ugly as molars.

Daily, a man known as the Captain parked his Chevy Nova on Fourth Street and paced these bluffs. Up and down he walked, swinging a substantial stick over his head and accosting anyone fool enough to talk to him, which was just about everyone. We, all of us who came to the bluffs at Esperanza Point, listened to his tales, endured his harangues, answered his trivia questions. Winter and summer he wore a thick sweater and a coat, and he walked briskly, swinging his stick and whistling "My Bonnie Lies Over the Ocean," or, possibly "My God How the Money Rolls In." The tunes are the same. On a particular April evening in 1973 he strode and whistled with especial relish, and if you had been there, he would have grabbed your arm and explained gleefully that Beg, the last of his enemies, lay dying in the concrete castle. *I've outlived my enemies!* the Captain would have told you, outlived the lawyers, three brothers he had impaled with the names Beg, Borrow, and Steal. But one day in 1977 the Captain himself would lie facedown in the ice plants, inert, his arms outspread on the bluff.

Seemingly born ancient, the Captain's face was weather-whipped and he cut his white hair with manicure scissors. His whole body was sinewy, stringy as a piece of hangman's hemp, and his character and convictions shared that same texture. He was catholic in his intolerance. He hated Democrats, developers, conservationists, unions, the Germans, the English, the Irish, the Japanese, Jews, Blacks, Reds, Mexicans, Italians, all religions, anyone in the legal, medical, or banking professions, drinkers, dope-smokers, every lying newspaper ever printed, all young people, surfers, the shiftless unemployed, and everyone on welfare—the Captain's enemies were legion. But only the lawyers, Beg, Borrow, and Steal, had actually got the better of him. He returned to these bluffs daily as a defeated commander might return to the battlefield.

He'd tell you how he once owned all this land, these

high bluffs at Esperanza Point, yes these and other tracts of California oceanfront property. *Hmm,* you might have said, since the evidence suggested he owned nothing but the Chevy Nova and the ancient trailer he lived in. But the Captain claimed to have made *mountains* of money, oh, long ago, back in the fifties, selling off his prime coastal property. Still, he swore, he would never ever have parted with these bluffs in Esperanza Point. Never. He had been tricked. He would tell you how in 1954 he had been brutally deceived by the lawyers, Beg, Borrow, and Steal in league with vile Japanese businessmen who now owned all this property, save for the small parcel on which sat the concrete castle.

Beg, Borrow, and Steal had taken the land as their commission from the Japanese businessmen. The brothers built the concrete castle, and lived there. The concrete castle had no yard or garden, only a smattering of the same rough grass and tough ice plants as would grow on the bluffs. Not so much as a potted geranium softened its contours and the harsh gray of unimproved concrete only dulled with time. It had an unfinished air, as though undecided if it were in the process of being developed or being demolished. With its high tower room and low stone wall, it was better suited altogether to the blustery North Sea than this balmy bit of the California central coast.

The Captain would tell you his tale as the truth. And over time, we, too, fashioned his tale as truth. He would tell his story to anyone who would listen and many who would not. In doing so, as well as besmirching the names of his enemies (as if Beg, Borrow, and Steal weren't smirch enough) he would rag and dump and rail against all those people he hated, but you could always bring him round to brighter topics if you knew what to ask. He was always eager, for instance, to wax on about his glorious Scots ancestry. He still had a Scot lilt to his voice. He was Alexander Seton, of *The* Setons, a Scottish family both noble and ancient.

He was actually born with an altogether duller name, James Robert Gray, a commonplace identity he jettisoned. (A citizen of nowhere is not bound. A citizen of nowhere can choose. Must choose, since he cannot inherit.) As a boy in Scotland, James Gray had inhaled stories of the Setons since the day he drew breath. Their stories were his stories. Truly. His favorite was the story of Captain Alexander Seton, the Scots military commander who, in 1651, had defended Tantallon Castle on the North Sea with a mere ninety-one men and fifteen guns, who held out for twelve days against Cromwell and his two thousand men, the New Model Army. Cromwell's troops massed there, their pennants snapping in the wind off the sea, their drummers marching through the fog, their artillery assaulting, their cannons bombarding Tantallon's ancient medieval walls, which had been built to withstand merely the slings and arrows of archers. The castle walls shook and shuddered, blew apart. Cromwell's artillery wracked the masonry, cracked the escarpments, reduced two towers to stumps. Cannons made castles obsolete. After 1651, Tantallon Castle—once thought to be unvanquishable—was abandoned on the cliff above the North Sea. Silent ruin though it was, you could still imagine them dying at Tantallon Castle. You could not imagine them living. That's what the Captain would tell you. As a child he had lived nearby, played there, the red stone walls behind him, his face to the sea.

This 1651 obscure siege of an unknown castle in Scotland became a well-known tale in Esperanza Point, California. Over time it passed, percolated really, amongst those of us who walked the bluffs, those who sat there staring out to sea, or feeding the ubiquitous seagulls. It rattled around the bank, the post office, Alfredo's Mexican Restaurant, the Daily Double Bar, the pumps at Phil's Mobil, the ovens at the DeLite Bakery, the watercooler at Lillian's Salon of Beauty. The story of this siege on the North Sea got told over the whine of powertools in the hands of workingmen, over coffee, over counters, and over time. A few of us wondered if it were not the Captain's fondness for this story of Tantallon's siege, his way of telling it, exactly the same way each time, same wording, that had afforded Beg, Borrow, and Steal the artillery (you might say) to fight the slander. After all, they had lost their very names.

Beg, Borrow, and Steal were three bachelor brothers, lawyers all, with degrees from some lackluster institution commensurate with their unambitious lives. In 1934 they opened a law office in the town of Esperanza Point, then a mere bump in the road. Pacific Coast Highway was called First Street. Their office was on Second Street. Third Street had some houses overgrown with hydrangeas and a Baptist church. Fourth Street fronted the bluffs. There was no Fifth Street, only a two-hundred-foot drop to the ocean, the beach below. By the Second World War, Esperanza Point had expanded a bit to the east of Pacific Coast Highway, and in the mid-1950s it experienced a short-lived boom before settling back into torpor. During this boom-ette the lawyer brothers were approached by a Japanese firm who asked them to act as intermediaries, to set themselves up as a dummy corporation of white men to buy the Captain's oceanfront bluffs. The Japanese, being no dummies themselves, had done their homework on the Captain and knew his aversion to people of their country.

The Captain hated everyone, yes, but for the Japanese he reserved especial loathing, rabid and inflexible, linked to his own glorious role in the Second World War. He liked to tell people on the bluffs (brokenhearted girls, unemployed men, mothers, grandmothers, kids with important kites to fly), during the War there had been a lookout tower, built to scout Japanese subs prowling the California coastal waters. The Captain had manned the tower himself, faithfully, as part of the Civil Defense effort (which of course namby-pamby ingrate young people couldn't possibly understand since they had no concept of work or responsibility). Patriotically, day after day, throughout World War II, the Captain had climbed up into the high wooden tower and scanned the horizon for any sign of a Japanese sub. If, on hearing this story in winter, you jumped up and pointed into the distance where gray whales gamboled, their flukes and fins splashing, catching the light, and if you had the bad sense to remark that gray whales might have been mistaken for subs, the Captain would walk away in disgust. He would have nothing to do with someone too goddamn dumb to know a submarine from a goddamn fish. He'd swing his stick and snag someone else, march that person over to the wide threadbare spot where the lookout tower had been, right there, very close to the edge of the bluff. Go on, look down there, you can still see where the tower's drainage pipe lay. See the line of erosion the drainage pipe made?

Maybe, but the bluffs were riddled with jagged lines of erosion, scarred up and down, like God had sharpened His nails there, and the place where the drainage pipe had lain looked sadly undifferentiated, merely one more ragged rib of crumbling stone.

The Captain told lurid tales: how the Japanese would have released empires of enemies onto these very shores, but for his vigilance, there in a tall wooden tower outfitted with two telescopes, a hotplate, a kettle, a waterbarrel, a telephone, a radio, and an unencumbered view of the vast Pacific. He usually concluded this soliloquy with the imputation that he had singlehandedly defended the central California coast from Japanese attack. He sometimes added that his task was rather like that of the soldiers in Captain Seton's 1651 army, keeping watch those twelve days on the battlements of Tantallon Castle. After the Scots' defeat, only the wind whistled through Tantallon's silent ruins. After the Second World War ended, the wooden tower at Esperanza Point vanished altogether, but the Captain remained its witness, walking where it had stood, whistling "My Bonnie Lies Over the Ocean," or maybe "My God How the Money Rolls In."

Supposing you believed him at all, you might ask (and people did) how a man who lived in a trailer park and drove a Chevy Nova had ever had money to buy great chunks of California oceanfront property. You might even be so bold as to inquire after his title, Captain. Was it honorary, military, or nautical? Irascibly he would inform you he was a nautical captain. But he had become nautical by avoiding the military altogether.

By 1916 the British government began conscripting men to fight. Two years into the Great War, and the government could no longer fill the trenches, nor strew No-Man's-Land with the bodies of men who would go, willingly, to die on the Western Front. James Robert Gray, eighteen years old in 1916, strong, fit, a seasoned sailor since boyhood, was obliged to register for the draft. Lanky, five-foot-eleven, he towered over the other conscripts, most of them narrow-chested walking testaments to the inadequacies of their diets for the past four hundred years. After he registered for conscription, James Gray returned home where his mother had laid his tea, places for two. (His father had died of drink, drowned, actually, but drowned drunk when James was ten. James and his mother were teetotalers.) He told his mother he would not bloody go to bloody war if he were called. Which he surely would be. He vowed he would not fight for the bloody British, nor be drafted into their bloody army. He was a Scotsman, native to East Lothian, born, his whole life lived at the confluence of the Firth of Forth and the North Sea, where Tantallon Castle, that monumental ruin, silently testified that ninety-one Scotsmen held out against bloody Cromwell's cannons, against artillery, against two thousand soldiers of the New Model bloody Army. He vowed he would never fight in an army that had once included the likes of Cromwell. His mother agreed; she felt as strongly as he did against Cromwell and the British, but these were perilous times and her only child's refusal to serve might get him imprisoned for treason. James told her this would never happen. He finished his tea, packed his few things, and bolted that night. He never saw his mother again.

He made his way across Scotland to the Western Isles and eventually to Ireland (where of course he hated the Papist Irish and was none too fond of the Protestant Irish either, though at least the Irish had the sense not to join the Brits). His seagoing skills got him onboard a vessel bound for Nova Scotia—no questions asked—and he was in Boston, Massachusetts, a citizen of nowhere, when the Armistice was declared in November 1918. Twenty years old, his character had already been cast: skinflint and flint-skinned, a pinch-hearted teetotaler if ever there was one. He took his new name, Seton, from his old life, Scotland.

How would such a man have arrived in sunny California a year later, in 1919? The story could only be cut from a bolt of impossible cloth and he would tell it to you. Did tell it. Told anyone on the bluffs gazing at the ocean, throwing scraps to seagulls, even if they were young and shiftless and unemployed. (Why else would they be on the bluff during the day? Real people work.) He kept toffees in his pockets and he would quiz us all: surfers with their blond locks and sun-strained eyes, knocked-up girls with tear-stained faces, beer drinkers, joint-smokers, bank tellers, day laborers, harmonica players whom he would stop in midmeasure. If we answered his strange, persistent questions correctly, we got toffees. (If we couldn't, it confirmed his belief that the American educational system raised up ignorant brats who thought the world owed them a living.) *When did Prohibition begin?* he would demand. And if you answered him that the Noble Experiment began in America in July 1919, you would have got a toffee in exchange for this otherwise worthless piece of information. You might not have thought Prohibition would matter to a teetotaler, but Alexander Seton was an anomaly: a temperance man in the seafaring trades where drinking was as much a part of the vocation as praying is to a priest. Temperance, in Alexander Seton's case, was the hinge on which his life (though not his character) turned.

In 1919 a Boston millionaire—a teetotaling contributor to the coffers of William Jennings Bryan, who was running on the Prohibition platform—wanted his yacht sailed round to San Francisco. He wanted a crew of temperance men. No drinkers need apply. Alexander Seton—experienced, seaworthy, and a teetotaler—was handpicked to be the captain of this yacht, though he was very young. He assured the millionaire that the crew would be teetotalers to a man. Then he hired competent sailors, asking no questions about their drinking propensities. When the yacht was offshore the Carolina coast, he took all the alcohol onboard and flung it into the Atlantic. He was not a popular captain.

Pity the poor sailors of Captain Seton's voyage! The yacht sailed at last into San Francisco in the fall of 1919, to find the city gripped in the fist of the Noble Experiment, Prohibition. It was enough to make a grown man cry. Late one night, strolling back to his hotel, the Captain overheard a man weeping, singing, embracing the lampposts as he warbled to the indifferent sky that beloved old Scots tune "My Bonnie Lies Over the Ocean." Or was it?

Alexander Seton listened more attentively. The tune was "My Bonnie Lies Over the Ocean," but the words (they hardly qualify as lyrics) were very different. "My God How the Money Rolls In" tells the poignant story of an impoverished family trying to make ends meet. The poor father makes book in the backroom (illegal gambling was of no interest to Alexander Seton). The degraded sister makes love for a dollar (equally, of little interest; Alexander Seton was averse to paying for his women in that he was averse to parting with money. When he paid for women, he asked only for release. He got what he paid for, nothing more. He wanted nothing more of women). It was the resourceful mother in the song who most attracted Alexander's attention, set him thinking. The mother made illegal gin. Bathtub gin for a thirsty world. Alexander remembered his erstwhile crew. Deprived of liquor, did they become better men? More attentive? Stronger? Healthier, wealthier, more wise? Clearly, Prohibition would never result in virtue, and vice must have a means to market.

Alexander Seton invested every nickel he had in a prim little schooner, the *Halcyon*. He lived on the boat by day, and by night he piloted her up and down the California coast, rum-running Canadian whiskey (sometimes mere bootleg hooch) for whomever would pay him to do so. And pay him well. His sailor's hands were hard and the only emollient they responded to was Greenback Salve. He took no liquor in trade and accepted no IOUs. Cash. No bill larger than a hundred. So swift, so experienced, so clever was Captain Seton that in all the glory days of the Noble Experiment, he lost only two cargoes and was only once arrested by Customs men. He secured his own quick release (if not justice) by applying that effective emollient, Greenback Salve, in small bills to the hands of the Customs' men. He secured Customs' continued cooperation in the same way.

His adventures ended with Prohibition, but the Captain had ploughed his seagoing savings into coastal property, and after the *Halcyon* smashed up during a storm, he moved to the beach town of Esperanza Point. Though he owned ocean-view bluffs and could have built a home there, instead he bought a trailer in the Cee-Vue Trailer Park where he lived cheaply and alone, few friends, no family, a citizen of nowhere. He could not return to Scotland (and why should he? His mother had died; the minister had returned his last letter to her with a brief description of her final unhappy days). A man of no indulgences and few wants, World War II was Captain's Seton's finest hour, though all he did was look out upon the Pacific from the high wooden tower. After the war, the tower proved an endless temptation to nasty boys. The County declared the structure unsafe and against the Captain's ardent protest, it came down. The bluffs he owned stood empty, save for the tough, wind-flattened junipers, the ice plants and coarse grass, the nasturtium curtains falling toward the ocean. There, with his back to the town and his face to the Pacific, Captain Seton stood where the tower once stood and told himself one woman is very like another and the sea is the sea is the sea.

Perhaps. But the land is not always the land. After he had been tricked into selling his land to the Japanese, the Captain suffered perfect orgasms of self-loathing. Tooth and claw, he told all of us, he should have hung onto this land, his fingernails dug into the sandstone cliffs, swinging on the long ropes of nasturtiums if necessary. Hell, he should have held onto all his coastal property so he could have reaped the astronomical profits others did. By the midsixties, coastal California became so valuable it might as well have been leafed in gold. Bid! Buy! Rezone! Build! Sell! Develop! And what had once been merely wild and beautiful was profitable beyond belief. So why didn't the Japanese—who now owned the bluffs at Esperanza Point (through the complicity, the skullduggery of Beg, Borrow, and Steal)—why did they not build, rezone, sell, or develop? *Why?* The Captain would demand of us, *Why don't they build?* We shrugged. We came here grateful for the wind, the perspective afforded nowhere else. We didn't care why the Japanese did not develop. The Captain cared. Moreover, the Captain knew why. He would chuckle bitterly and tell us that nature—indeed God himself—had bested the hated Japanese.

Never mind what had brought you to the bluff, whether you were adult, adulterer, truant, or teacher, the Captain would take your arm, face you west, point out that when *he* bought this property the bluff stretched far, far out into the almighty distance. When *he* bought it, there were acres—really! Acres more—off to the west. It had all eroded, fallen into the sea. The Captain would add that surveys could only be done on three sides of this land, the north, south, and east. The rugged west belonged to God. (Perhaps the Captain even believed in God, some vindictive and egregious deity Captain Seton made in his own image.) And because of God—the Captain would tighten his grip on your arm—the Japanese would never profit by their low trick. Look how God had eroded the bluffs! You can see where chunks of earth and rock have fallen. Long jagged gullies, like the vertebrae of dinosaurs, ran all the way down the cliffs to the beach, two hundred feet below. Nasturtium curtains barely concealed erosion so severe the cliff would never support another building. The San Angelo County Planning Commission had said so. The concrete castle, of course, as it was already there, could stand. But nothing new could be built on the west side of Fourth Street due to the dangers posed by the ongoing erosion. It was, the Captain would conclude triumphantly, geologically speaking, God's revenge on the wily Japanese. The site could not be developed. The land was worthless.

You might have said, *Is that so?* and gone back to your perch overlooking the Pacific, reflecting that the land was not worthless to you. It was not worthless to those of us suffering broken hearts or broken homes, to girls who gave up loving men who moved on, to the stoned, the staid, the flamboyant, the failures; it was not worthless to the aged, the unemployed, the unrequited, to surfers, clerks, cooks, poets, and fruit pickers alike. It was not worthless to women who came, their hair whipped round their faces and their skirts ruffled by the wind, not worthless to mothers clutching toddlers' hands as they flung scraps to the seagulls, not worthless to whale-watchers and kite flyers, nor to workingmen who brought their six-packs and their girlfriends to watch the most dramatic show in town: sunset from the bluffs and the green flash that illuminated the sky the very instant the sun crashed below the horizon. Lovers alone could see the green flash. That's what people said. But even if you weren't in love, even if you had just been dumped, divorced, or deserted, two-timed, or knocked-up, if you'd lost your car or your job, or your younger brother, indeed if all you wanted was an extraordinary moment in an ordinary day, on these bluffs you could have it. You could have the wind and the sea, the rhythm, wave after wave crashing on the beach below; you could call the wild sky your own, look to the horizon, and enjoy an unimpeded perspective granted nowhere else.

The Captain did not give a tinker's damn for perspective. He parked his Chevy Nova, winter and summer, took out his big stick, swung it overhead, walked, cursing Beg, Borrow, and Steal who sometimes watched him from their uncurtained tower window. The brothers had the land. The brothers held the castle. History belongs to the victors, doesn't it? Did not the New Model Army trounce the Scots? But whom do we admire: Cromwell? Or Alexander Seton and the men who held out against him for twelve days? Cromwell or Alexander Seton? History may be eroded by story, as land may be eroded by water. So completely had the Captain drubbed and dubbed the brothers Beg, Borrow, and Steal, that those seemed to be their very names. That's what we called them, called their law firm: *Oh yes,* we would say, *you mean the firm of Beg, Borrow, and Steal*. And then we'd tell the Captain's story. We were the Captain's ragtag army of believers.

However in 1961, the lawyers Beg, Borrow, and Steal took action against the Captain. Not in the courts, however. They used history against him. His story. They hoisted the hated Union Jack atop their concrete castle. The flag of the United Kingdom flapped there, the emblem of Scotland's failure. And just inside the low stone wall that marked their property off from the rest of the bluff, they erected a wooden sign, four feet across, three feet tall. In red, white, and blue letters, very imposing, quite unmistakable:

CROMWELL'S CASTLE

At their high window the next morning, Beg and Steal watched as the Captain, bundled up, walked to the sign, stood there, momentarily transfixed, as a just-caught fish is transfixed, unable to believe its own bad luck. Then he leaped over the low stone wall and struck the sign again and again with his stick. Beg and Steal nodded to Borrow who picked up the phone and called the San Angelo County Sheriff's Office (Esperanza Point being too small to have its own police force) and said private property was being vandalized on Fourth Street and they wished to press charges.

The Captain often skipped this part of the story, how his upraised stick had been halted, as it were, in midair by a young Sheriff's Deputy who explained to him that if he did not cease and desist, step off this property and stay off, the brothers could have him arrested. They would have every right to. They wanted to. The Deputy was giving him fair warning this once.

The Captain did not hear him. The Captain, in confronting Cromwell's Castle, was still fighting the flag that flew over it, as Alexander Seton and ninety-one others had fought, held out against the New Model Army, who, in the mind of this Captain, all had Japanese faces. In 1651 Alexander Seton and his men had so bedeviled the British that Cromwell sent two thousand soldiers, pikes, muskets, and six battering cannons to stop them, once and for all, at the edge of the North Sea where the Scots had staked their lives to Tantallon Castle, crumbling under cannonade. Explosion after explosion disintegrated battlements built to withstand arrows. For twelve days the Scots endured this murderous barrage without being taken. Without surrender. Their faces to the North Sea, their backs to walls eroding under fire, that Captain Seton knew the same hot defeat this one knew as he stood on the eroding bluffs at Esperanza Point, where he heard not at all the voice of the young Deputy, but another voice, a young soldier, his dirty face lit by the fire they had built that eleventh night, who asks of Captain Seton (whose hands are black with gunpowder, his rough clothes rouged from blasted stone), the young soldier asks: *We're all going to die, aren't we?*

And Alexander Seton replies, *Yes, we're all going to die, and those men out there, Cromwell's men, the men of the New Model Army, they're all going to die, too. We're all going to die.*

But, says the young soldier, *we're going to die first.*

Captain Alexander Seton repeats grimly, *We're all going to die.*

And he was right. None of those men from 1651 are alive in 1961 to hear Captain Seton cry out toward Cromwell's Castle, "You're all going to die! You're all going to die!" As the young Deputy leads him away from the stone wall, warns him against trespassing on private property, the Captain, his white hair whipping in the wind, raises his stick. "We're all going to die, but you're going to die first, you bastards! You bastards will die first!"

Borrow died first. Haunting the cliffs as he did, the Captain chuckled one afternoon in 1965 to see the ambulance come to Cromwell's Castle and the attendants remove one of the brothers, not yet dead, and take him to the hospital. The Captain yelled over the ambulance wail, "What did I tell you, you traitorous bastards! You're going to die first."

A week later, drinking thirty-weight coffee in Alfredo's Mexican Restaurant where he went for breakfast every morning, the Captain read the obituary in the San Angelo paper. He turned to everyone eating at the counter, to the cheerful waitresses, to Alfredo himself, laughed, and said Borrow was dead. And perhaps the truly sad thing is, we all knew who he meant.

The Captain celebrated Borrow's death by doing something he'd never done before. He bought a pint of Scotch and invited his neighbors at the Cee-Vue, Grizzle, Gizzard, and Gravel Gertie to his trailer for a drink. He himself did not drink. These were not his neighbors' real names, but that's what the Captain called them. Gizzard got his name from his croaking voice, Grizzle from his grizzled gray hair. Gravel Gertie came by hers by virtue of her platinum hair, thin, lank, and her aged skin tanned, tough, her skinny little body, in short, her resemblance to the character in Dick Tracy comics. Gravel and the Captain had been friends for many years. They had been more than friends. Lovers—if the tongue can quite wrap itself around that word and the Captain's name in the same breath. The Captain did not love Gravel, in fact, he liked her better when he was not sleeping with her. Then he owed her nothing, not even gratitude for her affection. The gratitude he could not express mingled with the poignancy he could not deny as Gravel's matchstick arms pulled him close against her bony chest, her skinny hips, and down into her bed, down down into the past, that other past, that other woman. The woman. *Sarah*. Plain, perhaps. Married, certainly. *Sarah, Sarah,* married to a man who had gone off to war, fighting in the Pacific. *Sarah,* say it like a song or whisper, *Sarah,* whose contribution to the war effort was to volunteer for Civil Defense, four years of long hours spent in the high wooden tower. *Oh, we have loved and graced this place, Alexander, we have graced and hallowed* the submarine-lookout station with its two telescopes, hot-plate, kettle, waterbarrel, its radio, and telephone and view of the vast Pacific. Four years of damp autumnal dawns, of fiery dusks as the summer sun crashed into the horizon with the green flash only lovers see. *Oh, Sarah, Sarah*. Alexander beheld the green flash and knew his life would never be the same.

On the day of Borrow's funeral, the Captain stood upon the vanished tower's very patch of balding ground, as the undertaker's limo delivered Beg and Steal back home. The Captain grabbed the arm of a nearby young surfer, blond, blue-eyed, who had just smoked a whole joint, stoned mindless and happy as a clam. He shook this boy and pointed, cackling, to the two old bachelors who resembled a pair of waistcoated moles. They emerged from the limo and went into Cromwell's Castle. The Captain told the surfer the story of the brothers' treachery, their pact with the Japanese, and how God Himself had eroded these bluffs so as to defeat them. "What profiteth it," concluded the Captain grandly, "if a man should lose his soul?"

"Far out," said the surfer, "who's Cromwell?"

The Captain heard of Steal's death in 1968 from Gravel Gertie who came to his trailer with that news and the announcement that she was leaving the Cee-Vue and Esperanza Point forever: she was going to Oakland to move in with her daughter. The Captain's eyes lit on Gravel, her carefully tended platinum roots, her lined, leathery skin, knobby little breasts poking through her blouse, and for a moment he suffered what might have been a pang of loss. The feeling passed so swiftly he was not obliged to assess it. The Captain was not the sort to root through loss, to grub about in longing, to ask Gravel to stay. He was not the sort to weep when a woman left him. He was not the kind of man who would protest when she said her husband was coming home from the war, moving to Arizona, far from the Pacific. Tragic? Was it tragic? Did he beg her not to leave him? *Don't leave me, Sarah*. Did he hold and rage and rail to keep her by his side? *Don't. Please don't leave me*. Did he even care that she left? *Go then, and be damned*, said Alexander Seton as she left him. *One woman's very like another*. He did not believe it and it was not true. Some five years after the war, there arrived an envelope addressed in Sarah's neat hand, no letter, a snapshot of a little boy fitted out for his first day at kindergarten. He wore corduroy overalls and carried a lunch bucket. He looked just like her. Didn't he? He had Sarah's brown eyes and Alexander's smile. If Alexander had had a smile. He went to the bathroom mirror in his trailer at the Cee-Vue. Stood there. Smiled. Or tried to. Turned the snapshot over. *Alan, born February 17, 1946*. The picture (which he taped to the bathroom mirror where it yellowed and paled and cracked) greeted him ever after with Sarah's reproachful eyes and the ghost of his own smile.

After Steal died, Beg stepped up the struggle: he had the sign repainted and hoisted a brand new Union Jack. It snapped in the strong winds off the Pacific, winds so fine and reliable that hang gliders discovered these bluffs. On weekend mornings, hang gliders jumped and swooped, flying, their faces rapt with concentration, ecstatic human kites, delighting everyone who came to watch.

The Captain reacted to Beg's salvo—the refurbished sign, the new Union Jack—by redoubling his wrath and accosting even more people. Captain Alexander Seton did not falter any more than the 1651 Captain Seton had faltered. Knowing that he and his ninety-one men had wreaked havoc on the New Model Army (and why else would Cromwell have sent two thousand men and six cannons?) must have given that doomed Scotsman satisfaction, even pride. Captain Alexander Seton of Esperanza Point, too, refused to surrender: he too took pride. And yet . . .

And yet, his satisfactions receded, running out as though borne away on an ebbing tide. For all his righteous wrath and passion, he could not seem, anymore, quite, to properly, to truly convey the whole *fundamental injustice* and *monstrous insult* that had been inflicted by the Japanese, in league with Beg and the late Borrow and Steal. The Captain's audience expanded as Esperanza Point grew (it became a regular hippie-haven, cheap rent, no cops, great views), but the toffees went stale in his pockets. His listeners knew nothing of Cromwell, of Prohibition or Civil Defense, cared less. They did not think a Japanese invasion of California possible, and did not care that he had thwarted it. People who came to the cliffs to marvel at the hang gliders ignored him, their rapt attention on the hang gliders. They applauded their breathless defiance, their freedom from gravity as they jumped off the cliffs and were borne aloft.

After Steal's death and Gravel's desertion (for that's how he came to think of her leaving), the Captain sometimes lingered at the bluffs long after sunset. The lights in Cromwell's Castle came on. Behind him, on the east side of Fourth Street, windows lit and smells of supper cooking wafted from the crummy clapboards and the ramshackle apartments. Laughter rippled out. Music. The Captain snorted at such commonplace comforts. He was not a sentimental man. He stood there and he thought about the

Japanese. He thought how—but for his vigilance—they might have run their subs aground on the narrow beach. And then he thought how they might have shimmied up these cliffs, climbing the nasturtium ropes, how the Japanese might have skulked eastward from the bluffs, stalked the town of Esperanza Point, overrun the whole California coast, and won the Second World War and he would not have known or seen or cared, because in the wooden lookout tower, he was in the arms of the only woman who had ever stirred him, loved him, demanded and returned his love, who had ever seen or made him cry. When the War ended and Sarah returned to her husband and moved to Arizona, Alexander Seton did not try to stop her from going. Hell no. Men whose ancestors have held out against the New Model Army, such men do not beg women not to leave them. They do not cry, please don't leave me, please, Sarah, please. Oh Sarah, Oh Sarah, don't leave me, Sarah . . .

Beg's health failed. Eventually a young couple moved into Cromwell's Castle to look after him when he could no longer look after himself. When he was virtually bedridden and the doctor strongly suggested a convalescent home, Beg refused. How could he wage war from the disinfectant corridors of a convalescent home? Who would protect Cromwell's Castle? Who would carry on the fight? Beg had his bed moved up to the high tower room where it faced west and there, with his back to the wall and his face to the sea, Beg mulled over Captain Seton, the other Seton of the 1651 siege. Perhaps Beg, too, tasted defeat as well as death.

Perhaps not. Beg was a lawyer. Beg knew what lawyers have always known: spill all the blood you wish, fire the gunpowder, spew hot lead, light the fuse, plunge the saber, pull the pin, search and destroy, pillage and burn, put men before firing squads, their backs to adobe walls or black forests, or to dark alleys or snowy steppes. Never mind. The tale is never truly told in blood. The tale is told in ink. Blood, once dried, powders up and blows away. Ink, once dried, can be used powerfully, as forcibly, as effectively as Cromwell's artillery shattered the towers of Tantallon Castle, which, after 1651, lay abandoned. A mere ruin. Mute. Ink, on the other hand, speaks. Volumes. The victor is he who lives to put his pen, his ink, to the treaty, to the will, or the writ of execution. The deed *is* the deed. The Japanese held the deed. They would surely build on these bluffs. Beg was certain the Captain would be deprived, not simply of victory, but of territory; Beg believed the Captain would literally have the ground taken from under him.

Then in the fall of 1972 the voters of the State of California approved the California Coastal Commission. It was a grand victory for conservationists and created a frenzy of joy in the hippie-haven of Esperanza Point. Dancing in the street. The Coastal Commission would safeguard oceanfront assets that belonged to The People, to future generations. The California Coastal Commission would protect and preserve natural beauty from greedy capitalists and developers who cared nothing, etc., etc. In any event, put into law, it was supposed to function thus: henceforth no coastal development could be undertaken and nothing built on coastal property without geological assessment, environmental reports, the bureaucratic approbation of science, the law, the judiciary, and eight designated committees who must each unanimously approve all new development. The California Coastal Commission killed Beg.

Beg's heart failed him. Not just literally—which is to say that after languishing for years, eaten up by heart disease, his heart merely attacked him one last time and won—but more particularly. Beg had so hoped, believed, that time and greed would do their old assured work, achieve their old assumed victory: eventually the erosion of the cliffs would not matter one damn bit. Greed would win. If there was money to be made, greed would prevail. The Japanese would build upon the bluffs, wouldn't they? Expensive, high-rise, high-class condos. *O Say Can You See the Japanese Condos at Esperanza Point?* Now, with the California Coastal Commission, the eight designated committees would never approve this development. The condos would never be built. Moreover, Beg knew for a fact that the cliffs were unstable; erosion had caused long cracks in his concrete walls and threadline fissures in his concrete floor.

Beg died in January 1973. Cromwell's Castle and the parcel of land on which it stood, he willed to San Angelo County. For a park. Acknowledging this gift, the County Commissioners came to Beg's funeral where he was buried alongside his brothers. Marking all three graves, a single stone bears this epitaph, chosen by the brothers:

Men of righteous heart and eye
Easy live and quiet die.

The Captain was having none of it. Neither easy live nor quiet die. Within five days of Beg's death, the sign CROMWELL'S CASTLE was not merely torn down, but blown up in the middle of the night.

Two Sheriff's squad cars came to the Cee-Vue Trailer Park immediately after the blast had shattered all the castle windows and many across Fourth Street, had knocked down every flapping beach towel in a half-mile radius. The cliffs had suffered too; another chunk of land dropped to the beach below, and still more loosened, ready to slide into the sea. The deputies found the Captain in his trailer. The cup of tea in his hand was cold and the engine of his Chevy Nova was warm, but nothing else connected him conclusively to the vandalism. They arrested him just the same, but the charges were thrown out. Insufficient evidence.

But oddly, Beg's death did not fundamentally alter the Captain's life. Although he could no longer walk and whistle at the same time, he continued pacing, swinging a stick, telling his tales, complaining, haranguing, quizzing, accosting, offending all of us. He was there, joyful, ecstatic, passing out toffees as we all stood on Fourth Street and watched the wrecking ball smash Cromwell's Castle, raze it to the ground. And still he continued, as ever, up and down the wild bluffs, until one day in 1977 when a long, black limousine turned onto Fourth Street, parked right behind the Chevy Nova. A chauffeur jumped out, opened the back door for a quartet of Japanese businessmen as the Captain, his heart pounding, mouth dry, veins constricting, watched helplessly, breathlessly. The Japanese businessmen strolled out to the edge and stood overlooking the ocean, their backs to the town, and the old man staggering toward them, his arms flapping, falling, facedown in the ice plants, his jaw wordlessly working over *No! No! No!* as they stood on the very spot where once there had been a tall wooden lookout tower. Once a man and woman had scanned the horizon, watched the sea and the green flash at sunset to make certain the Japanese would never reach these shores.

Put bluntly, the argument developers put before the California Coastal Commission was this: technology made erosion obsolete. By 1980, the California Coastal Commission had been convinced, and a team of experts concurred. Permission was given the Japanese businessmen to develop, to build on the bluffs at Esperanza Point. Approval was happily unanimous. (In fact Beg had been right: the California Coastal Commission had itself succumbed to erosion. Time and greed had done their old assured work.)

And so, eventually up they went: four stories of splendor, high-class condos on the west side of Fourth Street. (And soon after, down came the crummy clapboards, the bougainvillea vines, and ramshackle apartments—the beach-towel pennants flew no more. One condo begot another.) But before the actual construction began, naturally, all the junipers were chainsawed, bulldozed, their roots plowed up, and the tough ice plants were torn out with backhoes. Then contractors set to work on the cliffs themselves. These long ribs of erosion (seemingly scratched out by God's own fingers as He etched and clawed) were smoothed and buttressed with reinforced concrete and steel beams, girders to support the Cromwell Condominiums that jut out over the ocean. At night, in four stories of high-class splendor, sleepers rest soundly, trusting to technology while, two hundred feet below them, the sea crashes, as it always has and will, flinging itself, wave after wave, washing over the base of the sandstone cliffs, alternately ebbing and flooding the narrow beach.

And beside this vast condo complex there is a manicured little hanky of a park where once stood the concrete castle. A sign says Cromwell Park. A thin sidewalk leads to a single unshaded concrete picnic table and a metal plaque on which the County congratulates itself for maintaining this tiny spitwad of land for the people's enjoyment. Hang gliding is forbidden. The ice plants are all a uniform color. There are no nasturtiums. The grass is mowed once a week.

The Delinquent Virgin

THE REVEREND HAMILTON REEDY often wrestled with uncharitable thoughts. For instance, he wondered—uncharitably—if seventeen-year-old Lisa Kellogg ought to have the role of the Virgin in the church's Christmas pageant. Then he dismissed the question as needlessly legalistic. Of his superior, Bishop Throckmorton, Hamilton Reedy believed (uncharitably, but correctly) that the Bishop used sincerity to mask his colossal ineptitude and gross opportunism. However, as Hamilton sat in the church study penning one of his usual defensive letters to the Bishop, he took a rather different tone, explaining his unorthodox attitudes (as the unorthodox always do) in lofty terms. He had crumpled this draft and trashed it just before the church secretary, Mrs. Leila Doggett, tapped at his door and announced that the police were here.

The Reverend rose to greet the two officers who identified themselves as Washington and Green, the former a black man, about forty with a lined face and graying hair. Green, a much younger white man, suffered from a weak chin. "Thank you for coming so quickly," the Reverend extended a hand to each man. "Would you like some coffee?"

"I don't think we have time," said Officer Washington, whipping out an official set of forms in triplicate and poising his pen over them.

"You've seen the empty Nativity scene in front of the church, I take it," the Reverend said gravely. "It's a sad testament to the tenor of our times, gentlemen, that someone would actually steal the Holy Family from in front of the church itself." At that moment he considered dispensing with the Christmas Eve meditation he'd already written and substituting something along these lines—but then again, no. Too grim. Christmas was about uplift. "Hark! The Herald Angels Sing." Christmas was about glory, not theft. Leave the thieves for Easter, Good Friday, darkness at noon, that sort of . . .

Officer Washington cleared his throat, calling the Reverend's attention back to the topic at hand. "You'll be happy to know, Reverend, that we've found your Holy Family."

"You have? Well, this is good news." Hamilton rubbed his hands together and smiled.

Green and Washington glanced nervously at each other. Green continued. "The Holy Family was on the steps of the city jail, the downtown police station, this morning when our shift came on. We didn't know, until we got your call, where they'd come from."

"On the steps of the police station?" inquired Hamilton. "That's a very odd place for thieves to leave them."

"We suspect kids. Malicious mischief."

"Rather nervy kids to leave them on the police-station steps, don't you think? This sounds graver than mere mischief."

Rather than reply, Officer Washington began asking a series of predictable questions. Naturally the Reverend's answers were unsatisfactory: he had driven past the front of the church this morning, noticed, to his alarm, that the Holy Family was missing from the Nativity scene and called the police. Simple.

Completing his form, Washington stuck his pen back in his pocket, gave a copy to Reedy, and assured the Reverend that no harm was done. "I'm afraid, though, you'll have to come down to the station to collect them. You'll have to sign. Stolen property, you know."

Green offered, "The duty officers took them off the station steps and brought them in the waiting room. They look mighty strange there among the derelicts and hookers and drunks."

The Reverend said he would pick the Holy Family up in the church van late that afternoon.

"The sooner the better," said Washington as they took their booted, uniformed selves from the Reverend's study.

"Nasty brats did this," announced Mrs. Doggett, refreshing the Reverend's coffee cup. She was a prim woman, fond of cardigans and polyester pants, overfond of chocolate toffees; the scent of chocolate toffee clung to everything she touched. Mrs. Doggett heaped calumny not only on the perpetrators of this crime, but on their parents and grandparents as well. "Is your letter to the Bishop ready for me to type?" she concluded.

"Not just yet, Leila. It must be perfect, you know—or as close to perfect as we can come in this imperfect world."

Leila Doggett gave him the look that had annoyed him for the whole twelve years of his tenure at the St. Elmo Episcopal Church: as if pearls had suddenly shot from his lips and she might scuttle to catch them.

"Well, since you're not finished, would you mind the phone for an hour or so while I do some last-minute Christmas shopping?"

"Of course, Leila."

After she left, Hamilton Reedy went back to struggling with his letter to the Bishop. His thoughts, however, wandered along more pleasant paths, toward the annual Winter Solstice cocktail party this evening at the holly-decked home of Dr. and Mrs. Gorman. Rachel Gorman was one of those tireless committee women and hostesses (like the Reverend's own wife, Catherine), but unlike Catherine, Rachel had the gift of making all her undertakings appear graceful, easy, effortless, fluid. Her parties were earthly pleasures. Hamilton Reedy enjoyed his earthly pleasures, perhaps too much so. He knew this. Indeed, he knew it so well that he had always cherished visions of himself leading a very different sort of life, a life physically and spiritually strenuous: Hamilton Reedy, the inner-city pastor, a sort of *Going My Way* cleric, ministering to street toughs, bringing drug addicts to God. He often longed, nostalgically, for the old Civil Rights days, the glorious days when religion had marched on the side of Right. He saw himself there too: Hamilton Reedy in shirtsleeves, leading the integration of buses and lunch counters. In fact, however, during those glorious days Hamilton Reedy had been a seminary student and the only thing he had done in his shirtsleeves was wash dishes in a restaurant for minimum wage.

He swivelled in his chair, watching the palm and pepper trees sway outside his window and wished that St. Elmo might offer him some grander theater of religious endeavor. Perhaps a few Central American refugees to whom he might give sanctuary, the huddled masses crouched in the shelter of his church. Imagine Bishop Throckmorton's response to that! He laughed out loud. He chewed on the end of his pen.

Hamilton Reedy was a stout man, with a fringe of gray, fraying hair, serious eyes, and a whimsical mouth. He had a trove of anecdotes (religious and otherwise), a gift for conviviality, a sonorous voice that extolled what he liked to think were inspirational sermons, though he knew they were not. A fundamentally honest man, Hamilton Reedy was aware that his sermons were well crafted, but seldom moving, and never disturbing or demanding. In a word, tidy. However, he exonerated himself from complacency: after all, his tidy sermons suited the tidy lives of his well-heeled congregation. St. Elmo Episcopal was in a fine old section of the city, with big trees and wide parkways and irrigated lawns emulating the nearby country club where Hamilton often played golf with Dr. Gorman and a few other parishioners. At St. Elmo Episcopal, the congregation was largely professional, lawyers, judges, bankers, administrators, city officials, teachers, everyone well-dressed on Sunday, and the rest of the week as well. St. Elmo Episcopal parishioners had swimming pools, three-car garages, and investment portfolios; they had good retirement plans, good jobs, good credit, and good marriages, or at least, durable unions. Their children played soccer and piano, violin and varsity football, honor-roll students. Occasionally someone's daughter got pregnant, or a boy might flunk out of the university, or find himself on social probation. Occasionally people got miffed, or indignant, but never outright nasty (though choir politics were known to be intense). But mostly these were the sort of people who taxed only the Reverend's power of eulogy when they died. They would not demand that Reverend Reedy wrestle with those chronic demons of American life: drugs, divorce, alcohol, adultery, broken homes, broken hearts, broken vows. His own life was equally and mercifully tidy: married to Catherine for thirty years, three children, all of them happily married, two grandchildren. The only true cross that Hamilton Reedy had to bear was Bishop Throckmorton. As long as the Bishop so disliked him, advancement would not come to Hamilton Reedy. Oh, well. He'd advanced quite far enough to suit himself. He was a contented man. But he was hungry.

He put the draft of his letter in the drawer, took up the

schedule Leila had left him, and decided to begin early on the round of seasonal calls that he and his curate, Tim Voight, traditionally made each Christmas season, dividing the congregation between them. No doubt his parishioners would offer him something good to eat.

He took the list, his coat and hat (to protect the bald spot on his head), put on the voice mail, locked up the office, and crossed the church courtyard, pleased to feel the wind coming down from the east, ruffling the lacy branches of the pepper trees, rattling the palm fronds. Hamilton Reedy never missed the gray and gloom of his Northwest boyhood; he loved Christmas in California. It was so, well, so cheerful and undemanding.

His first call was a Mrs. Robin Vance, a newcomer to the church, he remembered. Her address (he was surprised to note) was an apartment; not many of his parishioners lived in apartments, save for a few old ladies. He found Shadetree Gardens Apartments, parked in the lot, and wandered the huge unkempt complex, looking for 23B. He might never have found it at all, but he recognized the two Vance children, a boy and a girl, playing outside their apartment in the dirt, building roads for toy trucks. The girl ignored him, but the boy, Patrick, about five, recognized the Reverend Reedy. Patrick jumped up, opened the door, and ushered the Reverend into a room furnished with castoffs.

Led by Patrick to the kitchen, Hamilton was dismayed to find Mrs. Vance kneeling on the kitchen floor, crying, and another woman sitting at the table with the phone in her hand, looking at it as if it had just sprouted a goiter.

"Forgive me—" he began ineffectively, "—if I've—"

Mrs. Vance raised her eyes. She was young, thin, nervous; had it not been for her swollen eyes and tear-stained face, she might have been pretty. She was still wearing a blue bathrobe and her feet were bare. She pushed her hair away from her face and gazed at Reedy, who could only mumble that he called on all his parishioners at Christmas.

She mopped her face with a wadded Kleenex and rose unsteadily to her feet. "Well, you've just stumbled on a broken commandment, Reverend. Caught my sister and me in the middle of bearing false witness. A gross, sordid lie. A useless lie."

"Oh, Robin," the other woman pleaded, "please, don't—"

"What does it matter, Renee? What can it possibly matter now?"

"Can I be of some help, Mrs. Vance?" the Reverend inquired reflexively.

"Not unless you're God. Or Santa." She blew her nose. "All I want for Christmas is my husband. All I want is the gift that money can't buy. You know, one of those gifts? The happy family reunited around the Christmas tree." She scoffed, and wept some more as she walked to the window, stared past the dead geranium in the pot. "He was my husband and I loved him."

This was an untidy life, that much was clear. Hamilton could not think quite what to say, but he composed his features soberly.

She swallowed her tears and stared at her Kleenex. "Six months ago I left him. Jon was cheating on me. It was intolerable. But now all I want for Christmas is the chance to forgive him. It is the season of forgiveness, isn't it, Reverend, isn't it? But you can't say something like that on the phone." She turned to Hamilton and her sister beseechingly. "You have to be face-to-face. Jon could get a ticket, fly here in time for Christmas, there's time. If he'd only come, if he'd only see Heather as an angel and Patrick as a shepherd, he couldn't help but . . ."

"Oh, Robin," Renee sighed.

"But of course, I couldn't ask him myself, could I? So I had Renee call him, just now, like she was at her own house, like I knew nothing about the call. I had Renee tell him she was just sure, if only he'd fly out for Christmas, if only we could all be together, I'd forgive him and . . ." Robin Vance began to cry again.

"What did he say?" asked Hamilton, his curiosity not wholly professional.

Pain contorted Robin Vance's features. "He said he'd think about it."

"Well, that's something," Hamilton offered optimistically. "That means—"

"It means he won't be coming. He doesn't care if I forgive him. It means the season of forgiveness will pass and there won't be another chance. It means this is an irrevocable tragedy and not just a temporary separation. That's what it means."

Renee hugged her sister's quivering shoulders. "He might come yet and surprise you, honey. There's still three days. He might."

"He might," the Reverend offered hopefully. "It is Christmas."

The picture of Robin Vance in her robe, on her knees, crying on the kitchen floor troubled Hamilton Reedy for the rest of the day, troubled him as he drove the church's van (donated by Dewey Schultz of Dewey Schultz Chevrolet) to the police station where he filled out triplicate forms for the release of the Holy Family. As he stood at the desk, Hamilton glanced over, surprised, somehow, to see the figure of the Madonna (Baby Jesus in her lap) on the waiting-room bench. Beside her, standing, Joseph dispassionately regarded a young thug with rings gleaming in his nose, his lower lip, his eyebrow. He had a swastika carved into his haircut, handcuffs on his wrists, and a chain tattooed around his neck. Mucous bubbled at his nose and his pupils swam like black fish in his blue eyes.

A drunk, brought in as Hamilton was filling out his forms, fell on his knees before Mary and began to scream, to rage and wail and weep. All this exertion caused his ripe personal bouquet to fill the room. He peed himself. He had to be dragged to his feet.

"Sorry, Reverend," the duty officer offered. The articles were described as *1 Madonna, 1 Jesus, 1 Joseph* and Hamilton signed on the dotted line.

Two young officers hoisted the plaster figures of Mary and Joseph into the back of the van. Hamilton himself laid the Christ child on the passenger's seat. Mary had to be laid on her side so that she appeared to be curled into a fetal position and Joseph was laid on his back beside her. It crossed the Reverend's mind that they might have been lying in bed beside one another, but he chased the thought away.

With the help of Curtis Frett, the church's groundskeeper, Hamilton once again established the Holy Family at the Nativity scene there before the church. Enclosed on three sides by a plywood shed, the plaster, life-size Mary sat on an orange crate beside the manger (complete with straw) that held the Baby Jesus with His little outstretched arms. Joseph looked on reverently. Plastic baby lambs and calves regarded the Holy Family with smiling bovine indifference. The silver star, stuck on a long pole behind the little shed, trembled in the breeze.

Satisfied, the Reverend Reedy paid the rest of his seasonal calls for the day. He dawdled pleasurably so that they occupied the entire afternoon (thus freeing him from finishing his letter to Bishop Throckmorton). He chatted amiably, drank tea or coffee, nibbled cookies, gingerbread, or pound cake, at each home, all of these parishioners tidy, cheerful, downright fa la la la la. *We Wish You a Merry Christmas.* Tidy lives. None of them on the kitchen floor, barefoot, crying their eyes out, caught in a lie told to no avail.

From the last house on his list, he went directly to the Gormans' cocktail party where the specter of Robin Vance was all but dispelled in the flow of spirits (of all kinds), good cheer, the grace Rachel Gorman trailed in her wake. Her tree sparkled, her canapés artfully arranged, the glitter of her crystal punchbowl, all this filled him with seasonal pleasure as did the whispered invitation that he and Catherine should stay for dinner. Rachel Gorman had ham and rice, candied yams for those select half-dozen she always invited to stay after her cocktail parties.

Amongst the other guests so honored were Eleanor Kellogg and her husband (parents of the virginal Lisa). Lisa was there, too, since she was the girlfriend of the Gormans' oldest son, Michael. Lisa hung on Michael, played with his hair, snuggled up to him in a decidedly un-virginal way.

After dinner they reassembled in the living room for coffee, and as Eleanor was director of the children's choir and producer of the entire Christmas pageant, Hamilton took the opportunity to ask after Robin Vance's children, Patrick and Heather. Eleanor Kellogg could not place them. "The family is new to the church," he added. "They only started coming this fall."

"What does the husband do?" asked Eleanor, stirring her coffee.

Hamilton hesitated. "I don't think there is a husband. I mean, there was, there still is, but he lives far away, he doesn't—of course he might—"

"A broken home," Eleanor stated soberly.

It occurred to the Reverend Hamilton Reedy only then and for the first time that the term broken home was absolutely odious, pernicious, and wrong-headed, that as long as children were loved, a home could not be broken. Hearts got broken, but homes did not need to be. In Robin Vance's defense, he corrected Eleanor Kellogg. "A fractured family, not a broken home."

The distinction was lost on Eleanor. She said she thought that yes, the Vance children were in the pageant and in fact Mrs. Vance had donated several afternoons in the church hall sewing angel and shepherd costumes. She added, beaming, that her daughter, Lisa, was sewing her own costume for her starring role as the Virgin Mary. "This will be the best pageant ever."

As Hamilton left the Gormans' and drove back to the church to park the van and pick up his own car, he noted that the electrical system was shorting again and that one of the spotlights on the Nativity scene was blinking on and off. He resolved to have it fixed tomorrow, parked the van, checked all the church doors, and was about to go to his own car when he felt impelled, oddly, to check on the Holy Family again. He was pleased to note they glowed serenely in the short-circuiting spotlight, their plaster faces rapt with adoration.

They were not there, serene or otherwise, the next morning. Again Reverend Reedy asked Mrs. Doggett to call the police. Again, officers Washington and Green arrived, took down the information in triplicate. The officers vowed to find the culprits, and stated moreover that the joke was no longer funny. The St. Elmo police would double their night patrols, that is, as soon as the Holy Family was recovered. With these assurances, they left the Reverend

Reedy, who continued work on his letter to the Bishop. Hamilton struggled for a full hour over a single paragraph in which he defended himself against the Bishop's unpleasant innuendos: that Hamilton Reedy was a *laissez-faire* pastor, that he was not sufficiently vigilant in routing out sin. The Bishop had further chastised Hamilton that commitment to Christ meant obedience to the church (i.e., the Bishop). Hamilton declared his fealty to Christ and to the church, at the same time reminding Throckmorton that historically it was the right of Protestants to approach God without benefit of an intermediary. That was as far as he got. Lunchtime.

Late that afternoon, surfeited with coffee, tea, spirits, Christmas cheer from his seasonal calls, Reverend Reedy drove home, picked up the St. Elmo *Herald* off the lawn, and greeted Catherine with a kiss. She was wearing an apron, picking up after a committee meeting in their living room. Hamilton loosened his collar, sat down, about to open the *Herald,* but just then the phone rang. It was Officer Washington. "You've seen the afternoon paper, I guess," the officer said.

Hamilton unraveled it in his hand and beheld the church's Virgin and Child sitting on the St. Elmo County courthouse steps. That is, the Virgin was sitting. The Child lay on the cold, hard flagstone. The caption read: *No Crib For A Bed.*

"She isn't at the courthouse anymore," Washington added. "I picked her up and took her in."

"For questioning?" the Reverend replied automatically.

There was a brief silence, as if the officer were uncertain of the joke. "For safekeeping."

"And Joseph?" Hamilton inquired. "Do you have him too?"

"No, just Mary and the Baby. We're still looking for Joseph."

The short December day had contracted into darkness by the time Hamilton arrived again at the downtown police station, the cop shop, he liked to call it. So much cheerier. He entered and found the Virgin in her same place on the bench, her blue robe soiled here, paint flecked off her outstretched hands; the Child's swaddling had grayed and His little nose was chipped.

The downtown police station was crowded this evening and Hamilton was told to take a number while the duty officers processed those before him. He tried to remember the last time he had been called by a number. Perhaps Cake Box Bakery on the day before Thanksgiving—last year. Here, he watched police process half a dozen kids arrested for shoplifting. They wore pants so huge they each looked like full-sail clipper ships and from the cargo holds of these ships there issued forth an astonishing array of stolen goods, including four videos from the boxer shorts of a boy who had refused to sit down. He had also refused to shut up. With his compatriots he spat and smirked and swore. All four gang members addressed one another and the cops—indeed everyone present, male or female—as *puta,* whore, bitch, inviting them to suck various substances, and informing them they all sucked in general. Their oaths counterpointed the yelps of a dreadlocked, gray-bearded veteran (wearing a VFW denim jacket) who alternately protested and wept about a chain of human ears. At least that's what Reedy thought he said. The veteran was being charged with disturbing the peace, assault, and public nuisance. He didn't seem to care; he begged Reedy to look at the chain of human ears he wore around his neck. There was no such chain. There was nothing.

All this clattered against the ring of phones, the blip and natter of computers, the clank of handcuffs. Suddenly the waiting room split with the screech of a rumpled woman in a short dress and running shoes, dragged in by two armed officers while she clutched at, refused to relinquish, the handle of a baby carriage. She screamed that she wasn't going to steal the baby, just talk to it. To Hamilton's horror, as she wrestled with the cops, the baby carriage overturned, and garbage bags with her belongings tumbled out, as did a doll, a baby doll warmly clad in soiled jammies who bleated out a weak, *Maaa-Maaa, Maaa-Maaa.*

"Next! Number 56!" cried out the duty officer. "Number 56! Where are you?" Hamilton rose and went to the desk. "There she is, Reverend, your Madonna. Sign here and a couple of the guys will carry her out for you."

Hamilton signed for *1 Virgin* and *1 Child* and they were carried outside and slid in the back of the church van, Mary on her side. Basically the Virgin seemed none the worse for wear, still tranquil, even benign, Hamilton thought. Although, as he placed the Christ child on the passenger seat, he reminded himself these were only plaster statues *(no graven images)* and their expressions, painted on, were not likely to change, whatever their circumstances.

Officer Washington came to the window of the van. "My advice, Reverend, is to go the Home Center and pick up a couple of locks and chains. Chain Jesus to the manger and the Virgin to her seat, lock them up, and you won't be having this problem again. When you been a cop long as I have, you learn that you can't stop anyone from stealing. All you can do is make it hard for them. Lock 'em up, Reverend, make it hard for them. But I don't think it will happen again anyway. The patrol car is going by the church every hour tonight. If they try again, they'll get caught."

"Then I won't be needing the chains, will I?" Hamilton asked pleasantly.

The thought of a shackled Christ, a manacled Madonna, was repugnant to Hamilton, intolerable. You couldn't chain up the light of the world or the woman who had given that light flesh. He bade Officer Washington a Merry Christmas and drove to the Gormans where he engaged the good doctor and his two sons (Michael—varsity tennis, Paul—varsity baseball) to help him return the Virgin and Child to the Nativity scene in front of the church.

"What about Joseph?" Paul Gorman asked, after they had put them in place.

"It looks awfully weird without Joseph," Michael chuckled, "like maybe Mary is an unwed mother."

"That Child's father is in Heaven," the Reverend replied. Though he had not meant it as a pompous remark, it came out sounding that way. Hamilton flushed, thanked the Gormans, and then drove home, wondering not about Joseph, but about Jon Vance, not about the fractured Holy Family, but about the fractured family at 23B Shadetree Gardens. While, certainly, it was the historical right of all Protestants to approach God without an intermediary, he prayed for Robin Vance to get her Christmas wish, not as he might pray for world peace or an end to strife and starvation in the great theaters of the globe, but for the Christmas spirit to enact itself in the tiny darkened theater of the human heart. He prayed that the season of forgiveness would not pass in vain.

This—and every other thought—was blasted from the Reverend's mind the following morning when he opened the *Los Angeles Times* and gaped at the picture from the St. Elmo paper, plastered on the front page, complete with its caption: *No Crib For A Bed*. Indeed, the Associated Press had picked up the picture. It was running all over the country.

Driving to work, Hamilton saw a bevy of unfamiliar cars clustered near the church and so he turned, avoiding the front, and drove round to the back, parked. Unfamiliar figures milled in the church courtyard; he walked past them without comment and dodged into the large church office, but even here, reporters swarmed out of the wood-paneled walls. They assaulted him with questions and Leila Doggett could not protect him. To the clamoring hordes, Hamilton muttered something cheerfully inspecific and ducked into his study where the lights on the phone flashed and flurried. There was a sheaf of phone messages, some from as far away as New York, Cleveland, Miami, and Blytheville, Arkansas. Unwisely he picked up line 1. It was a stringer representing *People Magazine* who wanted to know how to get to St. Elmo. Gesticulating wildly from the door, Mrs. Doggett indicated that Bishop Throckmorton was on line 2.

The Bishop sputtered questions, accusations, and innuendos without a single pleasantry.

"The police have assured me," Hamilton began, hoping to put the onus on their secular shoulders, "that they will patrol the church every hour. They did so last night."

"Is that so?" snarled the Bishop. "Did they perchance then see who stole these things?"

The dreadful thought accosted Hamilton. He had not driven by the front this morning, had not seen the Nativity scene. Could it be . . . ? He lay the squawking phone down very gently on his desk and dashed to the outer office, *sotto voce* inquired of Mrs. Doggett if the Holy Family was missing again this morning.

"Why do you think all these people are here?" she wailed, pointing to the reporters, camera crews, photographers, and other assorted hangers-on who were swilling the church's coffee and munching the church's Christmas goodies. In a great mass they lunged toward Hamilton, but he escaped behind his study door, and picked up the phone just as the Bishop was demanding, *Well? Well?*

"What can I say," Hamilton replied prudently. "What would you have me do? Chain Jesus to the manger? Chain Mary to Joseph?"

"You'll have to find Joseph first, won't you?" the Bishop retorted. "Never mind. I'll call a firm here in L.A. and have one delivered this afternoon. And you better hang onto him, too. You can't have a Holy Family without Joseph."

Less prudently Hamilton added, "I don't know why not. There are lots of families without fathers these days. That doesn't make them any less families, does it?"

"Very funny, Reedy. You really are too much. You had better see that this doesn't happen again. This—" Hamilton heard the rattle of a newspaper in the phone "—is not what we like by way of publicity." The Bishop hung up.

From these inauspicious beginnings, Hamilton Reedy's morning deteriorated. The church—venerable institution that it was—degenerated into another venerable institution, the madhouse. Traffic snarled for blocks as reporters congealed and collected, minivans double-parked and Minicams taped the serious reflections of pretty men and well-coiffed women. Sound people adjusted the volume for these representatives of the four networks, CNN, and two independent L.A. stations. Cell phones buzzed and pinged, and people sought the privacy of the church's flower beds for inconsequential conversations. Standing sturdily before the TV cameras, on-the-spot reporters gravely told their anchorpersons on the morning news what anyone with a brain to play with could clearly see.

The newspeople's power needs plugged up all the church's outlets and thick cords snaked across the courtyard, over the lawn. Finally the uncertain electrical circuits blew altogether. The place shut down: computers died, lights went dark, nothing worked. A cameraman called the electrician on his cell phone. Mrs. Doggett's stash of chocolate-covered toffees had been raided and she chose this moment to bring the theft to Hamilton's attention. Just then one of the female reporters popped her head into Hamilton's study and told them the women's toilet was backed up.

Officers Washington and Green rescued Hamilton from Mrs. Doggett, from the plumbing and electrical problems. He regarded them hopefully and they did not disappoint him.

"Marconi and Tuttle found your Holy Family about 5 A.M."

"Where?" asked Hamilton weakly.

"County Hospital. Emergency Ward. Marconi and Tuttle were bringing in some suspects—"

"You couldn't call them suspects," Green argued. "Marconi and Tuttle saw it. Damn near got it themselves."

"It was a domestic violence call," Washington explained, "and when Marconi and Tuttle got there, they could hear the man beating on the wife, threatening her with a gun and so they called out and kicked open the door, but the guy fired once at the door, turned back, and fired again at the woman. Hit her."

"And?" Hamilton asked urgently. "And?"

"She was OK."

"She's not OK," Green corrected Washington. "She's not dead. She's not seriously wounded, but she's not OK."

"Could have been a lot worse," said Washington. "By the time they called the ambulance for the victim, and they've read the guy his rights, got him handcuffed, Tuttle looks up, and there's the woman, up off the floor, bleeding and all, raging toward her husband with a butcher knife in her hand. She stabs him before anyone could stop her. Well, they couldn't put them in the same ambulance after that, could they? Not in that kind of murderous rage," Washington added soberly. "So they get to County Hospital, the ambulance with the wife, the squad car with the husband, and everyone's just struck dumb to find your Holy Family in the waiting room beside the potted palm, just like they're there waiting for word on their nearest and dearest."

"They're not my Holy Family," Hamilton protested without any particular verve. "Did anyone see them, well . . . arrive?"

"There was another guy there, a patient checked in just before the domestic violence, but they haven't asked him yet."

"Why not?"

"He was still having his stomach pumped, last I heard. Suicide."

"Attempted suicide," Green clarified. "Poison."

Hamilton paled, felt rather queasy himself, but he asked nonetheless if Joseph was with them, if Joseph had been found.

"No. Just the Mother and Child. We're still looking for the man."

"I guess I need to come down to the station and sign for them." Hamilton rose wearily, put his coat over his arm.

"Well, no, Reverend—"

"Listen!" Hamilton cried, surprise and delight wreathing his face. "It's quiet in the front office! The reporters have gone!"

Washington and Green exchanged uncomfortable glances. "They're not gone," Green said at last. "I think they're all out front of the church. You see, we have Christ and the Virgin in the squad car."

As Hamilton Reedy walked between the two cops (as though he were the one in custody), he positively kicked himself that he had ever wished for some grander, more dramatic theater of ministry. Gone was the picture of the shirtsleeved Hamilton integrating lunch counters and converting young toughs. He longed only for the tidiness of his placid congregation, Sunday School recitations, choir politics, and homebound ministries. Washington and Green protected Hamilton as microphones were thrust in his face, and cords and cameras barred his progress. Men and women shouted at him. Hamilton reminded himself of the sufferings of the Holy Martyrs. Torture.

Worse yet: there she was, locked in the squad car. Behind the thick grill in the squad car sat the delinquent Virgin, the blue in her robe chipped, but her expression unblemished, her eyes untarnished by anything she might have beheld—suicide, violence, vomit, poison, blood, bullet holes, stab wounds—in the Emergency Ward of County Hospital. The Reverend Reedy prayed to God to take this affliction from him, to protect the Holy Family from theft, to protect him from the Bishop's wrath. "All is calm," he murmured to himself, though clearly this was not true. "All is bright."

Officer Green unlocked the squad car and out wafted the aroma of cigarette butts, spilled coffee, stale hamburgers, and apple cores as the two cops hoisted the Madonna from her sitting position and carried her to the Nativity scene, the humble plywood shack, where plaster animals gazed at straw in the empty manger. A reporter thrust the Baby Jesus into Hamilton's arms and took his picture. Lots of pictures. The crews and cameras tumbled over one another to follow Hamilton back to the Nativity scene where he lay Christ gently in the manger, there beneath His mother's benevolent gaze.

The Bishop was as good as his word and a Joseph was delivered to the church by the last light of afternoon and placed with the Holy Family. Joseph looked new to the job. Mary and Jesus showed signs of wear. Manicured newspersons and their cam-crews, their sound people, still milled through the huge crowd that had gathered round yon Virgin, mother and child. Everyone in St. Elmo, and some from afar, had thoughts on the matter, including Lisa Kellogg who told KNBC that all this stuff really made her, like, think a lot about her role as the Virgin in the Christmas pageant tomorrow night. The reporter then asked Lisa if she would join an all-night candlelight vigil that people planned to hold tonight at the church to protect the Holy Family from further mischief. Lisa said she had a date. But later, sure. Cool.

However, it rained that night, a torrential downpour that quashed all thought of a candlelight vigil, and cut off power to two-thirds of St. Elmo from 12:27 to 4:54 A.M. At 6:00 A.M., the Reverend Mr. Reedy was awakened by a phone call. A young voice, allying itself with the St. Elmo *Herald,* wanted to be the first to ask him if he had any idea where the Virgin might have got to this time, since she was not in front of the church when the power came back on.

"What about Jesus and Joseph?" Hamilton asked.

"They're there. It's just the Virgin who's gone off this time."

The Reverend rang off and slowly rose from his bed, rumpling what was left of his hair. For some reason a smile tugged at his lips, at least he thought he was smiling. The suspicion was confirmed by the bathroom mirror. As he shaved, Hamilton found himself wondering if he could find a Biblical citation to support the notion of Joseph baby-sitting Christ.

Despite Catherine's furrowed brow and anxious questions, Hamilton's feeling of well-being, perhaps downright euphoria, persisted through breakfast. Driving past the front of the church he felt no twinge of yesterday's tortures and apprehensions, yesterday's dismay. He was merely curious, and clucked inwardly over the damage done to the church's narcissus beds where the people were taking snapshots (this early!) of the Virgin-less Joseph and Jesus. He parked his car at the back, whistling "God Rest Ye Merry Gentlemen," and stepped lively toward the office, eager, full of good cheer and goodwill, as if last night's downpour had washed an accretion of invisible tarnish from his very soul. He felt somehow expanded. Ignoring the ringing phones and stuttering fax machine, he greeted Mrs. Doggett jovially. And when she asked if they'd found the Blessed Mother yet, Hamilton patted her hand and replied that she would certainly turn up. He did not doubt it for a moment. He smiled. Mrs. Doggett thought him unhinged.

She did turn up. By midmorning of Christmas Eve Day, every newspaper in California and beyond had been apprised that St. Elmo's Vanishing Virgin had been found on the steps of the State Hospital for the Criminally Insane, some twenty-five miles from St. Elmo proper, near a town called (of all things) Vassar.

Mrs. Doggett heard it on the radio and told the Reverend, who was calmly working on his letter to the Bishop. He thanked her and returned to the task. He finished the letter. He thought it one of his best, a model of defensive dignity. Then he tore it up and decided not to be defensive at all. His next draft was dignified, succinct, and completed in a matter of minutes. He handed it to Mrs. Doggett to be typed. He went outside and stood in front of his church, waiting, along with Joseph and Jesus, for the return of the Virgin Mary, as though Mary worked the graveyard shift at an all-night diner and would be home soon.

And soon she was. Brought by the police (sirens blaring), trailing a caravan of minivans, bearing Minicams and soundmen shepherding mannequin-reporters, followed by dozens of other cars, all horns honking, the whole procession of pilgrims (as Hamilton thought of them) returned the errant Virgin from Vassar to the Episcopal church. As the cameras rolled and newspeople nattered into handheld mikes, police placed Mary back with her husband and God's son. And then, for the especial benefit of Channel 7, Mr. Will Dance of the St. Elmo Home Center volunteered free locks, free chains to keep her there. The cameras then panned to the Reverend Reedy who, despite the chill, was in his shirtsleeves, leaning against the church door. The reporter asked if St. Elmo Episcopal would take the Home Center up on their offer. The Reverend declined. He added, for all the world (to say nothing of Bishop Throckmorton) that you could not chain up the light of the world, or the woman who gave that light flesh. "If the Virgin wants to stray, to deviate from the paths mere mortals have assigned her, who are we to insist she stay put?"

"Reverend Reedy," the reporter inquired gravely, "they're saying that maybe the Virgin Mary was never really stolen, sir. What do you think? Has there been a miracle here?"

Hamilton's eyebrows shot up. He regarded the reporter ruefully. "A miracle?" he said. "In St. Elmo?"

Some hours later for Christmas Eve services, Reverend Reedy, clad in his vestments, stopped off in the church hall to see all the little shepherds and angels getting ready for their procession. They were subdued for a band of angels, and the shepherds clutched their fluffy sheep as much for comfort as for effect. Eleanor Kellogg was beside herself, issuing cues and instructions. Hamilton then took his customary place, and on the opening notes of "O Come All Ye Faithful," he entered the church following the acolytes, the brightly robed choir, and curate, Tim Voight. From the altar overlooking the congregation, Hamilton inwardly grinned; never had he seen so many faces in these pews. Standing room only. He blinked into the floodlights that had been set up at the back of the church to illuminate the pageant and when his eyes became accustomed to their glare, he searched for Robin Vance, finding her finally in the sixth row, sitting beside her sister. She kept turning toward the doors at the back, looking for her husband to appear, visibly disappointed when the church doors closed. She stared at her twisted hands.

Following the benediction, the pageant began, the littlest children leading the way into the church: shepherds and angels hand-in-hand, their little voices piping, "Angels We Have Heard on High." The choir took up the bright refrain and eased into "O Holy Night" and at that swelling chorus, *Fall! On your knees!* Michael Gorman as Joseph escorted Lisa (the Blessed Virgin) Kellogg down the aisle. Clad in a simple blue robe, her feet bare, her perky cheerleader's gait subdued, a satisfied smile played at Lisa's lips, but her gaze was straight ahead. Inexpertly she cradled a blanketed babydoll in her arms. Watching Lisa, Hamilton distantly heard the bleat of the babydoll in the cop shop where the sight of that homeless, childless, manless, jobless madwoman had shocked Hamilton, indeed, revolted him. But here in the context of the church, he was moved. Why was that, he asked himself. Why? The Three Wise Men followed behind Mary and Joseph, walking more like cadets than sages; these were boys Hamilton had known since their Sunday School years, watched them grow through Cub Scouts, the Science Olympiad, Junior Varsity, all that. But in these youths he so well knew, he saw, too, the clipper-ship shoplifters spewing defamation, the kid with the mucous bubbling from his nose ring, his empty eyes, his neck bearing a tattooed chain. In Michael Gorman who played Joseph (his hair all floured to make him look mature), Hamilton, quite against his will, saw the grizzled veteran, dreadlocked, mad, endlessly atoning for his chain of human ears. All this rang in Hamilton's head, in his heart, above the congregation's "It Came Upon a Midnight Clear." Hamilton forgot to stand. He sat rooted, looking out upon the crowded church as the carol ended, as the angels and shepherds ringed themselves round Mary and Joseph, and the narrator began the familiar tale. Suddenly, there was a crash at the back, and a tier of lamps smashed down and the church's eccentric electrical system gave out. The whole congregation was momentarily thrust into absolute blackness. The angels and shepherds began to cry.

Instantly Hamilton was on his feet, his sonorous voice booming out, "Do not be afraid!" Quickly, sharply, indelibly, understanding flooded over him, "This is the dark the world lived in for thousands of years!" he called out. "There will be light. Tonight, of all nights, there *will* be light and that light can never be shackled or chained or dimmed."

After considerable scuffling, the lights came back on. A man at the back shouted, "Nothing to worry about. A guy just came in late, tripped over the cord, and fell against the lights."

And with those words Hamilton Reedy saw Robin Vance bolt from her seat, start up the aisle toward the church door, and Hamilton's eyes, too, scanned the back of the church, looking for a man he pictured bearded as Joseph, searching, with Robin, for sight of Jon Vance, willing, as Robin must have willed, for that man to appear out of the darkness and step into the light.

So strong was the willing, the wish, the prayer, that Hamilton almost thought he saw Jon Vance, but the only man who came to meet Robin was Dr. Gorman who gently took her arm, murmuring that everything was all right.

Robin stared at the doctor for a moment. Then she allowed him to return her to her seat beside her sister. She picked up the hymnbook she had dropped and opened it. Her eyes met Hamilton's. His heart broke to see sorrow and disappointment drape her face. *It is the season for forgiveness and it will pass in vain.*

No, Hamilton thought. It cannot. It must not.

The sermon the Reverend Reedy delivered that night was not the one he had so tidily written days before. It was not tidy at all, but rather inchoate and incoherent, rambling, unconventional, alternately pompous and poetic, certainly impassioned, and judging from the puzzled faces of the congregation, he confused them. Perhaps that was all to the good.

Hamilton looked right at Robin when he began, saying

the reason Christmas was celebrated year after year, was so that we should remember that the season of forgiveness never passes away entirely. "Like all seasons, it returns. Like all seasons it brings the promise of renewal, shrouded in nostalgia." He said we should resist nostalgia and look "forward, to the promise of renewal, of forgiveness, to the goodwill we might yet spread in this sorry world." He opened up his arms; his gaze swept over the crowded church. "But first we must see that sorrow. For that we must look into the institutions. We must reach into the courthouse and the jail, the hospital for the criminally insane, the hospital for the terminally ill, for the suicide, for the wounded. We must wring that sorrow with our hands. Recognize it as our own sorrow. Who says we are immune? Do you think the Holy Family was immune from strife? From struggle? From anger? From anxiety? From heartbreak? The true beauty of the Holy Family, my friends, is not so much that they are holy, but they were a human family. As difficult as your own family. They were a fractured family, but not a broken home. Jesus was the original stepchild."

A quiver of outrage riddled the congregation and then Hamilton pointed out Jesus was in good company, Moses, too, was a foster child. Though this hardly mollified the faithful, Hamilton continued, unabashed.

"Jesus well knew the courthouse, the jail, the madhouse, and the hospital. Jesus suffered through all these institutions. You need only to read the New Testament to know He suffered. You need only to consult your heart to know His mother suffered with and for Him. At Christmas we acknowledge that He was born amongst the homeless. At Easter we acknowledge that He died amongst the thieves."

Hamilton then denied the rumor that there had been a

grand miracle in St. Elmo these past few days. "There are no more grand miracles," he told the faithful and the curious alike, "only tiny miracles enacted daily in the individual heart." He further confounded them, asserting that although there had been no miracle, neither had there been a theft. "There was no theft. The St. Elmo police will not find who fractured the Holy Family because families—even the Holy Family—exist in order to *be* fractured. By time if nothing else," he reasoned, "by death, finally and for certain. After all, children grow up, leave home, parents grow old, die. We might, any of us, you—or you—or you—" He pointed randomly into the crowded pews. "You might one day find yourself cast far from home, shackled in an uncongenial institution, in a jail, or a courtroom, or a hospital having your guts pumped out, your wounds sewed up, your heart still broken. None of that renders the family—any family—invalid. Flesh, blood, bone, life—these are finite! Love is not. Love is infinite and exists beyond time. My dear friends, time will make fools of us all, of our sufferings, indeed, even of our pleasures. Life is finite. Love is not. Love can bend like light!" The thought was so spectacular, so appropriate, so obvious, Hamilton marveled that he'd not understood before. He gazed out to the confused faces and concluded with a few random thoughts. He sat down. He was a little confused himself. The delinquent Virgin had shed her light, restored his vision.

The curate visibly checked Reverend Reedy's breath for alcohol when he whispered to him after the service that the police were waiting for him in his study. Hamilton crossed the church courtyard alone, up the flagstone paths, his cassock and surplice blowing in the cold winds that came off the desert, the vestments billowing until he closed the door of the office and then they seemingly died around his ankles.

Officers Washington and Green greeted him. With them they had four teenaged boys slouching on folding chairs. Hamilton judged them to be about fourteen and surly. Voluminous pants hung from their skinny hips and their enormous feet were planted defiantly apart. Permanent sneers twisted their features and one picked his nose with his third finger. Officer Washington made them stand up. "We caught them hanging around out front," said Washington. "We think they're the ones who have been stealing your Holy Family."

Hamilton considered telling Officer Washington once again that they were not his Holy Family, but he resisted. He turned to the biggest boy. "Have you been stealing the figures from in front of the church?"

"Hell no," said the boy. The others guffawed.

"Well, if you're lying—and I assume you are," Hamilton scrutinized their beardless faces, "allow me to congratulate you on your good work. Allow me to be the first to thank you for a job well done, men. Excellent! And please, I beg of you, in the name of the church, of Christians everywhere, on behalf of the Spirit of God and the message of Christ, go on stealing the Holy Family! Go on leaving them in places where people will notice them. I commend you! No one notices the Virgin and Child in front of the church, do they? Of course not. It's expected, isn't it? Conventional. Ordinary. But! The Virgin and Child in the mess and muck of the Emergency Room where people who have despaired of life are having their guts pumped out—now, no one could overlook the Virgin there! No one could miss the Virgin even if they were bleeding from knife wounds, riddled with bullets, or beaten in anger, could they?"

The boys rustled uncomfortably amongst themselves.

"And the Holy Family on the courthouse steps where families are dissolved every day, amidst all the wretchedness, the squalor of divorce—oh, boys, I tell you that was perfection! The courthouse where crime and degradation, desperation are every day judged. Oh, brilliantly thought out. I have to hand it to you. I am dazzled by your vision. And the madhouse? The *criminally insane?* What a coup! What imagination! Which of you men thought of taking her out there?"

The boys' sneers melted into disbelief. They glanced weirdly at one another. The tallest asked, "Are you fucking dicking with my head?"

"Shut up," commanded Washington. They shut up.

"The Virgin in the madhouse. That's where she belongs, isn't it? That's where she's needed," Hamilton continued. "Her tenderness and mercy amongst the criminally afflicted, the truly wretched of the earth. And I shall always be impressed with your conspicuous bravery in the first place, men, your certain foreknowledge in leading us, in taking the entire Holy Family, all three of them, and placing them on the steps of the downtown St. Elmo police station. You put her there. The pure, chaste Virgin there in the police waiting room. You are the kind of men our country needs. Men with bravery. Vision. Forgive me, men. I ask your forgiveness, truly. How could I have contradicted your wisdom? How could I have brought the Holy Family back to the church? Men—I beg of you—continue always in this great and glorious work! Merry Christmas. Go with God."

"What the hell, your Reverence!" cried Green. "You can't mean you don't want to press charges?"

"You can't mean you don't want us to take these guys in?" asked Washington.

"And have them spend Christmas Eve in Juvenile Hall? Yet another sordid institution? Never. Can it have escaped your notice, Officer Washington? It is the season of forgiveness." He gave them all a maddeningly benign smile.

The boys shuffled silently out. The cops stalked out, muttering. The Reverend took off his tippet and academic hood, his surplice and cassock, and hung them in the closet. As he put on his coat and turned out the lights, made ready to depart by the back door, Hamilton Reedy thought—at least he entertained the notion—that he heard a tiny round of applause in that darkest theater of all, that untidy chamber of hope and remorse, the human heart.

Moby-Jack

JACK LONDON CREATED JACK LONDON and Hemingway became him. Jack London could write about anything, from dogs to alcoholism, anything except women. Hemingway never acknowledged his debt to Jack London (though as we all know, he had nice things to say about Mark Twain). As a boy, however, Hemingway read all of Jack's collected works and learned from Jack London what Mark Twain could not teach him.

Hemingway's biographers cluck and bluster over his mother's sending him his father's fatal pistol, the gun his father had used to kill himself. They fail to notice that in that same box with the pistol, his mother sent Hem's boyhood collection of all of Jack London's novels. The gun upset Hem, naturally, but the books! He tore out all the flyleafs *(. . . Love, Mother, Christmas 1910)* and burned them. The books themselves he took deep-sea fishing and threw them off the boat, into the Gulf of Mexico, where they were read by all the fishes.

Thus, thanks to Hemingway, all of Jack London's stories imbue the briny deep. Borne on underwater currents from Key West to the Gulf of Mexico, Jack London's tales are taught in all schools of fish. Fish from the Baja Peninsula, up the California Coast, all along the Pacific Rim up to British Columbia and the tiny finger-islands off Alaska and on over to Siberia subscribe to Jack London's code of honor. From Jack London, fish learned the call of the wild, that fierce, horrid shriek they give when they are yanked from the sea, mauled in trawlers, strangled in gill nets, before they gasp and bleed on deck, tossed like shining coins, their blind eyes open to the sky before they are ignominiously iced and gutted, processed.

There was this one fish, however, who endured no such inglorious fate. His visceral understanding of Jack London was matched by that of his captor, his partner in struggle and narrative, Old Buck.

Tough, scrawny, bearded, and bathless, Old Buck fished the Puget Sound on a beat-up trawler named *Bessie* after his wife who had left him in 1949. Now Buck was too old to fish alone, but he was too mean to keep a crew, save for a single hapless college kid, Wyatt. Old Buck was chewing a cup of coffee one day on deck when he saw something huge leap, streak out of the sea. It caught the morning light, near-blinded him with its silvery flash, and when it plunged back beneath the waves, its wake near-swamped *Bessie*. Buck grinned knowingly, and tossed his coffee cup overboard. Old Buck knew his Jack London. This was a star-spangled, white whale of a fish! This was the biggest damn fish Old Buck had ever seen. On the food chain, this fish was the lock and key! This was the Leviathan all right. Buck had waited all his life for this fish. Buck called out to Wyatt, *Ready yourself, boy, we're going after Moby-Jack!*

For three days and three nights they fought with this fish, followed it out of the protected waters of the Sound and into the wild Pacific. Young Wyatt hadn't the mettle for this fight, hadn't the sheer sinew and endurance, the stamina or pith of the old man—or the fish, for that matter. The cold was killing. *Bessie* sprang a leak, the radio failed, and Wyatt had to throw all their gear overboard so the old tub could stay afloat and the old man could fight this fish to the finish.

On the third day, gloves shredded, his hands bleeding and raw from the lines, Wyatt called out over the screaming winds, *Hey, Buck! This reminds me of the story about that old man who went after a big fish and caught him and brought him in after this really fierce battle, but on the way to port, the sharks ate the whole thing and the guy had nothing to show for it. You know, Buck—a sort of metaphor for life—that story?*

Waves washed over the deck, *Bessie* listed perilously, but Old Buck knotted the lines around his wrists so he could stop struggling long enough to give Wyatt a long look of withering disdain and cry out, *This is no pasty-faced poseur, no Parisian Pamplona bullshit fish, you fool! This fish is not the figleaf of some metaphor-mongering imagination! This fish—*

But Buck's words were drowned out in Wyatt's screams. Wyatt was washed overboard.

The Coast Guard vessel *Rachel* rescued Wyatt. They wrapped him in blankets and listened to his story of Buck, *Bessie,* and the fish. The young lieutenant remarked to the captain, *That sounds like* The Old Man and the Sea, *sir.*

Forget Hemingway, the Captain scoffed. *Old Buck's in real trouble. This fish is schooled in Jack London. This is one white fang of a fish.*

In the morning calm, the *Rachel* found *Bessie* up to her portholes in water and sinking fast. The Captain hastened onboard to find Buck and the fish lying on the deck. Both goners. The huge fish, bigger than Buck, gleamed brilliantly in the sunlight. Buck still had the lines knotted round his wrists and his arm lay over the fish's fluttering gills.

Buck? The Captain asked gravely, *Buck, do you want Last Rites?*

Buck coughed and spat, reached up, and clawed the Captain's coat. *Do what you want with me, but show this fish some respect*. Buck smiled heavenward, gave the fish one final affectionate pat, and with his last breath added, *Promise me you'll give this fish to people whose literary taste isn't all under their tongues.*

Change at Empoli

You have no passion, only lust. No spirit, only appetite. Why have you come to Italy as students of art? You do not give a damn for art. Or, perhaps I should point to what one of you has so generously deposited in the hall, on the floor, point to that and say: that is what you give for art, for Italy, for love, for life. That. You are welcome to that. But I am leaving.

OH YES, THAT'S WHAT she should have said. Dignified, but its underlying tone unmistakable. She pulled her hat down a bit tighter and pressed her coat against her throat with a kind of dramatic savor, as though these words had actually traversed her lips in front of their intended audience. She was a woman best described as handsome, a face dominated by a firm jaw and wide green eyes, pale skin and dark hair. She checked her own wristwatch against that of the man across from her. He was deeply ensconced behind a newspaper, but his watch testified silently with hers, 9:34. The 9:20 should have left fourteen minutes ago. She pushed the train window down and scanned the platform, fearfully scouting for Giorgio. Silly. People like Giorgio could not command trains. Giorgio could not command his own cat, unless he could flatter and court and smarm. That's the way Giorgio dealt with everyone, except his wife, whom he bullied. Disgusting. Nonetheless, Corinne chided herself for having phoned him from the station. She should have waited, called him when she got to Empoli, when she changed there for Pisa.

She would not feel safe until the train pulled out. She kept a careful watch on the platform, prepared to vanish into the women's toilet if she saw Giorgio Carruthers running toward the 9:20. His coat would be flying, and he, terrified at the thought that he was about to cease being her assistant and now would inherit the directorship of the University's Institute for Italian Art. Giorgio would be sweating like a pig, would implore her, beg her not to leave the Institute and the filthy students. He would say they were young and thought it a mere harmless prank. Corinne would fix her green-eyed gaze on him, curl her lip in utter contempt, and ask: They are adults, are they not? Adult American students in a university program, guests in a foreign country? Giorgio would sputter here and she would continue mercilessly: I am—I was—Director of the Institute for Italian Art, not the crossing guard at an elementary school who must hold innocent hands. These students are drunken, disrespectful, irresponsible oafs. When I was their age, Giorgio, I had an infant daughter and a husband and I was in graduate school.

And , realizing he could not cajole her, Giorgio would next threaten: The University will sack you on sight. Your reputation as an administrator will be smashed. A woman as old as you will not be able to find another job.

Giorgio, you are young enough to be my son, though I thank God I am not your mother. Nevertheless, I am going to offer you this bit of wisdom: it is not my own. I got it from Max who is very wise indeed in these matters. You would do well to heed Max, Giorgio, though you do not know him. Max always said, *There are moments in life when all that is left to you is gesture*. You perform that gesture because without it, you are merely stranded and pathetic. The gesture is all that stands between you and pathos. Do you understand, Giorgio? Of course not. Ah well, your response to the students' thoughtful offering is your own affair, but I know why you and the other two instructors toady to them. Because these American students allow you to live in this beautiful medieval Tuscan town, to work for the Institute. It is, as they say, a very good gig. So of course you will chuckle and excuse this calculated heap of dung on the floor as a youthful, harmless prank. Fine, Giorgio, do so. But I shall not. I shall never. Never.

Her speech had gathered conviction and velocity as the train gathered conviction and velocity and by 10:05, it had rounded a curve that left the city itself behind. But at the time, the moment—yesterday morning—when this speech would have been best delivered, Corinne had been without words. Words—English or Italian—had failed her altogether. She sat in her office (door closed against the offending substance in front of it) and listened to Giorgio and the other two instructors in a classroom down the hall splutter and demand of the students: *Who did this?* Listened to the students giggle and rustle in response. Corinne knew who did it, knew with a kind of absolute imaginative certainty that Adam Green, vulgar, shiftless, shallow Adam Green had squatted there, defecated in front of her door while the rest of them, say a dozen or so of the thirty students in the program, watched, laughed. The picture, unthinkable as it was, did not defy the imagination. That's what was really appalling.

From her office she could hear Giorgio's fruitless and finally ridiculous harangue, heard him dismiss the students with vague (and as they well knew) empty threats. She kept her eyes on the voluptuous Annunciation angel painted by a less-than-masterful seventeenth-century hand in the arch of her ceiling and listened as the students' footsteps shuffled past her door to the staircase, listened to their giggling, casual obscenities, their overt contempt. *The old witch*. They did not even do her the honor of *bitch,* which at least implies malice aforethought. Witch. Hag. Sexless crone. *Strega Nona* in Italian, but they did not have enough Italian to know this. Their American voices echoed down the corridors of the old building, the broad staircase that led to medieval streets, their guffaws melded into the noises and cries from the street below. She brought her eyes from the angel on the ceiling and rested them on the shelves where her personal collection of slides, Renaissance and medieval art, were neatly catalogued and housed. Shelf after shelf. Corinne rose, picked up the nameplate from her desk: *Corinne Mackenzie, Director,* and dropped it fastidiously in the trash. That, by way of notice.

She had never taken off her coat. Her gloves lay on the desk. She drew them on, and in leaving the office (as she had in entering) she walked over, around, beyond the excremental token at her door. She held her breath and darted quickly down the broad staircase. At the bottom, she let her breath escape, then pulled the brass bolt on the heavy door and stepped outside, swept into the currents of the city.

These narrow medieval streets, thick with shadow at their base, alight with brilliant sunshine at the housetops, thronged with the life and vitality Corinne had always cherished. Despite the midmorning cold, people stood about smoking, talking, gesticulating broadly. Old men engaged in heated political quarrels, while women chatted on their way to market. Messengers on motorscooters plied the streets like small noisy skiffs, cutting through a sea of people, mothers pulling hapless children in their wake, and workingmen brushing masonry dust from their shoulders as they all stood about in the shadow of the

Italian national bird: the restoration crane. Overhead clothesline pulleys squealed and ancient shutters creaked open in the morning air. Cathedral bells tolled, making their august presence felt in the very stones as Corinne hurried to the sunny square. The chestnut vendor there, who knew her for a good customer, was surprised, even offended when she hastened right by, running for the Number 10 bus chugging at the stop.

It was market day and well-dressed women laden with parcels, flowers, and gossip pushed and shoved to get on the bus. In front of Corinne an aged woman, so stooped over as to form a sort of crescent, hoisted herself up the steps. A young man rose to give her a seat near the door. He pushed toward the back with Corinne right behind him. In the lilt and legato, the staccato of Italian all around her, she feared she yet heard the students, their flat American voices, their coarse contempt, their menacing laughter. She clung to the pole and rocked with the bus, closed her eyes tight, willed herself to hear Max's voice, Max's story. Like a quilt for comfort, a fable to hide under, she told herself Max's story. She, too, was fleeing, reduced to being a refugee, just like Max's family, fleeing Germany with the advent of the Nazis.

Not surprisingly, Max came from a mixed marriage, his mother a Christian, a painter, and a cellist; his father a renowned historian axed from the university because he was a Jew. They had become prisoners in their own country and so, they elected instead to become refugees. They bundled up and fled one night in a carefully planned exodus, first to England where they lived for fourteen months, and then to America. Max was just a little boy, and as the three prepared to leave their flat, their German life, Max had clutched an armful of toys to take with him. His father took them away. Little Max had cried as his father softly stroked his cheek, whispered, *This, Max, your skin, your flesh, this is what you get to take with you. It is all you get to take. Do not cry. You are lucky to escape with your skin*. Nonetheless, in a gesture of covert rebellion (entirely consistent with Max's adult character) he managed to secrete a single toy beneath his many jackets and when his father found out, he got angry.

Max's family's flight, some sixty years ago, put her own immediate circumstances in a comforting historical perspective. Corinne was fleeing, escaping obscenity, vulgarity, stupidity, and undeserved contempt, all implicit there before her office door. She had built this program, the Institute for Italian Art, worked day after day, contributed. And now, they had forced her to this cutthroat gesture. But it was all that was left and she would carry it off. Like Max would have. Fitting, that Max should somehow aid her when he was not actually here to help.

Ordinarily Corinne Mackenzie was not a woman who did things in haste. She preferred always the slow and voluptuous enjoyment of endeavor. She cared nothing for efficiency, and yet, when she reached the sunny, spacious flat she'd lived in for two years, she tore off her coat and gloves, and with frantic, unseemly haste, she flew, pulling clothes from the closets, cosmetics from the bathroom shelves. She moved swiftly through the flat, dashing through the bedroom, bathroom, study, sitting room with its balcony where potted flowers were already crunchy from the autumn frosts. She flung things into two open-mawed suitcases and when they would not zip shut, she flung things out. She ransacked her own flat. She took the phone off the hook and refused to answer the bell when it rang from the street. Giorgio. Of course it would be Giorgio.

Packed at last, that afternoon, she jammed her books

into shopping bags and hauled them downstairs and across the street to the greengrocers, the ever-obliging, aging, courtly Signor Vitti. She gave him (to his open-mouthed amazement) four hundred forty thousand lire and asked him to surface freight the books to America and to keep the change. Then she went home, and without eating, popped some pills to make her sleep.

The following morning she phoned Giorgio from the station where she awaited the 9:20 to Empoli. She told him she was about to board the train, to change at Empoli, and get the train for the Pisa airport. He said she was making a mistake, a silly gesture. It was only a harmless student prank, he said. All in the past. He begged her to reconsider. He said it had been cleaned up.

II

To be capable of gesture is to be assured that one's imagination is alive and well. For a woman of Corinne's age, it testified as well to vitality of spirit. Of course she did not look her age. Good health, good habits, good genes, and discreet applications of the dye bottle worked in unison to create the artistic impression of a woman on the sunny side of fifty. She felt no compunction about the dye bottle. By profession, temperament, and training, Corinne Mackenzie was dedicated to art and so, naturally, though she was an American, she was more at home in Italy than anywhere in the world. Italy shared her values: *Honor artifice, presentation is everything.* Honoring artifice, Corinne's personal presentation was such that you never would have believed her to be the mother of a woman as old as Allegra. Indeed, mother and daughter might have been transposed in the sense that women Corinne's age were supposed to be shrewd, practical, cautionary unto calculating, and utterly without imagination. Such a description better suited

Allegra who, despite all Corinne's efforts (beginning with the flamboyant name, ballet lessons, piano lessons, and European travel) had grown up to be a tremendous disappointment: married, middle-class, matronly, the mother of a dreary boy. Mention art to Allegra and she thinks it's a new caddy at the country club. Disgusting. Allegra, her hideous husband and her ineffectual father always playing revolting bridge. Always looking for a fourth. Well, wait till the boy grew up. The boy was the image of his insurance-mongering father. No doubt he'd play bridge with them. Rubbers.

"Mi scusi, Signora, ma non parlo Inglese."

The man across from her emerged from behind his newspaper and she realized she'd actually been talking aloud. To him. She laughed, "Non importante," she said, "niente."

He was well dressed, well fed, and exuded a sturdy sort of well-being so attractive in a man. His hair was dark, heavily salted with gray, and she reckoned him to be on the sunny side of fifty. No matter that he did not speak English, Corinne spoke beautiful Italian and of course he said so. People always said so. From Poggibonsi on, Corinne and her fellow passenger, Paolo Branchi, enjoyed their conversation, sitting in the shuttering squares of sunlight as the train plunged into the countryside where rags of November tattered the trees. On the hillsides the leafless vineyards lined up, row after row of them, their skinny arms twisted round wire and one another, synchronized as anorexic chorus girls. Corinne and Signor Branchi relaxed against their seats, speaking languidly as though they had time and time and time in front of them, none of it bounded by the railway's timetable. She found herself forgetting all about Allegra and Giorgio and the filthy students and basking in this man's attentions. There are some things only a man can do for you.

He was an engineer, returning home after business in Roma. He gave her his card: *Dottore Ing. Paolo Branchi*. Naturally she was impressed. She would have given him her card, but she was no longer Director of the Institute for Italian Art. She could not say that she was leaving because of a pile of student dung, so she said simply she was an artist, a student, a devotee of Renaissance angels, and after two years in Italy, on her way to the Pisa airport to return to America.

Paolo leaned forward. He was clean-shaven except for a manicured goatee framing his voluptuous lips. He smelled of something discreet, yet tangy. His eyes were rich with experience and he had the air of a man who rose from contented beds. He wore a wedding ring. He said, as an artist, Corinne should never leave Italy. As a woman, he added, she should never leave Tuscany. His voice was low, ripe with respect and innuendo, as though he, Paolo, recognized that Corinne and Italy were worthy of each other. Then he said he must get off at the very next stop. The one before Empoli.

He alighted from the carriage, carrying his briefcase and an overnight bag. She watched from the window as the autumn wind snatched at his coat. Pausing at the station door, Paolo Branchi turned and waved and for a single moment—until the train pulled sluggishly forward—she thought he might just . . .

Sad. He might have been an amusing companion, someone to have a coffee with at the bar of the Empoli station while she waited to change trains. She might have had more than a coffee with him. After all, she had no plans. No tickets as yet. No one waiting for her at some foreordained destination. She might have had many things with Paolo Branchi. Her sorrow at leaving him deepened into a sorrow at losing him, more intense than if he had been her lover. As lovers they would have had a past to cherish mutually, something like the toy Max secreted under his many coats. But as it was, they exchanged a wave and bid each other good-bye, *ciao* to all the might-have-beens, *ciao* to possibilities spun of tissue so fine, so fragile she could almost hear them shred and tear, catch on the metacarpal branches as the train hurtled over the November landscape. Earth and sky neutralized each other, as though hammered out by some ancient, expert hand into that singular color you could only think of as Tuscan blond, the very gold of those fat, pale persimmons still clinging to the blue-black trees.

Corinne Mackenzie made it a point of honor never to complain about the trains running late in Italy. To do so would have displayed a foreigner's too-tidy sense of values and played (historically speaking) into Mussolini's arms. Of course it was no accident that the great Italian railway stations had all been built in the fascist era and why—given that era's values—they all had the ring, the flavor of vast movie stages, sets decorated in the manner of the Kordas, where anything from battles to bedrooms might have been successfully choreographed, as long as they were false, immense, and costly.

The railway station at Empoli, on the other hand, had been entirely overlooked. It still retained its sleepy, intimate, well-tended air. The date on the ornate iron grillwork was 1890. The platforms were flagstone rather than concrete. Under rounded, eye-pleasing arches of peach-colored stucco, planters full of geraniums pinched in the chill. Doors leading to the bar, the waiting room, porter's office, and the station itself were neat square panes of glass framed in green paint. Corinne pushed the station door open and, once inside, her heels tapped on a floor of polished marble, an odd, velvety maroon color. So well-maintained was the Empoli station, you might have thought it a myth—and given that it predated Mussolini, perhaps it was.

Yes, the man at the ticket window said, because her train had been late into Empoli, she would now have a lengthy wait for the train to Pisa. Two hours. At least. His shrug indicated three hours at least.

Corinne gave her two bags to a tiny muscle-bound porter (with a tip; she knew what language was really spoken here) and said she would collect them in time for the Pisa train. The prospect of the wait was not so bad. She had no plans. No airline ticket as yet. No destination firmly in mind and no one waiting there. She might get to the Pisa airport, decide not to go back to America. She might instead say simply, give me a ticket on the first plane to Paris. To Milano. To Frankfurt. Hang the expense. Isn't that what credit cards are for?

"Signora?" The station *capo* addressed her as though she had been speaking to him. Perhaps she had. He was a burly man of forty or so with that Italian air of lewd gallantry. Italian men left you no choice: if you responded to the gallantry, you also automatically responded to the lewdness as well. With characteristic panache, Corinne informed him it was *non importante,* absolutely *niente,* and left him nurturing an air of bewilderment unbecoming in a man.

Suddenly famished, she went into the station bar where she ordered a *pannino* and *dolce*. Make that two. Of each. *Caffè machiatto.* In the warm, bright bar she loosened her scarf and coat and bolted her coffee in the Italian fashion.

Ordered another. She noticed for the first time the bar had two sets of doors. One led to the platform. One led to the street, to the town of Empoli. In all the years she had been coming to Italy, in the countless times she had changed trains at Empoli and had a drink in this bar, Corinne had never stepped outside those other doors. She wondered fleetingly what the town of Empoli was like. She moved to the doors, peering through the green-framed panes of glass. She did not open them, knowing somehow to do so would have been an irrevocable step.

Corinne returned to the bar, ordered another coffee, and watched the reflections of four other people in the mirror behind her. The mirror gleamed, colorful bottles of every stripe and hue were set on high shelves of thick greenish glass. The young bartender, ruddy, expressive, convivial, washed glassware and carried on a spirited conversation with an older woman and two men. They all seemed to know one another. Under discussion was the woman's worthless son who was breaking his mother's heart. Talk about broken hearts! What about your own daughter? Your only child who spurns all art, all understanding, emotion, and possibility, and marries a man who plays bridge and sells insurance! Grubbing money off people's fears? A vile, low profession, insurance—of course, everyone has to have insurance. I have it through the University, or at least I do for the moment. Did. But can you imagine living, *sleeping* with a man who gets people to spend money not on what they can taste or hold or relish or remember, but against the possibility, the absolute certainty of death. Death insurance. To barter in *morte, si?* He's no better than Allegra deserves, really. Not a single ambition, that girl, not beyond tennis and shopping, golf and her bridge game. Insufferable. Just like her father.

Allegra's father had no other name. That was all he was, Allegra's father. In some ways, all he had ever been. How could Corinne have married such a man? Trying to explain was like confessing to a youthful, inexplicable passion for rutabagas. He best resembled a rutabaga. In retrospect anyway. She could only ascribe her first marriage to a blinding assault of hormones. She recognized the fatal mistake quickly, but Allegra was on the way. Well, all right, though motherhood did not really engage her passions. Instead Corinne poured her considerable energies into graduate school, fell in love (though not into bed) with Max. Allegra's father knew this, but their union still endured, a puddle of marital inertia. Not coincidentally Max gave her the ticket out of the marriage. He got her an interview (and the job) at the museum where he worked in Philly. Allegra's father did not want to move to Philly. Corinne did. She divorced him and took Allegra to Philly. But even with divorce she could not get rid of the man. He pined mercilessly for Allegra. Called her all the time, finally moved to Philly to be near his daughter. Visitation every other weekend. And then, *Would you mind, Corinne?* Every weekend. *No, of course not. If that's what Allegra wants.* Corinne was not heartbroken. After all she was then free on the weekends, free to work if she chose, to be Max's accomplice, to exult in love affairs, emotionally extravagant love affairs or even swift physical episodes. Gratifying if not especially rewarding. But, you see, you could do that in those days. People did. Fell in and out of love. Fell in and out of bed. Often. It was only a question of stamina and imagination then. Not having to ask grim questions or take blood tests. The very term *safe sex* would have sounded ludicrous. Ludicrous, I tell you! Like something missionaries would do once a month whether they needed it or not. A woman would no more think of carrying a condom in her purse than a man would carry a tampon in his pocket!

Still, every Sunday evening Corinne would experience a slightly bitter metallic taste when Allegra placidly returned, holding her father's hand. Corinne resented their affection and camaraderie all the more as Allegra became a young woman. The female version of her father. So much so that Corinne suspected father and daughter had played a nasty trick on her, used her body to incubate, and that done, dispensed with her. They seemed to watch Corinne from a great distance, neutrally, expressing neither admiration nor condemnation for her, only a perpetually innocent perplexity. Allegra and her father preferred the neat foursquare confines of the tennis court and the bridge table. Then Allegra married and her husband joined them. And no doubt, so would Allegra's son. They had no special affection for Corinne, they only tolerated her on family occasions. And, since that's all it was, toleration, they scarcely noticed one Thanksgiving when she (purposely) had too much to drink and said, loudly and for the benefit of the other guests (all card players, naturally) how much she despised bridge, hated it. In a very large voice she announced that the shuffle of the cards reminded her always of flatulence. They went right on shuffling, shuffling, shuffling

"Signora? Signora? Allegra?"

She explained to the bartender that Allegra was her daughter and she was about to turn to the woman whose son had broken her heart, but the woman was gone.

A man came into the bar. A working man, judging from his cap and paint-flecked clothes. He ordered a drink and from one of the high shelves lining the mirror, the bartender took down a bottle of thick metallic-looking liquor, maroon as the marble floor. The man took the drink down in one gulp. Winced hard. Shivered. Tipped his cap. Smiled and left.

It was not a drink Corinne knew. She had seen the label of course. One does not come to Italy time and time again over thirty years and well, of course she'd seen the label. Her eyes swept over the bottles sparkling invitationally in the warm light and the high mirror. Fifty or sixty of them. Maybe more. She counted carefully; she had perhaps tasted a dozen. Maybe two dozen. The other thirty-odd she had never tasted and there wasn't time now. Not before the train came. There might never be time. The gleaming Unknown inside the bottles seemed to wink and tease her in the light, to glisten with the same imputation of lost possibility, like Paolo Branchi's sad wave.

The young bartender put a glass of mineral water in front of her while he made exaggerated drinking motions. He picked up a paper napkin and thrust it at her. He wiped his own eyes with it in broad gestures and then handed her a clean one. He put it in her hand. She watched him—as though at a great distance—pinking with exertion and the steam from the dishwater, his arms up high indicating *drink drink* and she felt suddenly flushed and weakened, terrified at what she'd done. At what she'd done and left undone. The flat unlocked. The hot-water heater still on. The laundry still flapping on the balcony lines. She had forgotten the laundry. Yes and forgotten something else urgent and important, something she was powerless to change or effect. She patted her face with the paper napkin and drank the water, thanked the bartender, but declined his insistent advice that she should sit. She would feel better outside.

Once on the platform she buttoned up her coat and paced in long, quick strides, troubled by thoughts of the unlocked flat and laundry on the balcony line. Unthinkable that Giorgio Carruthers should find her stockings and slips and panties flapping on the balcony in a sort of brazen, come-hither way. But she certainly couldn't go back and collect them, turn off the hot-water heater. She'd left that on, too. Too? Was there something else? The wind rattled and shook her, like an angry parent to get her to confess, like Max's father had shaken him when he found out Max hid the toy in spite of his father's prohibition against toys, in spite of his father's assertion that Max was lucky to have escaped with his skin.

Shivering, she pulled leather gloves from her pocket and put them on her fine, long fingers. Artist's fingers. That's what Max always said. He would turn her hand over in his and say she had artist's fingers and hands. An artist's mind and eye and imagination. And then he would laugh in that peculiar, jagged way, and add that she had a model's body as well. She rather took offense at this. If he had slept with her, she could have absorbed it as a compliment, but since he never had, the observation smacked of the clinical and faintly obscene. Though one couldn't really, actually take offense at Max. He was so funny and urbane. The most civilized man in America. Difficult. Of course. But civilized. And like any civilized person, very few things were good enough for Max. Over the years even this paltry number had dwindled until talking with Max was like clinging to a slippery rock in a sea of mediocrity, holding on so that one should not be swept into that vast ocean of what was tacky and vulgar and beneath contempt, as though these things were constantly nibbling at your ankles and if you once slipped or lost your vigilance, they could suck you in. You could drown in a sea of mediocrity. Max could wear you out.

She had met him in graduate school. She was still married to Allegra's father, but the real love of her life she had just discovered: Renaissance angels, so muscular, handsome, and ineffably gentle. How then to account for her falling in love with Max as well? Max was a snob, even then, but so powerful a personality, so blond and fastidious and funny and arch. Such a delight. He was two years ahead of her in the graduate program and after he left, moved to Philly and his museum job, Corinne's life passed in a gray Max-less fog, framed in the faces of the Renaissance angels and punctuated by his frothy acerbic letters and long-distance telephone calls. So consummate were Max's political skills—even then—that when she graduated, he had ushered her right into the museum's European Art Department. An enviable position. Great. Corinne divorced her husband. Fine. Grand. Wonderful. She was convinced: once relieved of her ineffectual husband, Max would surely return her love.

But he didn't. True, he squired her about everywhere, and on the arm of the most civilized man in America, Corinne found herself dining in celebrated company, artists, scholars, curators, actors, authors, patrons of the arts. Society. The best society. She became, in effect, Max's accomplice and went everywhere with him. She remained his accomplice while she fell in love with other men, gorgeous great love affairs with men who, one by one, dropped from her life with nasty crashes, resounding like shingles falling from a steep roof. She remained Max's accomplice even when she fell in love with Dennis, besotted by Dennis, about to die of cirrhosis of the heart for Dennis. And even when she married Dennis, she could not quite vow off Max. She tried. He always wooed her back. The snob. Flattery. He said (and it was true) Corinne was the only person in the world not frightened of him. Offended, yes. (Wasn't everyone?) But Corinne was always ready with a quick repartee, never frightened of Max's lacerating wit.

Corinne instinctively knew how to fence (verbally), to thrust and parry, kick and duck. She got occasionally hurt, but never really wounded. Not until that night. That night Max himself seemed to slip, to lose his balance, to tumble, snatch and claw at everything and everyone in his path. Even Corinne. Especially Corinne.

It was the usual gathering, Corinne and Dennis amongst others invited to dinner by an art patron, sitting at a burnished table surrounded by educated, civilized people who agreed with Max that America was a grubby place where nothing worked right. Everything in America was commercial, shallow, and vulgar. England—England was even worse. Max confessed to having lived in England and to being an Anglophile. (And their hostess, smiling, said she had always been an Anglophile because England was so—) Not anymore, Max cut in. He vowed he would never go back to England. The strikes. The breakdowns. The general despair of society and had you ever seen anything more jingoistic and preposterous than that Falklands (so-called) War? What a lot of posturing! All that sodding worship of Princess Diana and the orgy when she died? No, England had gone to pot: a narrow, tawdry little country where nothing worked and everything was inefficient. Europeans in general, but the English in particular were living off their past—Max continued, having got up a great sail of hyperbole and invention fueled by the conviction of his own uncontested wit—the English served up their past like a huge dead bird without having taken the trouble to fully pluck or bleed it, or cook it either for that matter, just putting it, neck wrung and dead eyes staring on a silver platter, the pale, feathered carcass still sort of oozing.

This vivid unfortunate metaphor over dinner made everyone blanch. Dennis looked positively ill. The mouth of their hostess twitched as she tried to daunt the conversation over to gardens or something, but it was no good (Corinne could have told them this, all of them) trying to stop Max once he'd got going. It was no good trying to dampen or avert Max. He was so very funny, wasn't he? Even if he was angry, even with that little golden gleam of malice twinkling in Max's brittle wit. Oh, maybe he sometimes went too far. Brutal. That night, of course, he did. Caustic. Increasingly vicious. Corinne, vaguely desperate, exerted herself on behalf of the others, interrupted (she was the only one who could interrupt) his soliloquy on the great, oozing feathered lifeless bird of the past, and she said—*Ah yes, well with all this decay everywhere else, at least we have Italy, yes? Tuscany. At least we have that.* Closing her eyes and under the spell of the wine and the candlelight, she willed herself away from the dreary dining room to the golden poplars, dusky cypresses, the yellow light of the Arno.

Max's jagged laughter sliced, ripped right up the middle of that illusion and that's what he said it was: A stupid illusion, Corinne, because the Italians do not deserve their beautiful country, which was going to hell anyway. The Italians did not offer up their past. No. They sold it. They would sell the Sistine Chapel if the price were right. Slavering after tourist dollars, the Italians all posed and simpered and all that nasty greed made it plain that from the Medici, Michelangelo, and Leonardo right on down to the beggars and urchins, they were all peasants or pickpockets. They would weep at the feet of the Virgin while they picked your pocket in the church. You'd have to be stupid not to know that. To believe anything else.

Corinne's face stung. As though Max had slapped her cheek. Hard.

My roses have the blight this year, their hostess said. At our home in the country the roses have withered . . .

Corinne rubbed her cheek, feeling for welts. As little Max must have, all those years ago. At that moment she knew, swiftly, absolutely, and correctly that Max had lied about his father. His father had not stroked his cheek. His father had slapped him hard across the face, sent him spinning. His father had flung down the toys, smashed them, shouting, *You can take nothing with you! You are lucky to escape with your skin!*

None of them escaped. They're very old rose bushes.

Corinne peered across the candlelight. Amazing. Max had grown old. She could see it in his still-handsome face. Some crucial change. Max had rounded a curve in time, after which the world lost savor. Beyond that pivotal moment, all change was—and henceforth ever would be—for the worse. Nothing would be the same or as good as it once was. Not men or women or food or sex or wine or music, not books or movies or countries. Nothing. Max had been somehow shipwrecked in the present. Sputtering, angry (look at him), beached in the present with his civilized wit while the future sailed off without him and the past vanished golden in the haze. *Max is going to die.*

She and Dennis left almost immediately. Once home, Corinne went into the bathroom, turned on the harsh light, and regarded herself in the mirror. Had she, too, grown old without knowing it? In spite of good sense, good health, good habits, and the dye bottle?

Corinne made love with Dennis that night: rich, slow, voluptuous love, the way Corinne liked to make love, like whales make love, she always thought, like whales' warm-blooded bodies heat up the ocean around them, like whales savor the succulent present.

But then. What happened then: everything? Everything so fast. After that night, within, say six weeks of that night, Dennis had left her. Gone before she could utter a wordless *what?* Dennis gone. Out of her life after a brief chat in front of the fireplace (*what? what?*) followed by the click of the closing door. Dennis's key on the kitchen table and soon—immediately?—a letter from his lawyer. Odd clunky Latinate phrases which, when you finally translated them, meant that Dennis had got rid of the old wife so as to marry a new one. Younger.

And where was Max when she needed him? When she needed his cutting ability to say nasty things about Dennis and how Dennis had never deserved her in the first place? Oh, Max was gone. Not simply gone from Philly, but from America, gone without a word of explanation or farewell, gone to Switzerland or Sweden or Scandinavia. Some cold place. *Why* couldn't she remember where Max had gone? Impossible! Anyway, she had it in her address book. If she'd brought it. If she'd remembered it. Had she forgotten? Left it in the center desk drawer in the flat? Even so, it was engraved on her heart and mind where Max went. Wasn't it? He had been her friend for thirty years. Friends, colleagues, accomplices, though never—no, they had never been lovers.

Anyway, she'd long since quit lusting after Max. A little abashed however to say how long she had lusted after him. Hungered for him without ever guessing, well, guessing, maybe. Yes, guessing. But not *knowing*. And not wanting to know. And anyway, in those days, things were different. You couldn't possibly pop yourself out of the closet and expect all your straight friends to applaud. You couldn't pop into court and whine because you'd lost your job, say you'd been discriminated against. In those days it was different. Well, some things were different. Some things stayed the same, like the way Max could persistently fire her imagination. The sly smile. The half-hooded eyes. The air of intimacy Max spun, as though he pulled thread from his body, like a spider, bound her imagination somehow with that silken, gorgeous cord. *Oh, Max, Max*. He drove all night to be present at her dissertation defense. *Renaissance Angels*. And though the seminar room was filled with friends and fellow students (to say nothing of Allegra's father and the hulking, heavily judgmental faculty), once Max was in the audience, Corinne was speaking to and for and with Max alone. As though they were in bed together and she wanted his approval. And she got it. There are some things only a man can do for you.

He got her the job, didn't he? Those early months at the museum were filled with richness, luster, wonder. Oh, there was the job itself, the city, its pace and excitement, and of course, the pride in going about with Max, in being Max's accomplice. Then too, she'd got rid of Allegra's father and fallen in love with Barry, wonderful, slow, voluptuous love with Barry. Of course it didn't last. The shingles all fell, crashed down from the roof, and she was crazy with grief because there are some things only a man can do for you. To you.

Never mind Barry, Max counseled. Barry never deserved you anyway. You were always too good for him. Come to Sunday brunch, Corinne.

That Sunday brunch, with the snow flurrying thickly at the apartment window, where all this emerged, for sure, for knowing and never again simply guessing, even if you did not want to know, never guessing how (oh, remember, in those days if you were found out, you could be ruined; it was the kind of thing people tolerated only if they did not know and only guessed). If it emerged at all, it should be like some tropical, exotic flower. Like an antherium, she thought. Not at the time. At the time she had thought no such poetic thing, but later she thought of that brunch—snow and all—like an emerging antherium, with its hard little yellow phallic tongue wagging out, *I fooled you I fooled you I fooled you* (not that it made a damn bit of difference, so passionate and powerful was her attachment to Max, so powerful was his personality that it made no difference ever to Corinne who went on loving him even after) that snowy Sunday. She had not brought antheriums. Common freesias. Hothouse. Yellow.

And rather confused, she stupidly offered the yellow freesias to Max's friend—oh bloody say it, his lover. She held out her hand with the yellow freesias to Max's just-risen—like slow, warm-blooded, just-risen whales, male not beautiful or even especially young—lover, already balding with a pronounced overbite and a mole on his head that his receding hair uncovered. He had answered the door. He introduced himself: I'm Woody.

From the kitchen Max called out gaily and asked if she would like a hit of brandy in her coffee. Against the cold. Of course she would like it. Against the cold. Get Corinne some coffee and brandy, called Max.

Sugar? asked Woody, who could not have looked less Woody-like if he had been a woodpecker. So to speak.

Yes. Sugar. Please. Sweeten it.

I take my coffee black, said Woody.

After this initial blundering, bovine beginning, however, she rather thought she had carried it off. With panache, actually. (Panache and daring were Max's two favorite words. Anything without panache and daring could only be dismal.) In fact, she was relieved. Even rather buoyed. Because it meant that Max had not spurned her, Corinne Mackenzie, in particular. But women in general. She could not take offense or have her feelings hurt that he had never gone to bed with her. It was not personal. Quite the contrary. Her friendship with Max testified to . . . to . . . to whatever it was friendship testified to when you did not go to bed together. Women were not Max's cup of tea. It made sense to her, naturally he had dated as long as it was politically incumbent on him to do so for advancement in the museum hierarchy, but he had not bedded those other women either because they were not his cup of tea. He might even have phrased it exactly thus. Did. His wrist flicked and the starched cuff peeked out and the cufflink gleamed. He was, even then, the most civilized man in America.

But now Max didn't live in America anymore because it was crass and commercial and shallow and nothing worked and England was impossible because nothing worked there either and they picked your pocket in Italy. All Europe was living on its glorious past, nothing else. Europe laid out its past like a giant, still-feathered carcass for the Americans (and now, of course, the Japanese) to prey on, peck its dead unseeing eyes and

She sat down on one of the wooden platform benches, breathless after her incessant pacing, and looked up the empty tracks and wires leading away from Empoli toward Pisa. And the airport. Escape. She rubbed her throbbing temples, took off her hat, and shook her dark hair, undid the top button on her coat. There. That was better. The easier to breathe. Inhale. Exhale. Inhale. Yes. And of course it was silly to—exhale—get worked up because she would simply look Max up in the address book. She would not have left something that important behind in the center desk drawer. She would call Max before she flew out of Pisa because he was someplace in Europe. Some cold place. He had moved someplace where things presumably did work. Switzerland or Scandinavia. Some cold place that had an air of efficiency. Rather like a hospital.

III

Over the crackling loudspeaker, set in high wooden cabinets, came a voice announcing the train to Firenze. Corinne began to gather herself until she realized that was the Pisa-Firenze train. Going the wrong way. As in a slow and noisy, random dance, passengers for this Firenze train gathered on the platform, their advent and recession predictable as the tide and the timetable posted low, eye-level on the wall outside. And one inside, high above the ticket booth. High and low. Ebb and flow. The Firenze train blasted in and passengers got swept on and dusted off (because the Empoli station was nothing if not well maintained). Those disembarking at Empoli ebbed from the platform as the train pulled out, absorbed into their families or into the station or the bar, or simply, with the porters, leaning against the peach-colored arches, smoking, waiting, like actors whose cues are a long way off.

She was chilled clear through and realized she must have been outside for a very long time. The thought of coffee appealed to her, but not the cozy crowded bar with its bottles filled with experience she would never taste and the door that led irrevocably to the town of Empoli. She stood and walked to the waiting room. It had only one door. To and from the platform. No other possibilities. No lost possibilities.

The waiting room was broad, high and drafty, lined on three sides with polished benches and a single inadequate heater. The marble floor was so clean you could see your reflection and though the walls were bare, they were not painted institutional green, but a sort of pale vanilla color with fluted plaster piping at the ceiling. Whimsical. A single slab of sunlight cut into panes fell from the door and Corinne unbuttoned her coat and sat within its picketed confines, amongst, oh, possibly a dozen other people scattered along the walls. No good-looking men though. With or without newspapers.

A cleaning woman hunkered in a corner with her broom and barrel, daring anyone (with her eyes) to dirty her floor. One young man (a German judging from the stickers on his backpack) did, tossed a used ticket down. She swooped on him, crying out for all the world to hear that this young man came from a family of pigs. Look at him! No respect! Young people today were thoughtless and thankless. The cleaning woman turned to three old huddled grandmas, each the perfect *Strega Nona,* each with the single-seam mouth of the toothless. They solemnly corroborated the cleaning woman's assessment of young people in general, this German boy in particular. He stalked out of the waiting room. Amongst themselves the three old dragons and the cleaning lady agreed it was good riddance to bad rubbish. They exchanged heated views on the general uselessness of the young.

Oh yes. Corinne could have told them a thing or two. How truly vile young people can be. All they want is sex and money, but no responsibilities. And thankless? Thankless! Here we are, offering them a program that allows them to study art in Italy. A sacred opportunity! Truly! Sacred! What do they do? They defecate on it. No, it's true. I swear. One of them actually crouched, squatted in the hall, oozed *merda*. And his peers—no better. The girls laughed. Crass. In my day, things were different. I do not say we were angels, but we revered art and life and love. These kids—but it is a mistake to call them kids. They are not cute and little. They are adults. They are a menace. Listen, in America you get three of them on the bus and people get off. It's true. On the subway, you clutch your bag and keep your eyes on the ads. You step aside at their offensive arrogance. Offensive. I tell you, offensive. But they thought it was funny, that—that pile. *Merda*. Could I continue to deal with such dogs? Dogs might defecate on the floor, yes, but dogs would not laugh. They are worse than dogs. I am done with them. Finished. But when I return to the University, they will fire me. It will be very hard to get another job at my age. And everyone, it's a small field really, everyone will know I broke my contract and just walked out on the Institute. *Ciao*. Left my responsibilities. Well, I'll point to the contract and I'll demand of them: Where does it say a thing about *merda*? Where?

Where?

There, in the center desk drawer. I left it there along with the address book. I know that now. I accept it. I must. Giorgio Carruthers will paw through that, too. (Giorgio is as American as they come, even if his mother couldn't speak a word of English. Giorgio is insufferable.) But he will paw through the desk and my underwear. I can't do anything about it. I took what I could. I was lucky to escape with my skin.

She rubbed her cheek thoughtfully. Sadly. As Max had said his father touched his. A lie. His father had slapped him. But after all these years, what could it possibly matter? After more than half a century, *aqua passata, non macina più, si?* She smiled at the three old black-clad women in the waiting room, all of them staring at her with piercing eyes, the absolutely unabashed gaze of dragons. They had no one to fear. No one to answer to. These women reigned supreme over as much of the world as they cared about. Corinne bit her lip. "I've been thinking aloud, I guess. Well, you can imagine the shock of it. To come in and find—terrible. Terrible what these young people will do."

The cleaning woman had returned to her barrel and the old dragons hunkered down amongst themselves. Words blew up from their enclave like smoke, like three crones huddled, hunched over a boiling pasta pot. *Strega Nona*. Grandma Witch. The three fell, as witches will, to fearlessly muttering of death and husbands, of children, weddings, errant girls and wayward boys, difficult births and swift, fatal illnesses. Corinne understood all. All. *Tutti*. She wondered if she put on a black dress and thirty pounds, stooped over, abjured the dye bottle, might she too qualify as an old dragon? Like these women, she had had husbands and weddings and difficult births—well, one, a daughter, that wayward girl, Allegra. She had known men, lain down with them at night, risen with them in the morning, lied to them, lied for them, cried for them, bent double and beat her head on the floor for them. Oh, not for her first dim and ineffectual husband, Allegra's father, but the others. Lovers. Cherished, vanished lovers. She had lied and cried and wept for them and for the other husband, Dennis. Dennis.

When Dennis left her (and she was at an age when such passion is utterly unbecoming in a woman, when a woman is supposed, expected—the hell you say, *required*—to exude grandmotherly serenity unto senility) Corinne Mackenzie had bent double, beat her head on the floor, gasped, wailed. She took so many sleeping pills she saw double when she got up the next morning. She got stoned, not on pills, but stoned, beaten, smacked in the face, back, belly, groin, hit with chunky Latinate phrases from Dennis's lawyer, stoned like the woman taken in adultery would have been. Though it was the man in this case,

Dennis, taken in adultery. Taken. Smitten. Succumbed to adultery and moved right in with her, married her as soon as the divorce was final from Corinne who tried everything she could think of to hang onto him. Money. Moral obligation. Threats. Pity. Tears. The grandeur, sweep, and longevity of her love. Every lofty principle and every low trick in the Book of Love (and no need to wonder who wrote the Book of Love. Not anymore. Lawyers. They wrote it, relished it: the swine). Corinne lay stoned and bleeding, making long expensive transatlantic calls to Max on those crackling phone lines that always make you feel like you have to shout: I'M DYING, MAX.

No, you're not. You've known he was cheating on you for years.

NO! I NEVER KNEW.

You never wanted to know. There's a difference. Everyone thought you were so brave, tolerating his infidelities.

I NEVER TOLERATED HIS INFIDELITIES.

You deluded yourself then. And it's all the same thing, Corinne.

WHAT IS?

The truth of it is, Corinne, that what people call strength is only an endless capacity for self-delusion, for imagining things otherwise.

I'M NOT DELUDED! I'M TIRED OF BEING STRONG. I WANT . . . I WANT . . .

All you need is a new man. Someone new to occupy your imagination. Someone other than Dennis. That's the trouble.

THAT'S NOT THE TROUBLE! I'M TOO OLD FOR A NEW MAN.

Bullshit, my dear.

I'M DYING! I'M DYING OF THE PAIN, MAX

Corinne only knew for certain she was not dead when there came to her office at the museum a wholly unexpected phone call from the University and a man asked her to have coffee with him that afternoon at a discreet restaurant to discuss the Institute for Italian Art they were founding in Tuscany. They needed a director.

You come highly recommended as a Renaissance authority and an administrator, said the wispy, bald man before her. He had an overbite and a mole at what was once his hairline. He passed the sugar. *You take sugar, I believe.*

Woody?

Max says you are the perfect Director for our program. He says you have a first-rate mind, that you are fearless, imaginative, able, and speak fluent Italian. Woody sipped his black coffee. *Max says you have panache.*

He is fond of that word.

But he is sparing in his praise. I thought it best to approach you informally in case you did not wish to leave the museum, after all these years, for what would be a brand new undertaking in every sense of the word.

I would welcome the new undertaking. I do welcome. I

Do, she had said to Italy, the land of Honor Artifice and Presentation Being Everything. The perfect place for Corinne. The perfect job. Perfect. Except for the students. Unused to dealing with students, Corinne did not know (as Giorgio did) how to please them. She had not the happy faculty of appearing egalitarian and accessible. She was the Director, after all. They were the students. Moreover Corinne did not see them as winsome youngsters; she refused to indulge or mollify them or pat their little hands or heads. She was appalled at their bad manners. It seemed clear to her that one would practice good manners in someone else's country as one would in someone else's house. They had no manners at all. Giorgio made excuses for them, and Corinne thought him a great toady to offer himself as chum, troubleshooter, and all-around Good Guy. She thought Giorgio downright spread-eagled himself to the students. And of course, that's why the turds were not at his door. The pile of indignity and obscenity was at her door. Oh, was there ever

"Lady? Hey, Lady—are you all right? Can I get you something, Lady? Can I help you put your coat back on?"

He was a young man, a student, clearly. You could tell. He was the age of Adam Green and for a moment she feared it was Adam Green and he was about to squat

"Lady, can I bring you something from the bar? A glass of water, maybe?" He reached out and brought Corinne's coat up over her shoulders. "You're shaking all over, Lady, and I could hear your teeth chattering all the way down there." He nodded down the bench where his girlfriend, who had stringy hair and wide eyes, watched. He patted Corinne's shoulder. "I knew you were an American."

"Of course I'm an American," Corinne snapped. "I'm more American than you will ever be. I have had to defend, to define myself every day for two years as an American. For two years, every day, someone says how well I speak the language and I must be an American and I have to say: Yes. YES! I am an American!" She glanced from the young man to the three Italian crones, looked from one to the other as though she'd been asked to choose with whom she best belonged. Define. Defend. She was suddenly very tired.

She patted the boy's hand, smiled. "Thank you. Thank you. It's nothing. It's been cleaned up. Thank you," very much, gentlemen, but I shall not leave this post under an undeserved cloud. My reputation, my whole professional life is at stake. You believe that since the *merda* was cleaned up, I should have stayed. How very American of you. How very American to think that the past, once addressed, however shallowly, in whatever sort of namby-pamby manner you care to call good faith, that such paltry efforts will vanquish the past. You believe that in tidying and dusting the past, you can defeat it. How American. To say, *It's all in the past,* is exactly the same as if you'd said, *It never existed at all*. This is as American as the Pledge of Allegiance. It might as well BE the Pledge of Allegiance, *It's all in the past, dear, and so it cannot matter. Let us merely clean it up, turn our backs, and march forward. The present creates itself afresh each day. The pristine present, sprung forth on the half shell.*

I stand before you gentlemen, to testify to the contrary. Giorgio may have cleaned up the *merda*—oh, let us say it! Let us say it was shit, *shit* gentlemen, there before my office door. Giorgio may have cleaned up that shit with his own fair hands, but the shit existed. The past *can* contaminate the present! And the future? Oh, the future is the vassal of the past. To vanquish shit, the past, you must do more than clean it up. You must do what Max did: You must twist and writhe it, clip and force, *insist* that the past fit the present you envision. It is not a matter of cleaning it up, denial ever after, but reconstruction. Don't you see? It is a matter of imaginative conviction.

I do not wholly indict you, gentlemen. I am an American, too. I am more American than you could ever dream of being, there in your safe little university berths. I have been defining and defending myself and my country—daily—for two years to people like those three dragons over there. Look at them, gentlemen. In Italia, *Strega Nona* is a powerful person. In Italia, these old women (on the sunless side of fifty) are fearless. Ride any bus and see what I mean. The young people snap to around these old women. But for me? Adam Green leaves his shit at my door and his peers concur in this action, even if they did not themselves squat. Adam Green will go unpunished. But I shall be punished because he shat in front of my door. I did not imagine this, gentlemen, I heard them, laughing and chatting, their endless coarse and boring babble all the way down the corridor and into the street, riding the bus, and even at home as I so hurriedly packed, because nothing could make their voices stop except the pills I knew would drop me down down down into that sweet and dreamless well of forgetting the center desk drawer and the laundry on the balcony and the hot-water heater. Because *to clean it up*—and I do not mean to mock poor Giorgio's voice unduly—but to clean up the shit is *not to say it never existed* stinking before my door, not to say I can keep it from contaminating everything I have worked for here. I mean

There.

Because by the time she got round to this speech, she would be back in America.

Probably. The great loudspeakers echoed in the waiting room, announcing the train to Pisa would be delayed. Several travelers in the waiting room jumped up (as travelers will) as though their jumping up and making a fuss will somehow hasten or make some other damned bit of difference. The American boy who had been so kind to her looked patiently at his girlfriend. The girlfriend took the maternal line, patted his hand. The three old women went on obliviously with their smoky babble. Dragon talk. Perhaps they were not going to Pisa. More likely, they knew the train would get here when it got here, and there was not a damned thing they could do about it. It simply didn't matter

It certainly didn't matter to Corinne Mackenzie. She was going to Pisa, yes. The airport, *si*. But she had no airline ticket as yet. No plans. No foreordained destination with someone waiting. Only one thing matters to the refugee: escape. Escape from the students and the center desk drawer and Giorgio. The dreaded thought occurred to her: perhaps Giorgio had phoned ahead, told them to hold the Pisa train while he jumped in his car and drove like a wild man to Empoli. He would know she would change in Empoli. Everyone changed in Empoli.

She could see him now, parked illegally before the station, flying in, his coat like wings, flying out to the platform, looking wildly, finding her in the waiting room, appealing before her on bended knee (like some skinny, unlovely Annunciation angel) to return to the Institute.

Nothing can induce me (oh, that was grand, fine, simple, distinguished), nothing can induce me to return, Giorgio, even if you tell me you will find my underwear waving bye-bye on the balcony, even if you go through my flat as though I had died, moving toward the center desk drawer where there, yes, beside the address book, I put it there yesterday (it could not have been yesterday, could it?), yesterday I put it in the desk drawer: that last anguished letter from Max who guessed, who knew from the night of the dead-bird dinner party. Knew, not guessing. Knew. Even if you find the hot-water heater on and the flat unlocked, Giorgio, I shall have escaped with my skin. I have fled. I have given four hundred and forty thousand lire to the greengrocer across the street who will never in a million years mail my books, but keep the money, knowing he will never see me again, never mind that Signor Vitti has been always courteous, friendly, gentle, and protective, a pleasure to deal with for two full years. Never mind. That's how those Italians are, Giorgio, pickpockets! Peasants! They kneel at the feet of the Virgin while they rob you in the church.

IV

"Signora, prego!" He took her arm, this man, gently, but firmly. He led her out.

"I must find the porter. It's time for the Pisa train. I must have my—"

"Signora, guarda—" He pointed to the sign.

Two choices presented themselves to Corinne. She could blush, falter, *die on the spot,* that she had wandered into the men's room while looking for the porter. Or—rather like an old dragon—she could assume she had a perfect right to go wherever she wished. She chose to be gracious about it, to allow the man (whose hand was light on her arm, a whiff of wine on his breath) to escort her to a bench outside. As they walked, she chatted with him in her fluent, musical Italian and then he was all deference and understanding. Oh, after that, he was all paste and wax. The wax would give the paste substance. The paste would hold the wax when it wanted to melt. Men were like that. All men.

He asked her to wait on the bench and returned with the tiny muscle-bound porter who explained that it was too early to bring out her bags for the Pisa train. Had she not heard? It had been delayed. Yes, delayed again, if you like, Signora, but delayed. She should go into the warm waiting room until it was announced. She should not sit here on this outside bench where it was so cold.

It wasn't, though. The wind had made a truce with the sun. Or perhaps the sun had seduced the wind, lulled it into submission. In November it would be a short seduction, but what of it? It was time for lunch. *Il pranzo.* How nice, the prospects of *il pranzo,* that lovely big meal followed by *il riposo.* Soon, one by one the shops would close and everyone would go home for a big meal and a nap. The affirmation of the personal life. Commercial life would not resume until four when the awnings rolled back up. Till then there would be no life on the streets, only noise from the restaurants and cooking smells, perhaps sleepy children's voice, perhaps tender laughter from behind the shutters of second-story windows. *Il pranzo* and *il riposo.* Was that why so many of them—like Paolo Branchi, like the young bartender, like this man, whoever he was, though he had gone now, even like the old dragons—all had the look of people who had risen from contented beds? Because they rose from those beds twice a day instead of once. They slept after lunch and returned to work late in the afternoon and then meandered home at eight.

Hopelessly inefficient. That's what Max said of the Italian way of life. He had come to visit her just a few months ago. August. Late in August and for one afternoon only and would not hear of staying a moment longer. One afternoon he stayed before turning around and going right back to wherever it was he had gone to. They had a slow, pleasurable lunch on her shaded balcony, clothesline down altogether, thank you, everything spruced up, looking its best for Max. Presentation Being Everything. The potted geraniums waved languidly, responsive to whatever miscreant breeze might care to waft up from the street below. The narrow street was lined with skinny crepe myrtles, their pastel papery blossoms the colors of sashes on young girls' dresses a hundred years ago, said Max. Or maybe a hundred thousand years ago.

On the white tablecloth tiny tears of spilled Chianti stained. They each held an amber glass of *vinsanto* and the sticky dessert plates lay in a kind of afterglowing afternoon abandon between them. The balcony had a lattice on each side and shadows played through their interstices, played over Corinne's fuchsia cotton dress, caught at the smoke that rose from Max's cigarette, which he held in the

European fashion, though she knew very well he affected this. Max was more American than he cared to admit. Although the effort had cost him a good deal of imaginative energy, he had effectively vanquished his refugee past, the life of squalor and necessity, living over a stinking furrier's shop in Philly, his father rising daily, pulling on his pants and a moth-bitten sweater and going downstairs to work in the furrier's shop because without the English language, all his gorgeous German learning was worthless. His father was stubborn and did not wish to learn English. He did not learn it at all until after Max's mother—lacking paint, cello, and family—had died. She had worked for the furrier, too. She kept the accounts. Max, politic as he was polite, shrewd as he was charming, put his parents and the furrier behind him. Swiftly and without regret. So tidied, dusted, and cleaned up was his refugee past that it might never have existed. His father's angry smack, the slap across Max's boyish cheek transmuted, transubstantiated into a caress. So much better. Yes, that's better. So befitting the most civilized man in America. Probably the most civilized man in Italy now, Max. Here, on her balcony. They watched the greengrocer across the street reopen his shop.

Hopelessly inefficient, said Max, as the greengrocer's awnings rolled up in a thunderous rattle. Old Signor Vitti began hauling his boxes of produce out again in the afternoon as he had hauled them before seven this morning, stacking them neatly, artfully in front of his shop. *Hopelessly inefficient*. He should stack them once a day, in the morning, Max said, work till five and go home for a nice long uninterrupted evening. Not go to all this effort twice a day. Max pointed to Signor Vitti who (unaware of their eyes) stood wiping his brow.

That's very American of you, Max, Corinne chided him.

But you are in Italy and here you have to relinquish efficiency. You must shrug at the future, savor the past and the present. As it were.

Oh, my dear Corinne. Only you could take that ridiculous phrase—as it were—and invest it with such, what? Seductiveness. Truly. You make it sound like an invitation.

Don't flatter yourself, she replied breezily. (That was the sort of tone you took with Max after thirty years, after you guessed but did not know. Guessed all the things you did not want to know.)

Italy suits you, Corinne.

Italy saved my life. You did, actually. After Dennis. Getting me this directorship.

Oh, it was nothing. A word to the wise. I was not lying. You are superb. Anyway, you wouldn't have died. You're just being dramatic.

It felt like death to me.

Max smoked thoughtfully: Love is like that. Overrated. Like travel or Godiva chocolates.

They watched as Signor Vitti, perspiring in the August heat, heaved his bins of Tuscan tomatoes out to the sidewalk. His son came by with his little daughter. They gave the child a peach and the son told the father to go into the cool of the shop. The son, lithe, strong, well proportioned, effortlessly brought out the bins and boxes, muscles straining against his damp shirt.

You should have been a man, Corinne. You have lived the way a man lives.

Max spoke without a false note and this ring of utter sincerity was so foreign to his voice that Corinne was stunned.

Men do as they please, he went on. Men always find a reason, if one is needed, before or after, but men live as they please. Women don't. Women always live the way someone else wants them to. They conduct their lives along a sort of railway timetable which dictates that things must be done at a certain time and in a certain order. But men say, you can't confine or constrain me by what you think I ought to be. You've lived like that, Corinne.

It has cost me, she said evenly and after a deep breath.

Of course it has! It will cost you more as you get older. That's the universal rule: things get easier for men as they get older. Things get harder for women.

Dennis, I suppose, is a case in point.

Don't look at me like that, Corinne. I didn't make the rule. I'm only reciting it.

Smoke curled from his nose and a smile curled on his lips. The sun moved through the lattice and light struck his cheek.

I knew you should have been a man when I first met you, he continued. Oh, it's not a sexual judgment, for God's sake, it's intellectual. Really.

And how did you know?

Max chuckled: All those Renaissance angels. Most women who go in for art, they flail and coo over the Impressionists, which—he snorted contemptuously—is art for Kleenex boxes. The gorge rises. Only a woman with real balls takes on the Renaissance.

I don't recall having taken it on.

That's why you should have been a man! You were, you always have been unaware of your own courage. You're quite beautiful to watch. Not at all posturing the way women usually do when they undertake something brave. His voice minced high and false, Oh, look at me! I'm being so brave! You, Corinne—he put out his cigarette by breaking the ash off. A clean break—you simply did it. You didn't even know you were brave.

It was a dissertation, that's all. I think.

He shook his head: You see, when most people talk about the Renaissance, they offer up all that textbook tripe, that humbug about humanity and the human body and so on. Bullshit. All of it. The Renaissance was not about Man or Mankind. It was by, for, and about men. Men's bodies and men's thoughts and men's laws and battles and politics and the religion men fashioned. Men, not mankind. And certainly not women! All those Botticelli beauties aside.

That's quite a large aside.

You know exactly what I'm talking about. He lit up again, Don't you?

Why didn't we have this conversation in graduate school, Max?

There was no need to then.

She sipped her vinsanto: Do we need to now?

Max fanned the smoke and laughed his jagged laugh: Think of all those Renaissance Annunciations, Corinne. Does the eye rest on the vapid Virgin about to get the news? No. Of course not. It's the angel that draws, keeps, delights the eye. The angels' sinews, those strong-fingered, strong-winged angels with the bodies of men, their rippling courses, their strong flanks, their draped planes. Angels, perhaps, but still, the unmistakable bodies of men.

Signor Vitti's son, finished with the cartons of produce, swung his little daughter (now finished with her peach) up easily on his shoulder, and with a cheerful farewell to his father, set off down the street.

Most women haven't the stomach for the Renaissance for that very reason, Corinne. That's how I knew you were remarkable from the beginning. Of course, then, all those years ago, I did not know, I could not guess you would be ongoingly interesting. You have been, you know. I have watched your life with ongoing interest, even fascination.

You have done more than watch, she said drily, adding: But less than you might have.

The sun, inching forward, beyond the lattice, fell harshly on Max's face: bony, the skin thin and fragile, mottled. His hair was entirely gray and not at all blond. Dark splotches dotted his hands.

Perhaps we've been fortunate that you weren't a man, Corinne. Our friendship has been fortunate in that.

Perhaps *you* have been fortunate, she said with more bitterness than she intended.

He seemed not to notice, chose not to. He continued: If familiarity breeds contempt, you can imagine what intimacy breeds. You've had lovers. You've had husbands—he did not take his steadfast blue eyes from her—you've lived the way a man lives and that's why you've suffered so much. That's what your lovers, your husbands could not endure. Your courage and imagination, your insistence on living like a man. They hated you for it. You were too much, too intense for them. But I loved all that. I admired your courage, your imagination, your passion. Most men can't abide that in women. Anything else they will tolerate. Literally, Corinne, *anything*. But not that. That's why they left you, my dear. From that first, dreary, what was his name?

Barry.

From him till Dennis. Everyone in between and everyone since.

There hasn't been anyone since.

Pity.

On the street below the other merchants ran their awnings up on rackety metal runners and in the afternoon allegro, Corinne said, If you so admired me, why did you never love me? I loved you. You never loved me.

Of course I loved you. Didn't you know that?

He looked at his watch. His cufflinks gleamed in the light. Even in the heat of a Tuscan August, he wore cufflinks: But I must leave now. I have a train to catch if I'm to get the plane at Pisa.

You're sure you won't—

I'm sure.

She rose. Odd, she should just now notice they were virtually the same height. He always seemed taller. He'd grown so thin. She outweighed him. She spoke slowly and sadly: That train will take you directly to the Pisa airport. You change at Empoli.

I'm glad to know it.

I didn't know that, Max.

But you just told me, I change at Empoli and that train will—

I didn't know you loved me.

Of course you did. You've always known it. You just didn't know I'd say it. Ordinarily, I might not have.

Let me come with you.

Absolutely not! No, don't even get up. Stay here. I can find the door, Corinne. You stay here so when I get down to the street, I can look up and see you here on the balcony with a glass of vinsanto. Pour another glass of vinsanto. Please. Do as I ask. Let me see you here at the last. Let me take this picture of you with me to the

> *. . . grave, that is my next, my foreordained destination. But please, do not for one moment mistake this for some sort of tacky, vulgar suicide note written in a drunken stupor. I am as sober as I can be, what with the pain, the pills, all that medical mess. That's why I came here in the first place. I heard they had a cure. Perhaps I did not hear quite cure. I might have heard treatment, maybe not that even. Maybe I heard drugs they do not*

allow in America. So I came to this cold, efficient place and I shall do the efficient thing.

Ultimately one wishes for efficiency. Dying is very difficult, ugly, graceless, ungainly. Whereas death—what could be simpler? There are some moments in life when all that is left to you is gesture.

I am about to become, once again, a refugee. This time I will not escape with my skin. I shall take it off—the flesh—like the tattered, dirty, crumbling old shirt that it is.

Do not fear for me, my dear. It will all be swift and easy. Do not cry, my dear, my love.

V

The three old dragons roused themselves from the clean, warm public splendor of the waiting room as the train to Pisa was announced. Every porter not actively engaged in cadging tips hopped to, lifted the old women's bags for them as they hobbled toward the platform. Corinne rose from her bench, hoisting her own two suitcases, and joined the other passengers. People seemed suddenly to emerge from all over the station, clustering forward expectantly, listening for the approach of the train. You could tell—just to look—who was getting off at Pisa Centrale and who was going on to the Aeroporto. Look at those people: a family of five surrounded by a perfect forest of baggage. Americans, of course. No European would pack up that many children and think it fun to travel. Europeans would only do that if they had to, if they were refugees, lucky to escape with their skins.

Corinne peered forward, looking for the Pisa train, happy, confident that Giorgo would never catch her now. Perhaps he had not even pursued her to Empoli. Perhaps he was, even now, at her flat, pushing open the unlocked door, walking through the deserted rooms, the bedroom, the study, bathroom, sitting room where he had found the laundry flapping on the balcony line, on into the kitchen, turning the hot-water heater off. Walking in and through her flat, her life, the things she'd left undone, the letter in the center of the desk drawer, Giorgio treating her things as though she had died. Like Max had died, already dead by the time the letter arrived. Day before yesterday. Max. Already dead. Dead.

"Ah well," she turned to the old dragon by her side. The woman came up to Corinne's shoulder. Corinne smiled. "Aqua passata, non macina più, si?"

Strega Nona agreed it was all water under the bridge, though she could not have known this was a very American sentiment and ultimately correct. *Ultima*—literally: in the end—correct. The process of living is that of accumulation: friends, lovers, family, goods, experience, memories. The process of dying is that of letting go. Not in any orderly or efficient fashion, but release. The change, from one process to the other, was that of a curve in time; you rounded this curve in time and the one process was behind you; life lost its savor. Nothing—not food, not wine, not sex or music or men or women or the pleasures of paint or words—would ever be as good as it once was. You got on this train and you could not get off. You rounded the curve whether you wished to or not. Did people know when they rounded this curve? Did most people know? You would think so. Such a fundamental moment. Although perhaps it came on you slowly, and slowly the things you'd accumulated fell from your life, and the people you'd accumulated fell from your life, the experiences you'd accumulated fell from your life, the knowledge, the significance of memory. And then your life fell from your life.

The train for Pisa galloped into Empoli, hurtling,

thrashing, a great swirl of noise and smoke, impatient, as though it had no wish to stop. It was already crowded. People were standing in the aisles.

Corinne followed the three old dragons on. As soon as they entered the car, four people stood so that the dragons might have a seat. The dragons accepted this gesture with a nod. Nothing more. Certainly no cloying thanks. It was their right. Corinne took a place opposite, a single place beside an old man who farted loudly, lifting one buttock for effect. The sound was that of the flaccid snap of a deck of old cards. The odor rose warmly up. Corinne seemed to wilt.

One of the dragons motioned to Corinne, *Come, join us, there is room here with us.*

The old man looked pleased. He had farted this seat empty all the way from Firenze.

Corinne sat beside the old woman, pulled off her gloves, folded her hands over her purse, and held her breath against that moment of heightened expectation and irrevocability: when the train goes into motion, pulls out of the station, and your chance to go backwards is forever lost and now denied you. When time dissolved like a great lozenge in a bath of *what if.*

What if, for instance, Paolo Branchi had not waved his sad and simple farewell this morning? What if he had got back on the train and come to Empoli with her? Would Corinne be with Paolo Branchi now, rippling over a musky bed in some Empoli hotel room? Or, what if Corinne had said to the young bartender, there in the station bar, pointing to each of the thirty or forty liquors she had never tasted: one shot of each, *per favore,* I don't care what it costs and I don't care how long it takes. Now *that* would have been a grand gesture! Really, immensely satisfying. Worthy of Max. Courageous. Imaginative. This—the mere desertion of Giorgio, the Institute, her job, and the filthy students—paled beside a gesture like that! Line them up—she should have told the young bartender—put them all along the bar. One bottle, and beside it, one glass. I shall taste them, each one, slowly. I shall savor. I shall not be rushed, but savor slowly as a just-risen, warm-blooded whale, move along the bar and through this experience. It is absolutely *non importante* to me how long it takes. *Niente*. Perhaps when I finish, I shall turn away from the bar, walk to the front door, fling open that door, and step, irrevocably, into the streets of Empoli itself. After all, I have no plans as yet. No tickets. No one waiting for me at some foreordained destination.

LAURA KALPAKIAN is the author most recently of *Steps and Exes.* Three of her earlier novels, *These Latter Days, Caveat,* and *Graced Land* are set in the fictional town of St. Elmo, California, a place best described as east of L.A. and west of the rest of the world. She has as well two collections of short stories, *Dark Continent* and *Fair Augusto* (Graywolf Press, 1987), which won the PEN West Best Short Fiction Award that year. She has received a National Endowment for the Arts Fellowship in Fiction and was twice awarded the Pacific Northwest Bookseller's Prize. Her stories and nonfiction are widely published in England and America. A native Californian, she was educated on both the East and West Coasts. She lives in Washington State.

This book was designed by Donna Burch. It is set in Apollo type by Stanton Publication Services, Inc., and manufactured by Maple Vail Book Manufacturing on acid-free paper.

Graywolf Press is dedicated to the creation and promotion of thoughtful and imaginative contemporary literature essential to a vital and diverse culture. For further information, visit us online at: **www.graywolfpress.org**.

Other Graywolf titles you might enjoy are:

Salvation and Other Disasters by Josip Novakovich
The Wedding Jester by Steve Stern
How the Dead Live by Alvin Greenberg
The Loom and Other Stories by R.A. Sasaki
A Gravestone Made of Wheat by Will Weaver
We Are Not in This Together by William Kittredge
The Graywolf Silver Anthology